Reginald Horsley

The blue balloon

A tale of the Shenandoah Valley

Reginald Horsley

The blue balloon
A tale of the Shenandoah Valley

ISBN/EAN: 9783337136000

Printed in Europe, USA, Canada, Australia, Japan

Cover: Foto ©Andreas Hilbeck / pixelio.de

More available books at **www.hansebooks**.com

Down came Ephraim's rifle to the charge again.

Page 153.

THE BLUE BALLOON

A TALE OF

THE SHENANDOAH VALLEY

BY

REGINALD HORSLEY

AUTHOR OF 'THE YELLOW GOD;' ETC.

WITH SIX ILLUSTRATIONS
BY
W. S. STACEY

NEW YORK
E. P. DUTTON AND COMPANY
31 WEST TWENTY-THIRD STREET
1896

CONTENTS.

LIST OF ILLUSTRATIONS.

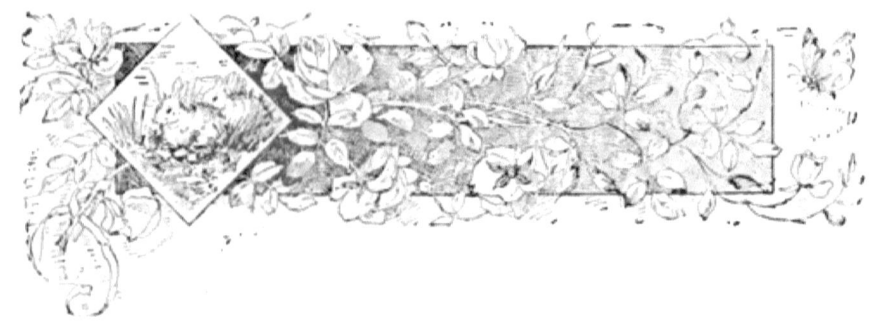

THE BLUE BALLOON.

CHAPTER I.

OLD GRIZZLY.

THIRTY-THREE years ago, or, to be quite exact, in the month of May 1862, the great civil war in the United States of America was in full swing. The Federals had discovered that their boast that they would finish the whole affair in ninety days had been an empty one; while the Confederates, brave as they were, and fighting with all the vigour of men goaded to fury by the horrors of invasion, were learning by slow degrees, and in the teeth of their successes, that one Southerner could *not* whip five Yankees.

The short remnant of summer which followed the first battle of Bull Run, or Manassas, as it was named in the South, had come to an end without startling incident; the dreary winter had dragged itself to a close, unmarked by aught but skirmishes and conflicts of minor importance; but in the spring of '62 immense armies took the field, and campaigns were begun,

compared with which all that had gone before was
merely an insignificant prelude.

At the first rumour that McClellan, stirring at last
from his long and inglorious inactivity, was about to
advance upon Richmond, the Confederate General
Johnston at once evacuated Manassas, and fell back
towards the threatened point; while Stonewall Jackson,
who commanded the army of the Shenandoah, moved
up the valley, so as to keep communication open with
the defenders of the capital.

In the valley lay the town of Staunton, the capital
of Augusta county, Virginia, and the presumed
objective of one section of the Federal advance. Here,
when the war began, lived a youth named Ephraim
Sykes, more commonly known as 'Old Grizzly.' Not
that he at all resembled that ferocious animal either
in person or in disposition, for his manners were mild
and inoffensive; but since his Christian name happened
to coincide with the sobriquet usually bestowed upon
the grizzly bear—namely, 'Ephraim'—a happy thought
occurred one day to a youthful wag of Staunton.
So Ephraim Sykes was promptly dubbed 'Old Grizzly,'
and as such was known ever afterwards.

Ephraim was between nineteen and twenty years of
age, but looked much older, for he was tall and lank,
with a thoughtful face and a sallow complexion, while
an early and luxuriant crop of dark and curling hair
flourished upon his thin cheeks and square, resolute
chin. It was this chin, along with a pair of clear,
steady, gray eyes, which conveyed to the physiogno-
mist the impression that, shy and retiring as the lad
was, beneath his unassuming exterior lurked the spirit
of a lion, united to a will of iron.

Ephraim was a 'hand' in one of the large iron-works in Staunton, but he owned a soul above his humble calling, and his mechanical genius was little short of marvellous. He was for ever inventing curious toys and handy appliances, which he traded off among the Staunton boys for sums very far below their actual value. The money thus obtained he devoted partly to the support of an aged aunt, who had brought him up since the death of his father and mother, and partly to the purchase of material for the manu-facture of his inventions, or, as he himself styled them, his 'notions.' Education, in the ordinary sense of the word, he had never had, but he had managed, nevertheless, by his own efforts and quiet persistence, to acquire an extraordinary amount of general and useful information: a neatly made bookcase, which stood against the wall of his little room, held a supply of books on science, mathematics, and the mechanical arts, which seemed curiously out of place in the homely cabin. But that Ephraim knew their use, and profited by the information he derived from the study of them, was evidenced by the character of the work he turned out, and the increasing favour in which he was held by Mr Coulter, the master of the works in which he was employed.

By the boys who formed his chief customers Grizzly was popularly supposed to be very rich, and the one fault they had to find with him was that he hoarded his gains in a miserly fashion, spending not a cent more than was absolutely necessary to provide him-self and his aunt with the simple necessaries of life. Here, however, they misjudged Ephraim, for though it was true that he scraped and pinched and denied himself to put aside some small proportion of his not very extensive means, yet there was a purpose in what he did, and his motives were very different from those which the boys in their thoughtless way ascribed to him.

The fact was that poor Ephraim's soul was fired with one strong and overmastering ambition. He longed to rise in the world. He dimly recognised his own powers, and felt within himself a capacity for progress which he could not but see was denied to the bulk of his fellow-workers. His shrewdness early taught him the value of money as a means to this end, and while others spent and squandered, he added dollar after dollar to his little hoard, and watched with keen satisfaction the slowly accumulating pile.

He was known to almost everybody in Staunton— there being few homes which did not possess some proof of his skill in handicraft—and he was a general favourite on account of his unfailing good-nature. For though careful, or mean as some called it, with his money, he was always willing to give the work of his hands, and many were the small boys whose happiness had been rendered unbounded by the acquisition of some precious plaything, for which they could not afford to pay, but which Ephraim had not the heart to deny them.

Still, though many sought his acquaintance, Grizzly allowed himself the luxury of but one friend, the only boy, perhaps, in all Staunton who thoroughly understood and properly appreciated him, Lucius Markham. And him Ephraim simply worshipped. The contrast between the two was almost absurd, for Lucius was what is called a gentleman, and with his fair hair, blue eyes, and aristocratic bearing, stood out in curious relief beside the rough working-lad whom he had selected for his crony. Yet the two were inseparable, and Lucius, who was three years younger than Ephraim, and high-spirited and self-willed, would listen to no remonstrances on the part of his parents, who looked askance upon this ill-assorted companionship, but spent as much of his spare time as he possibly could by Ephraim's side, often in the latter's little workshop, where he watched admiringly the processes which neither could his head understand nor his hands execute.

As for Ephraim, Lucius was his hero, and he adored him with a dog-like affection, which the other, though he certainly returned it, yet received with a lofty air of patronage, as became the son and heir of so important a personage as Mr Markham of Markham Hall.

When the war broke out, the enthusiasm of the two lads knew no bounds. The Staunton artillery, in which Mr Markham held a commission, had been almost the first to take the field, and had played an important part in the capture of Harper's Ferry and the arsenal. Lucius had therefore a personal interest in the war from the very beginning, and great indeed was his delight when he was allowed to pay a visit to his father at the camp at Harper's Ferry, where the impetuous young Southerners were receiving their first lessons in the art of real war from generals and captains who were afterwards destined to write their names large upon the scroll of Fame.

On his return to Staunton, Lucius flew to the house of his friend, burning to impart his new experiences.

'Hello, Aunty Chris!' he shouted, bursting into the

little cabin where the old woman sat darning Ephraim's socks. 'Where 's Grizzly ?'

'Hyar I am,' said Ephraim, coming out of his den with a jack-plane in one hand and a piece of walnut wood in the other. 'How ye comin' along, Luce ?' he added, his eyes beaming affectionately upon his friend.

'Oh !' cried Lucius, not troubling to return the salute, 'I tell you I 've had such a time at the Ferry. They are all there—father, and General Harper, and General Harman, and Captain Imboden, and all the rest of them; and Major Jackson of the Military Institute way down in Lexington has been made a colonel and put in command over the whole lot of them. They didn't like it at first, but they 've got used to it now, and my ! don't he just make them work. They were having a picnic before he came, but I guess he didn't help to whip the Mexicans for nothing.'

'Do tell,' remarked Ephraim.

'I should say so,' went on Lucius. 'He's a stark fighter, he is, and he keeps them down to it. They 're drilling and marching, and marching and drilling, all day long; and at night they have camp-fires, and sentries, and everything. You never saw such a show. And oh ! Grizzly, what do you think ? Captain Imboden let me fire off a cannon.'

'Ye don't say so !' exclaimed Ephraim, his sallow face lighting up. 'How many Yanks did ye shoot ?'

Lucius burst out laughing. 'Why, it wasn't loaded, stupid,' he said, 'except with blank cartridge. But I touched her off, and she made an awful good row.'

'Hyar I am,' said Ephraim.

'I reckon,' said Ephraim simply, adding with some anxiety in his voice: 'Then ye warn't in no battle, Luce?'

'Battle! No,' answered Lucius. 'There hasn't been one so far, and I imagine they wouldn't have had me around while it was going on. There's sure to be one soon, though; so they all say. Don't I wish we could be there to see it. There'll only be one, you know,' he added confidently. 'We shall whip the Yanks, and then everybody will come home again.'

'Thet's so,' remarked Ephraim sententiously, ''ceptin' them as is killed, of co'se.' He fell to considering the piece of wood which he held in his hand.

'What are you making there?' demanded Lucius.

'A gun-stock. I got a bar'l in thar.'

'I'll come and watch you,' said Lucius, 'and then I can tell you all about the camp.'

He followed Ephraim into his workshop and sat down upon the edge of a small tub, in which were set two huge glass jars, partly filled with fluid.

'Don't ye set down thar,' cried Ephraim, pushing him off. 'Jerushy! A little more and ye'd have been through the roof.'

'Why, what's in them?' inquired Lucius, looking rather scared, as he shifted his seat to the dusty bench at which Ephraim worked.

'They're chemicals—different sorts, ye know,' explained Grizzly. 'Just's long as they're by themselves they're all right, ye onderstand; but wanst they come together there's the all-firedest kick-up ye ever see.'

'What a fellow you are!' said Lucius, glancing round the room with its mixture of tools, cog-wheels, small

engine bars, glass retorts, and what not. 'You'll blow
your own head off some of these fine days.'

'I nearly done it last Toosday,' grinned Ephraim
genially; 'and old Aunty Chris war thet skeert, she
run down the street hollerin' thieves and murder.' He
laughed quietly at the recollection.

'That's all very well,' said Lucius; 'but you
shouldn't leave them so close to one another if they
are so dangerous as you say they are.'

'Thet's so,' acquiesced Ephraim, removing one of
the jars to a corner of the room. 'It don't matter a
cob of corn what goes wrong with me, but I 'low I'd
never forgive myself if harm came to you.'

'How's the pile, Grizzly?' asked Lucius irrelevantly.

'It's growing, sonny; it's growing. It ain't the
wuth of a gold mine yet; but it's coming along.
War ye wanting a trifle, maybe?'

'Who, me?' answered Lucius loftily. 'I should
say not. I've got plenty.' He rattled the money in
his pocket as he spoke. 'But I say, Grizzly, when do
you think it will be big enough to let you go to
college?'

Ephraim's eyes glistened. 'Maybe two years,'
he replied; 'that is, ef trade keeps steady. It
seems a long time, don't it? But it's a little while
when ye reckon I've worked and waited five years
for 't already.'

Lucius looked at him admiringly. 'You'll do big
things yet, if only you get the chance, Grizzly,' he
said. 'And if you weren't so mighty proud, you could
have had the chance long ago. Father would give me
the money for you, if you'd let me ask him. I know
he would.'

'No, Luce,' returned Ephraim, laying a hairy paw affectionately on his friend's shoulder. 'I know ye'd do it and willin', jest ez I'd give you the best I had; but I med up my mind long ago thet ef I couldn't work it out myself I wouldn't be wuth no one's workin' it out for me, and thet's the fact. It'll come in time, I know thet. And besides I'm used to waitin'.' He sighed, though, as he said it.

'It does seem a shame,' burst out Lucius, 'that a great empty-headed noodle like me should have more money than he knows what to do with, while a clever, enterprising fellow like you, with a brain full of notions, should be kept back because you haven't got any. I'——

'Oh, shet yer head, Luce,' interrupted Ephraim goodhumouredly. 'Ef I war all ye make me out ter be, I'd hev been thar long ago, dollars or no dollars. Maybe it's best as it is,' he concluded; 'for ef I war ready ter go now, I reckon this old war would come in the way of it.'

'Pooh! the war,' ejaculated Lucius contemptuously. 'I tell you there's going to be no war. Father says there'll be a battle likely—just one, and that will settle the Yankees and their bounce for good and all.'

'Maybe,' nodded Ephraim. 'We're going ter see.'

'Well, if there is a war,' proclaimed Lucius, 'I am going to join in. So there.'

'You!' exclaimed Ephraim in unaffected astonishment. 'Why, Luce, they wouldn't have ye. Ye're too young.'

'What of that?' retorted Lucius, flushing. 'I am sixteen. I can carry a gun. What more do they want?'

B

'A heap, I reckon,' said Ephraim, eyeing him along the gun-stock he was planing. 'But no matter for that, Luce. Yer par would never let ye go.'

'Maybe then I'd go without asking him,' muttered Lucius rebelliously.

Ephraim laid down the gun-stock and approached him. 'See hyar, Luce,' he said anxiously, 'ye ain't got no idees in yer head, hev ye?'

Lucius burst out laughing. 'Well, you have a way of putting things,' he cried. 'I believe I have just one, and that is, I am going to be a soldier.'

Ephraim considered a moment. 'Waal,' he said at last, 'ef thet's so, I believe I'll hev to volunteer ter look after ye.'

Lucius roared afresh at this. 'A pretty soldier you would make, Grizzly,' he shouted. 'I fancy I see you ambling along with a gun over your shoulder. Why, I believe you'd be scared to death the moment you let it off.'

'Maybe I would,' admitted Ephraim candidly. 'I 'low I han't been used to shootin'. But anyway, Luce, whar ye kin lead, I reckon I'll do my best ter foller.'

CHAPTER II.

STONEWALL JACKSON'S WAY.

THE months rolled on, the battle of Manassas had been fought and won, and the Federals, driven back upon Washington in hopeless rout, with the immediate result that thousands of volunteers left the Confederate service and returned to their homes and their ordinary vocations, thinking that an enemy so easily whipped could be as easily finished off without their further help. Many officers, too, who had hastened to the front at the first call of the trumpet, leaving their plantations or their businesses to look after themselves, gladly took advantage of the temporary lull to snatch a short furlough. Among these latter was Major Markham, who since the first sudden rush upon Harper's Ferry in April had never once left the field. Now, however, a wound received at Bull Run incapacitating him from further service for the present, he rejoined his wife and son at Markham Hall.

The picturesque descriptions which his father gave him of the leading features of the battle, along with many incidents of personal adventure and heroism, so fired Lucius's already ardent spirit, that from that

time onwards he lived in imagination the life of a
soldier. He begged, he prayed, he implored, he even
went on his knees to his father to allow him to join
the army as a drummer-boy, as a bugler, as a mule-
driver, as anything at all, in any capacity whatsoever.
Major Markham laughed at his son at first, but when
he realised how absolutely in earnest Lucius was, he
bade him, with what show of sternness he could
muster—for he could not but admire the boy's high
spirit—never to mention the subject again.

Thwarted at home, Lucius sought consolation from
his friend Ephraim, and so worked upon his slower
nature with tales of deeds of daring, drawn almost
entirely from his own perfervid imagination, that even
Grizzly was stirred to enthusiasm, and flourished his
long arms over his head as he declared his intention
of annihilating whole regiments of Yankees at one fell
blow, by means of some devastating compound, the
first idea of which was germinating in his fertile brain.

At the same time, Ephraim's common sense stood
both him and Lucius in good stead, and held the
younger boy back more effectually than the commands
of his father or the pleadings of his mother. But
when Major Markham rejoined his regiment in December, to take part in the terrible expedition to Romney,
Lucius could bear the restraint no longer, and one cold,
snowy night he astonished Ephraim by suddenly
appearing and boldly proposing that they should run
away together.

'Whar ye gwine ter run ter?' inquired common-
sense Ephraim, looking up from the calculations on
which he was engaged.

'How do I know?' flashed Lucius the fervid.

'We'll just go on until we come to one of our armies. They'll be mighty glad to let us join.'

'A stark fighter sech ez ye would be!' said Ephraim with beaming admiration, and without the least trace of irony.

'Yes,' assented Lucius complacently; 'they'll not refuse two such strong and active lads as you and '——

'Sho!' interrupted Ephraim. 'Don't ye count on me. I warn ye.'

'What!' exclaimed Lucius, in a voice of mingled surprise and grief. 'Do you mean to say that, after all I have told you, you will let me go alone?'

'I ain't gwine ter let ye go at all, Luce,' returned Ephraim, placing a long, hairy arm affectionately round the boy's neck. 'See hyar, now,' he went on, as Lucius shook himself angrily free, 'thar ain't nuthin' ter call fightin' goin' on jest now. Nothin' but marchin' round and round, and up and down in the snow and the slush. Now, thar ain't no fun in thet, I reckon.'

'Well, no,' admitted Lucius reluctantly. He thought for a moment or two, and then burst out: 'Look here, Grizzly, the real fighting is sure to begin again in spring. If I promise to wait, will you promise to come with me then?'

'I 'low we'll wait till spring comes along,' answered Ephraim oracularly. 'Ef ye're ez sot upon it then ez ye air now, I'll see what I kin do.'

'That's a bargain, then,' said Lucius. 'I just long to see a real good battle. Mind, if you go back on me now, I'll call you a coward and start without you.'

'I ain't any coward,' answered Ephraim quietly, though his pale face flushed slightly; 'leastways ez fur ez goin' along with ye is consarned. Ye don't imagine I'd go fer ter lose sight of ye, Luce?' he finished, with a catch in his voice.

'Oh no,' said Lucius, mollified. 'Only I thought that maybe you couldn't understand my feelings. You're a dear old thing, Grizzly; but you're a rough bit of stick, you know, and you haven't so much at stake as people like us.' And the young aristocrat drew himself proudly up.

'Thet's a fact,' nodded Ephraim; 'though I ain't heard ez the fust families hez been doin' all the fightin'.' There was a subdued grin on his face as he spoke.

'Of course not,' said Lucius hastily. 'Our fellows are stark fighters all round; but it's men like my father and Jackson and the rest who lead the way. You know that well enough.'

Ephraim stretched out his brown hairy paw and drew Lucius towards him. 'I only know I'd die fer ye glad and willin' ef ye war ahead, Luce,' he said tenderly.

'Shucks!' exclaimed Lucius impatiently; 'who said anything about dying? Now it's all settled, and you'll come.'

'I'll be on time,' said Ephraim. He was silent for a moment, during which he thought deeply. Finally he said, 'Ye air jest sot ter see a battle, ain't ye, Luce?'

'Yes,' answered Lucius. 'Didn't I tell you so?'

'Waal,' resumed Ephraim, 'wouldn't ye be content jest ter see wan, without arskin' ter take a hand in the fightin'?'

'Whatever do you mean by that?' queried Lucius. 'I don't understand you.'

'Waal, it don't matter,' said Ephraim, 'fer I reckon I han't got no very cl'ar idee of what I mean myself ez yet. Anyway thar's heaps of time. We're on'y beginnin' December now, and thar'll be nuthin' this long while. Ef ye're still sot in spring, why, we'll see.'

'See what?' demanded Lucius impatiently. 'Can't you explain?'

But Ephraim either could not or would not, and presently Lucius took his departure in high dudgeon.

Ephraim sat thinking to himself for a long while, and finally he took down a volume from his shelves and buried himself in it, until the voice of the old woman in the next room disturbed him by querulously demanding 'Ef he warn't never goin' to bed.'

'I b'lieve I could do it,' he thought to himself as he undressed; 'but'—— He pulled a trunk from under his bed, and unlocking it, drew out a small cash-box. This in turn he opened and studied the little pile of dollars it contained with an anxious face.

'Thet's the only way ter do it,' he muttered, passing the coins backwards and forwards through his fingers. 'Thar's not much more than enough thar, if thar is enough. Imagine! Only that little lot in five long years. Seems a pity, jest fer a whim. But it's fer Luce. It's ter pleasure Luce. He's that sot on it, and he nat'ally looks ter me. No matter, I guess I'll work it up again.'

He stood looking into the box with eyes that did not see, for he was far away in spirit in the little Massachusetts town, where stood the famous college he so ardently desired to enter.

Splash! A great tear fell into the box of dollars.

'What ye doin'?' Ephraim apostrophised himself with great vehemence. 'Ain't it fer Luce? Ain't he wuth it? Ef ye can't do a little thing like that fer yer friend, it's time ye'——

He broke off suddenly, snapped the lid of the box, and threw it back into the trunk.

'Ef ye can't do a little thing like that without makin' a fuss about it,' he repeated, 'it's time ye—it's time ye'——

He choked over the words, a rain of tears gushed from his eyes, and with a low cry he flung himself sobbing upon his bed.

The year came to an end, and plague and worry him as he would, Lucius could extract nothing from Ephraim to throw light on the mysterious remark. Indeed Grizzly was now seldom or never to be found in his workshop; nor could Aunty Chris explain his absence, or disclose his whereabouts, for, as she frankly confessed, she knew nothing whatever about him. Lucius, of course, whenever he could waylay him, questioned and cross-questioned him as to what he was engaged upon in his spare time and where; but Grizzly invariably replied with a wag of his head: 'Ye'll git thar in time, Luce. On'y ye'll hev ter hang on till the time comes.' With which Delphic utterance Lucius was obliged to be content.

Meantime the war was not standing still. Manassas had, after all, not crumpled up the North, and early in '62 the people of the valley were rudely awakened to the fact by the appearance among them of no less than three Federal generals, with an aggregate force of sixty-four thousand men. And to these Stonewall Jackson could oppose but thirteen thousand! But though the excitement was great, there was little anxiety; for the reputation which Jackson and his brigade had won at Manassas, and their stern and soldierly endurance of the terrible hardships of the severe winter just ended, inspired a confidence in their prowess, which would scarcely have been shaken had all the armies of the North been combined against them.

What were men's feelings then, when the astounding news spread like wildfire from town to town : 'Jackson has deserted us in our extremity. He has fled through the gaps to the east side of the Blue Ridge !'

The report was not unfounded. It certainly was true that Jackson had disappeared from the valley. Only Colonel Ashby, the famous cavalry leader, remained behind with a thousand sabres at his back.

Men laughed bitterly. What was this little force to do for their protection against an army so gigantic? But Ashby with scattered troops was here, there, and everywhere. Now at McDowell, now at Strasburg, now at Franklin, yesterday at Front Royal, to-morrow at Luray. But what he learned in his reconnaissances, and where he sent the information which he acquired, no man knew, no man had the heart to ask. In Staunton itself the wildest confusion reigned; for no sooner had the news of Jackson's flight been conveyed to the Federal generals, than they set their masses in motion, and began to advance along converging lines upon the little town. That it was to be occupied was regarded as certain, and in the universal terror much that was valuable in the way of military stores was removed or destroyed ; while General Johnson with six regiments retired from his strong position on the

Shenandoah Mountain, intent only on saving his small
force by effecting a junction with the vanished Jackson
wherever he might find him.

Then came the day when Staunton, abandoned and
defenceless, lay sullenly awaiting its fate, with Milroy
and twelve thousand Federals not two-and-twenty
miles away, and Fremont coming on with thirty
thousand more.

It was a Sunday, and the churches were full of
devout worshippers, praying doubtless that the chas-
tening rod held over them might be averted in its
descent.   Suddenly a strange and terrible sound arose
—a noise of trampling thousands, the clink of steel
against steel as scabbard and stirrup jangled together,
the clatter of squadrons upon the road, the hoarse
rumble and grumble of artillery wagons.   People
looked at one another in dismay.   Despite their
supplications the blow had fallen: they were in the
hands of the enemy.

Slowly, with mournful hearts and dejected mien,
they filed out of church, their downcast eyes refusing
to look at the bitter sight.   Then, as one head after
another was lifted, exclamations of deep surprise broke
forth here and there.

Where were the stars and stripes ?   Where was the
blue of the detested Federals ?   The marching columns
were *gray !*   The stars and bars waved proudly in the
breeze, and here and there in the midst of a regiment
the lone star shone upon flag and pennon.

What a shout of joy went up from the multitude:
'Confederates ! Confederates !   They are our own boys
back again !   Old Stonewall is here !   Thank God !
Hurrah !   Hurrah !'

The excitement was tremendous. Nerves were strung to highest tension; emotions touched the breaking point. Men leaped and danced for very joy. Women flung themselves into each other's arms and wept for sheer happiness. And through it all the gray hosts rolled steadily on.

Then, as suddenly as it had arisen, the hubbub subsided. Apprehension reigned once more, and the eager questions passed from lip to lip: 'What are they doing here? Have they been routed? Are they only in retreat?'

No, the soldiers answered, they were not running away. They had not seen or heard of the enemy for days. What were they doing here, then? Again they did not know. Nobody knew except old Stonewall. He knew of course. It was one of his tricks. He had got something under his hat.

Then the crowd surged to the railway station to watch the debarking troops as train after train rolled in. Here the same ignorance prevailed. Nobody knew; nobody could understand. To their personal friends the officers were dumb, for they were in darkness like the men. Only the General knew; and those who knew the General knew also how hopeless it would be to question him.

The dwellers in the country, who had come into town for church, hastened away, full of their news, to tell the folk who had been left at home. They did not get far. All around the town a strong cordon of soldiers had been drawn who forced them back. What! they asked, might they not even return to their own homes? No, they might not—at least, not yet. Why? Nobody knew. Simply the General had ordered it so. Probably he did not wish the news of his arrival to be spread abroad. But to everything, the one monotonous, exasperating answer, 'We do not know.'

Then at last the people understood. Silent as ever as to his plans, mysterious in his movements, Jackson's flight had been but a clever feint. He had stolen back swiftly and without attracting attention ; and now, while the Federals fondly supposed him east of the Blue Ridge, here he was, ready and able to deal them one of his slashing flank blows. It was 'Stonewall Jackson's way.'

As soon as the soldiers began to arrive, Lucius and Ephraim, who both sang in the choir of their church, hurried out and raced to the station. Long before they got there Lucius had shouted himself hoarse, while, though he took things more quietly, Ephraim's cheeks were burning, and his eyes blazing with unwonted fire.

'Say, Grizzly, isn't it splendid ?' panted Lucius.

Ephraim did not answer, for just then a roar of delight rent the air. 'Here he comes! Here's the General! Hurrah! Stonewall Jackson! Stonewall! Cheer, boys! Hurrah! God bless you, General! Hurrah! Hurrah!'

Clad in his old gray coat, soiled and smirched with the stains of the dreadful march to Romney in December, and with his queer slouched hat cocked askew over his forehead, 'Old Stonewall,' then but thirty-eight years of age, rode in the midst of his staff. His shrewd, kindly face wore a smile of almost womanly sweetness, and his keen blue eyes, which, it is said, glowed when the battle rage was upon him with a terrible light that appalled both friend and foe, now beamed mildly on the shouting crowd who sought to do him honour. He bowed continually right and left, and was evidently pleased at his welcome, as well as touched by the supreme confidence of the people in him.

So frantic was Lucius in his demonstrations that at last he attracted the notice of the General, who after regarding him good-naturedly for a moment, broke into an amused laugh, saying, as he nodded pleasantly: 'Thank you, my lad, for your welcome. It does one's heart good to see such a face as yours.' For a moment Lucius could not believe his ears. Then, as he realised that the General had indeed spoken to *him*, his face crimsoned with delight, and forgetting everything in his exaltation, he rushed into the road and clung to Jackson's stirrup leather, as though to detain him by main force.

'Take me with you, General!' he cried at the top of his voice. 'Take me with you. I want to fight, and they won't let me.'

'Hurrah!' shouted the crowd, moved by this novel sensation, while Ephraim, glowing with pride, craned his long neck to see his hero, as he fully expected, caught up in front of the General and borne away to the wars.

'By time!' he muttered, 'ain't he jest cl'ar grit? Ain't he noble? And he's my friend.' Great tears rose in his honest eyes and blurred his sight as the General reined in his charger and bent over to Lucius.

'Take you with me, my boy?' said Jackson kindly, laying his hand upon the fair, curly head as he spoke.

'Take you with me? God forbid! We don't want children amid such scenes as we are forced to go through.'

'Why not?' gasped Lucius. 'I'm sixteen; I'd make one more anyway. I don't mind being shot any more than the next man.'

'Gloryful gracious!' murmured Ephraim, his eyes fairly brimming over; while Jackson, bending lower still, said somewhat huskily: 'God bless you, lad, for your true heart.' Then straightening himself in his saddle, he cried in ringing tones to his officers: 'When our men grow from the stuff this boy is made of, gentlemen, it is no wonder that the victory is ours.'

The crowd cheered again lustily at this, and Jackson, turning once more to Lucius, said: 'Tell me your name, my boy. I should like to remember it.'

'Lucius Markham, sir,' replied the boy. 'That is my father coming up now.'

'What, the son of Major Markham!' said Jackson. 'Ha! a chip of the old block.—Major!' he hailed, as a fine-looking bronzed officer rode by with his battery. 'So this is your son?'

'I am afraid so, sir,' returned Major Markham, smiling and nodding at Lucius. 'What has the young scapegrace been doing? He is always wanting to follow the drum.'

'Nay,' protested Jackson, 'I won't allow you to call him names. He is a fine fellow, and wants to come and be a soldier under me.'

'May I, father?' asked Lucius eagerly. 'Do say yes.—I know most of the drill, sir,' he added to the General, 'and I can shoot pretty straight.'

There was a laugh among the officers at this, but

Jackson checked it with a look, and, turning to Lucius, said impressively: 'Listen to me, Lucius. You are too young to come with me, but still you can be a soldier, and a bold one, if you choose.'

'In what regiment, sir?' asked Lucius, looking up at him eagerly.

'In the faithful regiment,' answered Stonewall gravely, 'under the banner of the Cross, and with Christ for Commander. The war is the holy war, and the battles are fought for God and against self and the wrong every day. And remember, Lucius,' he concluded, 'the first duty of a soldier is obedience.'

He rode on, followed by the cheers of the crowd, while Major Markham slipped back to his place.

Lucius stared dreamily after them, heedless of the curious and interested looks cast at him, till all at once a hand gripped his arm, and Ephraim's voice whispered in his ear: 'Come away out of the crowd, Luce. I 'se suthin' mighty partic'ler to say ter ye.'

CHAPTER III.

THE BALLOON GOES UP.

STILL absorbed in his own thoughts, Lucius followed his friend in silence through the crowded streets until they reached a remote field or piece of waste land at the very outskirts of the town, and here Ephraim halted and spoke once more.

The pomp and circumstance of glorious war had laid hold of poor Grizzly, for his cheeks were still red and his eyes sparkling, while there was something intense in his voice as he said : 'Air ye sot, Luce? Air ye still sot like ye war?'

'Set on what?' asked Lucius, still dreaming.

'On seeing the fight.'

'Oh yes,' answered Lucius; but his expression plainly showed that he had scarcely heard, and certainly not comprehended Grizzly's remarks.

'Waal, come over hyar, then,' said Ephraim, 'and I'll show ye what I've been fixed onter for the last five months.'

He moved mysteriously towards an old shed of considerable size that stood in a corner of the field, and with many anxious glances all around unlocked the door. Though it chimed in with his mood, his caution was unnecessary, for not a civilian was in sight. Only in the near distance they could see part of the cordon of sentries pacing up and down with bayonets fixed, and ever and anon a patrol rode swiftly by. Occasionally a bugle blared in the town, and the hum of many voices came faintly to them. Except for these all was quiet, and they were quite alone.

'Come along, Luce,' said Ephraim, pulling him through the door, which he carefully shut and locked behind him. 'Ye won't know whar ye air, but I'll tell ye. This is my new workshop. I got it a bargain from Pete Taylor last December after us two had thet talk. I pinned him down not to let on that I had the place, fer I didn't want ter be followed and worried by the boys. And I been fixin' things hyar ever sence ye 'lowed ye war so sot.'

He flung the shutters wide as he spoke, and the light streamed through two windows upon a great heap of blue cotton material, apparently enveloped in a network of fine ropes. Here and there lay other ropes neatly coiled, and close beside the blue heap was what looked like a large round hamper without a cover.

'Waal,' demanded Ephraim anxiously, after a somewhat protracted pause, during which Lucius glanced vacantly around the workshop, 'what d' ye think of her? I 'lowed I 'd try and fix her up fer ye, seein' ye war so sot.'

'For me?' echoed Lucius. 'What is for me? I don't see anything.'

'Don't see nuthin', don't ye?' chuckled Ephraim. 'I reckon ye see without onderstandin'. What d' ye 'magine this is?'

C

He took up an armful of the blue fabric as he spoke
and let it fall again in a heap.

'I'm sure I don't know,' answered Lucius.

'Co'se ye don't; co'se ye don't,' said Ephraim, rubbing his hands together, and grinning delightedly.
'Ye never see nuthin' like her before, I bet.'

'I have not,' returned Lucius, now thoroughly awake,
and examining everything with great curiosity. 'What
a queer-looking—— Oh! why, Grizzly, if I don't
believe it's a balloon!'

Ephraim sprang off the ground and twirled round in
the air for joy. 'Thet's it,' he cried. 'Thet's it!
By time! ef ye ain't cute. Thet's jest what it is.'

'But—but—I don't understand,' said Lucius, finger-
ing the network. 'Where did you get it?'

Ephraim gave himself another spin. 'I done read
her up out of a book, and made her myself,' he said.

'Grizzly!' cried Lucius in profound admiration.
'You—made—it—yourself. Well, if you don't just
beat every one. You're a genius, that's what you are.
What put it into your head to make it? You clever
old stick!'

'You did,' answered Ephraim, glowing with pride
and pleasure.

'*I* did! Why? How? What is it for, then?'

Ephraim took a step forward and looked into his
eyes. '*Fer you and me to sail around in and watch
the war,*' he said.

Profound silence followed this extraordinary announcement, and then Lucius sat down on a heap of
shavings and rather feebly remarked, 'Oh!' There
really seemed nothing more to be said.

'Yas, sir,' went on Ephraim, still beaming with

satisfaction ; 'when ye said ye wuz so sot ter see some fightin', I began ter study and figger out what'd be the best way for ye ter do it 'thout ye gettin' in the track of the bullets.'

'Oh,' commented Lucius, ' you were afraid of being killed, were you ?'

' No, and I warn't neither,' returned Ephraim simply; 'but I wuz powerful frightened lest ye might be. Bullets is sech darned unpolites—they never stops ter inquire if ye b'long ter a fust fam'ly or if ye don't.'

'But you know,' explained Lucius, 'when I said that I wanted to see a battle, I meant that I wanted to take part in one.'

' I know ye did,' assented Ephraim. 'At the same time, ez fur ez I kin l'arn, that's about *the* most or'nery way of seein' a battle ez has ever been invented. I tell ye, a bullet is the meanes' thing alive.'

Lucius laughed. ' But we can't fight if we are up in the air, Grizzly,' he observed.

'Can't we ? I reckon we kin, though,' replied Ephraim. 'But ez fur ez that goes, who wants ter fight ? I don't, fer wun ; and I don't mean to let you, fer another. Ain't there enuff of 'em hammerin' away just now without you and me joinin' in ?'

'That's not very patriotic,' said Lucius with emphasis.

'Ain't it ?' answered Ephraim drily. 'I reckon it's sense all the same. Anyway, this is how I've fixed it up. If ye don't like my way, I promise ye, ye won't get a chance to go off on yer own, ef I have ter tie ye in a chair and keep ye at my own expense until the war is through.'

Lucius laughed again. 'You dear old Grizzly,' he

said, 'you are always thinking of me. I'd just love to go with you. It will be splendid fun. But, tell me, how ever did you manage to make such a wonderful thing all by yourself?'

'Waal, I don't say it war ez easy ez hoein' a row,' replied Ephraim, 'but it warn't so dreadful hard nuther. I got it all outern a book, as I was telling ye, and made her to measurement, and thar she is, ye see. Besides,' he added with an affectionate grin, 'seein' ez how it wuz fer ye I made her, Luce, I didn't take no count of trouble. Ef thar wuz any, I reckon it never come my way.'

'Upon my word, you are a good old Grizzly,' cried Lucius enthusiastically, and fetching Ephraim a sounding slap between the shoulders, which seemed to delight the assaulted one immensely. 'To think of your taking all that trouble just to please me. And the thing itself—why, it's magnificent! If you aren't clever! Say, Grizzly, are you sure it will hold us?'

'I reckon,' answered Ephraim. 'Git inter the kyar and see.'

'Yes, I see there's plenty of room in there,' said Lucius, but what I meant to say was, will it bear us, hold us up, or whatever you call it?'

'Waal, I should say so,' cried Ephraim joyously. 'Ye onderstand, Luce, thet's jest whar the hard part came in. I had ter cal'clate the strain and—— But d'ye know anythin' 'bout airy norties?'

'Airy who?' repeated Lucius, puzzled. 'Oh, I see, aeronautics.'

'Waal, I said so. D'ye know 'em?'

Lucius shook his head.

'Then I han't no time ter teach ye now. Ye kin

read 'em up twixt now and the time we go up, ef ye like.'

'I shouldn't understand it,' said Lucius. 'I guess I'll leave it to you. It means the way to handle a balloon, I suppose?'

'Thet's about it,' answered Ephraim sententiously. 'I 'magine it's easy 'nuff. I read her up, and if ye care to come, why, I ain't afraid ter be airy-nort.'

'I'll go with you fast enough,' said Lucius. 'It will be grand. When do you mean to start?'

'Waal, perhaps we'd better wait till we get a notion whar old Stonewall's goin' ter. Then we kin foller him up; fer, don't ye know, thar's bound ter be some mighty stark fightin' when old Stonewall is around.'

'Oh!' cried Lucius, flushing scarlet, as a sudden recollection struck him. 'I forgot. I won't—I mean I can't go with you.'

'What! what's thet ye say?' exclaimed Ephraim, too astonished for further speech.

'A soldier's first duty is obedience,' went on Lucius, speaking to himself. 'It's no use, Grizzly; I'll just have to stay behind.'

'What ails ye ter say such ez thet?' asked Ephraim, much aggrieved. 'Right now ye seemed willin' 'nuff, and ye looked right peart and chipper. Ye seemed ter ache ter come. Co'se ye mought have been funnin' bout'n thet; but ef thet's so, why, I give in I never war so fooled before.'

'No,' said Lucius, shaking his head sadly; 'you were not wrong. I did want to go. I do still, very much indeed.'

'Then why in thunder don't ye?' queried the mystified Ephraim.

'Well,' answered Lucius, growing very red again, and stirring a coil of ropes with his foot, 'you know what father said when I told him I wanted to join; and then *he* said—the General, I mean—"a soldier's first duty is obedience." And, oh! Grizzly,' he cried, flinging himself face downwards upon the blue heap, 'I'd just love to go now; for since he spoke to me, I'd follow him through fire and water all the world over. But I mustn't—I mustn't.'

Ephraim stood twining his long brown fingers together, the picture of distress at sight of Luce's grief. A blue vein which ran perpendicularly in the centre of his forehead, swelled out, a rugged bar, against which the waves of red which chased one another over his face broke and receded. His eyes were troubled, and swept rapidly up and down and round and round as if seeking inspiration, while so firmly were his lips compressed that the line of parting could barely be distinguished.

'Don't ye take on so, Luce. I can't abear it,' he muttered huskily, at last. Then, as if with the breaking of his silence the idea of which he had been in pursuit had been captured, he emitted a sudden cackle of satisfaction, and flinging himself down beside Lucius, drew the boy to him and hugged him like a grizzly indeed.

'Cheer up, Luce!' he cried. 'I done got the way. By time! what an or'nery fool I must hev been not ter remember thet.'

'Remember what?' asked Lucius, willing but unable to see a ray of comfort.

'What I been doin' ter let thet notion past me?' inquired Ephraim cheerfully of himself. 'I declar' I had her all along; on'y when ye up 'n said ye wouldn't come, I 'low I let her slip fer a minnit.'

'I wish you 'd explain,' said Lucius fretfully.

'Comin', Luce, comin'. Don't ye go fer ter knock thet idee out er my head agen with yer talk. Why, I war workin' along the very same lines myself when we began ter talk, if ye recollect. Now, see hyar. This is the way I put it up. Your par, he says ye 're not ter go fightin'—and I swow it 's the last thing *I* want ter do—Old Stonewall he 'lows ye orter do ez yer par says, and ye 'low ye orter agree with both of 'em. Ain't thet so ?'

'That 's so,' admitted Lucius forlornly.

'Ezacly ! Waal now, Luce. I 'll give ye the whole idee in a par'ble. Ye know thet black bull way down ter Holmes's place ?' Lucius nodded. 'Waal then, we 'll suppose yer par sez ter ye : " Luce," sez he, " that bull er Holmes's is powerful servigerous. I 'll not hev ye goin inter the field ter take him by the tail ! " '

'Well ?' laughed Lucius, as Ephraim paused to wrestle with his idea.

'Waal, ye 'low ye 'll do ez yer par sez ; but all the same ye hev an outrageous hankerin' ter see thet bull er Holmes's. Now, what d' ye reckon ye 'd do ?'

'Why, sit on the fence and look at him,' answered Lucius.

'Ezacly !' cried Ephraim joyously. 'Thet 's what I 'lowed ye 'd do. And think no harm of it ?' he finished anxiously.

'No,' said Lucius ; 'I wasn't told not to look at the bull. I don't see how there could be any harm in doing that.'

'Then thet 's all right. This hyar fight, thet stands

fer Holmes's bull, ye onderstand ; and the old balloon, she stands fer the ring fence. How does thet strike ye ?'

'You mean,' said Lucius thoughtfully,' that since we only intend to watch what is going on, I shall be doing no harm if I go with you.'

'Thet's it, I reckon. Why, don't ye know, I've been studyin' all the time how I could git ye thar, and give ye suthin' like what ye wanted, without ye runnin' no resks.' It did not appear to strike Ephraim that there could be any risk connected with the balloon itself. 'Waal,' he added after a pause, during which Lucius gave himself up to reflection, 'what d' ye 'low ye'll do ?'

'I'll come,' said Lucius, rising to his feet. 'There can't be anything wrong in this, for it's only a piece of fun.' There was a note of doubt in his voice ; but he was anxious to allow himself to be convinced.

'Then thet's fixed,' said Ephraim, with a sigh of relief. ''Tain't likely ez I'd ask ye ter do anythin' wrong, Luce.—Now we'll git outern this, and I'll let ye know when all's ready fer a start.'

'But how are you going to manage it ?' asked Lucius. 'What about the gas ?'

'I'll show ye,' answered Ephraim. 'See them two bar'ls ?'

'No,' said Lucius ; 'I don't see any barrels.'

'Thar, opposite the door, buried in the ground.'

'Oh yes ; filled with straw. What are they for ?'

'They ain't filled with straw, ye onderstand,' explained Ephraim. 'I'll show ye.'

He gathered up the straw from the top of one of the

barrels, and disclosed underneath a quantity of iron filings and borings.

'Why, that's iron,' exclaimed Lucius; 'what has that to do with gas?'

'Hold on,' replied Ephraim genially. 'I'll make it cl'ar ter ye in a jiffy. Ye see,' he pursued, 'this kind er thing goes on all the way down—a layer er straw and a layer er iron-filin's plumb down ter the bottom er the bar'l.'

'I see,' said Lucius, looking very wise, though, as a matter of fact, he was as much in the dark as ever.

'Now,' went on Ephraim, pointing to some carboys ranged against the wall, 'them things is full er sulphuric acid—vitriol, that is ter say; and ez soon ez ever I take and heave the acid on top er the iron-filin's, the gas—hydrergin it's called—begins ter come off.'

'Does it?' said Lucius, much interested. 'Let's see.'

Ephraim grinned. 'I reckon I han't been gatherin' the stuff all these months jest ter fire it off before the time,' he remarked; 'but I'll show ye the same thing in a little way, so ter speak.'

He took a glass flask from a shelf and placed a few iron-filings in it. He then poured some sulphuric acid into a cup, added some water thereto, and finally introduced it into the flask, completely covering the lumps of iron.

'Now,' said he, 'ye'll see what ye'll see.' He closed the mouth of the flask with a cork through which was set a glass tube, and to the free end of this latter he presently applied a lighted match. Instantly the gas which was issuing from the tube ignited, and burned with a pure, pale flame.

'Hooray!' shouted Lucius.   'That's wonderful.   I never saw anything like it.'

'Waal, it's been done before, ye know,' said Ephraim drily.   'I didn't invent it.'

'You're a marvel, all the same,' cried Lucius enthusiastically.   'My! what a splash you'll make when you get to college, Grizzly.'

Ephraim turned quickly away, and stooping down, replaced the straw which he had taken from the barrel.   When he looked up again, his face was very pale.

'Ye see, Luce,' he went on, concluding his explanation, but speaking with much less fire and animation, 'what went on in the flask is what'll go on in the bar'ls, and ez the hydrergin comes off it'll be led through these pipes, which I can fix onter the bar'ls, inter a tank er water, ye maybe noticed standin' outside.   Thar's a receiver in the tank, or thar will be wanst we're ready, and another pipe'll be led from thar to the balloon, and thar ye air.'

'What do you lead the gas under water for?' inquired Lucius.

'Ter cool it fer wan thing, and ter wash it fer another.'

'Well, it's wonderful!   That's all I can say,' repeated Lucius.   'And to think that you should have done everything all by yourself.   But, Grizzly, surely you can't fill the balloon and let her up without help.'

'I know thet; but don't ye fret,' returned Ephraim. 'I bet she'll be ready when we air.   There's two or three in the works ez I kin trust to tell about her 'thout them lettin' it go all over the town.   All ye hev ter do is ter go home and set still till I arsk ye ter git up.—Come on; let's be off out er this.' For some reason or other he was growing restless under Luce's perpetual fire of questions.

'How pretty the blue stuff looks, varnished,' said Lucius, adding suddenly : 'It must have cost an awful lot, Grizzly. Where did you get all the money to buy it with ?'

'Oh, hyar and thar,' answered Ephraim uncomfortably. 'I sold things. She ain't made er silk, ye know —only er cotton stuff.—Come on, Luce, it 's gittin' late, and Aunty Chris will be hollerin' fer her tea.'

But Lucius stood still, looking down upon the confused heap of material and cordage, and pondering deeply. All at once he swung round and faced Ephraim. 'Grizzly,' he said jerkily, 'I believe you have broken into the pile.'

Ephraim's face was a study If he had been caught robbing his master's till, he could not have looked more sheepish and ashamed. He shifted uneasily from one foot to the other, and twisted his long fingers in and out till all the joints cracked like a volley of small-arms. 'Waal, waal '—— he stuttered.

'You 've broken into the pile,' interrupted Lucius. 'For five years you 've been grubbing and saving all for one purpose, working overtime, and making odds and ends here and there for the boys, all for one purpose—that you might go to college. And now you 've gone and upset everything. I 'll bet you haven't a dollar left of all your savings. Now, have you ?'

'No,' mumbled Ephraim shamefacedly. 'But '——

'I know what you 're going to say,' broke in Lucius—' you did it for me. You are always doing things for me. But you 'd no right to do this. You 'd

no right to spoil your whole life just for me. What
can I do? I can't pay you back. And father'——

'Ez ter thet,' interjected Ephraim, 'it war my own.
I ain't askin' any wan ter put it back.'

'It wasn't your own,' burst out Lucius. 'At least it
wasn't your own to do as you liked with. It was to
help you on in the world. It was to give your brains
a chance. Oh! weren't there heaps of ways in which
we could have had our fun without this? If I'd
known it, if I'd dreamed of it, I'd have gone off and
'listed without a word to any one.'

'I know ye would, Luce,' said Ephraim quietly.
'Ye were mighty nigh doin' it thet snowy night when
ye came ter me. Thet sot me thinkin'. I sez ter
m'self, sez I, I reckon it's mostly froth on Luce's part.
Ef I ken git him pinned down ter come with me, I
guess I kin keep him out er harm's way. Lordy! Luce,
what would I hev done ef I'd gone and lost ye? Waal,
ez I sot thar thinkin' ter m'self, all at once thar comes
an idee. I dunno whar it came from, but thet's it'—
he pointed to the balloon—'and wanst I gripped it I
never let it go again, fer it jest seemed the best way
in all the world fer ter let ye see all ye wanted ter see,
and ter keep ye safe et the same time.' He held up
his hand as Lucius was about to speak.

'Don't say it again, Luce. It's done now, and
can't be undone. Maybe some folk'd think it war a
mad thing ter do; but it didn't seem so ter me, seein'
it war done fer you.'

Sometimes the step from the ridiculous to the
sublime is as easy as that in the opposite direction. It
was so now, when the rough, hard-handed mechanic,
whose brains, nevertheless, had been able to devise and

execute this wonderful thing, stood before the high-spirited, empty-headed boy, whom he loved, and for whose well-being, as he imagined, he had thrown away his substance and his worldly hopes.

For a few moments there was silence between the boys, Ephraim standing with his hand upon the bolt of the door, Lucius driving first the toe and then the heel of his boot into the ground. At last he shuffled over to Ephraim, glanced shyly up into the big gray eyes that beamed so affectionately down on him, and with something that sounded suspiciously like a sob, clasped Grizzly's free hand in both his own.

Ephraim flung wide the door. 'Garn away!' he said with a genial grin, and tenderly shoved Lucius out of the cabin.

On the following Wednesday Jackson marched his army out of Staunton, broke up the camp at West View, and started to attack General Milroy, whom he met and defeated with heavy loss at McDowell. Movement then followed movement so rapidly that the people of Staunton were bewildered. However, as all the news they received told of the success, they were also content. Meanwhile the month wore to an end without another word from Ephraim to Lucius on the subject of the balloon. But at last, one bright afternoon in early June, the long expected and desired summons came.

Lucius was sitting idly on his own gate, whittling a stick, when a working-man approached him, and after a cautious look up the avenue to see if any one else was in sight, observed interrogatively, 'Young Squire Markham?'

Lucius nodded, and the man went on : 'Ef that's so,

I've a message fer ye from the Grizzly. He sez ye're
ter jine him et the shed any time ye think fit after
midnight, and before day.'

'Is he—going up?' asked Lucius, with rounded
eyes.

'I 'low he is, ef the wind holds from the south-west,'
replied the man. 'Will I say ye'll be on hand?'

'Rather!' answered Lucius. 'Here's a dollar for
your trouble. I'm much obliged.—Hi! you won't say
anything about it?'

'I'm dumb, squire,' grinned the man as he moved
away, while Lucius, ablaze with excitement, stole into
the house and shut himself up in his room to think.

He knew perfectly well that he was about to do
wrong; but he tried to deceive himself into the belief
that Ephraim's casuistry afforded him a sufficient
excuse for going off without the leave which would
certainly never have been granted him. Moreover,
he argued that, after the sacrifice which Ephraim had
made just to give him pleasure, he could not now hang
back. In a word, as many a wise person has done
before and since, he set up objections like so many
men of straw, and deliberately proceeded to knock
them down again.

At last he succeeded in crowding his conscience into
a corner, and about eleven o'clock, when every one
else in the house was fast asleep, rose from the bed
where he had tossed and turned since nine, and slipping on his clothes, softly opened the window and got
out.

The night was very dark; a light breeze blew
from the south; and the waving branches of shrubs
and trees smote Lucius gently on the face as he stole

through the plantations to the turnpike. His heart thumped violently against his ribs, for it seemed to him as if unseen hands were laying hold of him and striving to draw him back to his duty. But all these sombre thoughts took flight when he reached the rendezvous, where Ephraim, with the aid of half a dozen of his fellow-workmen, was engaged in inflating the balloon.

Three or four great torches illuminated the scene, which was to Lucius at least sufficiently awe-inspiring, for what he had last seen a tangled heap upon the floor of the cabin, now rose a vast bulk, which, passing into the mirk above the flare of the torches, seemed to rear itself into the very vault of heaven. Lucius trembled as he watched it.

'Hello! Luce,' said Ephraim, coming forward. 'Ye're hyar on time.'

Lucius attempted to reply, but the words stuck in his throat, and he only gripped Ephraim nervously by the arm.

'Purty, ain't she?' asked Ephraim with pardonable pride, as he surveyed his handiwork, which, now nearly full, and securely anchored to the ground by strong ropes, swayed to and fro in the night wind.

'She ain't big, ye know,' went on Ephraim—big! she seemed to Lucius like a vast mountain—'she ain't big, ye know, but she'll carry the like er us two shore and easy. Say, Luce,' as he felt the latter shaken by a violent shiver, 'ye ain't afraid, air ye?'

'Not I,' answered Lucius, as well as he could for his chattering teeth. 'I'm cold—I'm excited; but I'm not in the least frightened. Shall we get into the car?'

'Not yet,' answered Ephraim. 'She ain't full yet. I'll tell ye when.'

But two intolerably long hours passed before Ephraim hailed him with: 'Now then, Luce, I reckon she's ready, ef ye air.'

At the sound of his voice Lucius started. To say that the boy was merely frightened would be incorrect. He was sick and faint with a deadly, paralysing fear. The terrors of the unknown had got hold upon him with a vengeance. However, he managed to stumble forward without knowing exactly how he did it, and assisted by one of the men, scrambled into the car, where Ephraim was already standing. The next moment the balloon, released from all its bonds save one, shot up to the extent of the remaining rope.

'We'll be off in a jiffy,' said Ephraim cheerfully. 'Good-bye, boys. Take keer on yersels till we see ye again. It don't matter who ye tell now. We'll bring ye the latest news from the seat er war. Cast her loose.'

'Wait!' gasped Lucius, rousing himself by a mighty effort. 'I meant to write a message before I left home; but I forgot. One of you go up to the Hall in the morning and tell my mother I'm all right, and that I'll be back in a day or two.'

He leaned over the side of the car as he spoke, and one of the men answered him. Then, even as he looked, the torches suddenly lessened to brightly twinkling points of light, then to mere sparks, and finally went out altogether.

CHAPTER IV.

THE BALLOON COMES DOWN.

'HELLO!' exclaimed Lucius. 'What have they put out the torches for, I wonder.'

'So they hev,' said Ephraim, peering over. 'Sh! keep mum! Maybe thar's some wan tryin' ter head us off. I wish they'd let her go.' Then, as no sound broke the stillness of the night, nor could any noise of footsteps be heard, he called softly, 'Let her go!'

Instantly came back a response in his own words, as a bo'sun repeats the orders of the mate, 'Let her go!'

But the balloon remained stationary, and at last, after waiting for a moment or two, Ephraim cast prudence to the winds and shouted at the top of his voice: 'Let her go, ye durned fools. Why don't ye let her go?'

'Ye durned fools, why don't ye let her go?' was hurled back at him with savage emphasis.

'By time!' began Ephraim—when Lucius interrupted with, 'That was echo, Grizzly.'

'Echo in this yer field!' retorted Ephraim. 'Thar ain't any echo. If thar war, why didn't she up 'n

answer when I gave the boys good-bye and ye
hollered out yer message?'

'Well, it sounded like it,' persisted Lucius. 'Try
again and make sure.'

'Let her go, can't ye?' howled Ephraim, unable, in
his anxiety to be quit of mother earth, to think of
any other test. But this time there was no reply.

'What'd I tell ye?' cried Ephraim excitedly. 'Thar
warn't no echo. The or'nery skunks hev been playin'
it back on us, and now they've skedaddled and left
us anchored hyar.'

'Perhaps some one came along and scared them,'
suggested Lucius.

'I'll scare 'em wanst I git down agen,' grumbled
Ephraim. 'However, it don't amount ter a cob er
corn. I'll soon cut her loose, though sutt'nly I didn't
want ter lose that extry bit er rope.'

'It's grown very cold all of a sudden,' remarked
Lucius, as Ephraim hunted round for the lantern he
had brought. 'And wet, too. Oh!' as the Grizzly
drew the slide and flashed the light here and there.
'It's raining hard, and never a sound on the balloon.
How very odd.'

'Hyar's the rope,' exclaimed Ephraim at this junc-
ture. 'Ketch hold on the light, Luce, while I cut
her through.'

He handed the lantern to Lucius, and having
opened a formidable clasp-knife, put his hand through
the cords which rose from the car, and laid hold of
the detaining rope.

Instantly an exclamation of deep surprise escaped
him. The rope was slack.

'What's wrong now?' inquired Lucius, still occupied in wondering why the rain had made no sound. 'It has stopped raining. I can see the stars again.'

For answer Ephraim broke into peal after peal of laughter. 'Co'se ye kin! Co'se ye kin!' he shouted. 'Why, don't ye know ye must be nigh on a mile nearer ter 'em than when ye started. Ho! ho! ho!'

'What do you mean?' asked Lucius. 'We can't have gone up so high just since you cut the rope.'

'Cut the rope!' cried Ephraim. 'I never did cut the rope. See hyar.' He hauled in the slack and flung it on the floor of the car. 'While us two fust-class samples er prize ijots hez been growlin' and howlin', ole Blue Bag hyar hez been cuttin' through space like a wheel-saw goin' through a block er pine.'

'My!' exclaimed Lucius. 'Then the torches were not put out by the men?'

'Not them,' chuckled Ephraim. 'The old balloon jest lit out fer the sky and left 'em.'

'I didn't feel any movement then, and I don't now,' said Lucius incredulously. 'Are you sure we are off?'

'You kin smile,' returned Ephraim. 'You've looked yer last on the old world fer a bit. Why, that echo might hev told me, fer I read about jest such a thing in my book; but I war that flabbergasted et what ye said about the torches that I clean forgot it.'

'Was the echo in the air then?' asked Lucius.

'It p'intedly war. Thar and nowhar else. Then we got out er that belt and whoosh! through thet cloud and rain-storm, and hyar we air bright and early, all ready to give howdy to the little twinklin' stars. Hurroo!'

'But are you sure?' persisted Lucius. 'I can't believe it.'

'Waal, it's so, sonny. Ye kin see fer yerself.' Ephraim tore up some paper and flung the pieces over the side of the car, and as he flashed the light upon them, Lucius observed that they appeared to be fluttering down. 'Thet shows we're goin' up, ye onderstand,' said Grizzly.

'No, I do not understand,' answered Lucius; 'and since you know so much about it, you'd better explain.'

Ephraim needed no second bidding, but at once began a learned discourse on ballast, valves, and everything pertaining to the manufacture and management of balloons, when Lucius suddenly shrieked out: 'My ears are beating like drums, and I think my head is going to burst.'

'Ye don't say so!' responded Ephraim in unaffected alarm. 'Hello! so's mine. We must be goin' up too high. Hold on! I'll fetch her down.'

He pulled the cord which opened the valve as he spoke, and presently they were conscious of pleasanter surroundings.

'That's better,' said Lucius. 'Do you know, I think it was rather rash to come up in the dark.'

'Maybe it war,' admitted Ephraim; 'but ef we'd tried ter start in the daytime, we'd never hev come up at all.'

'We should have been stopped, sure enough,' assented Lucius, who with the absence of motion on the part of the balloon had lost most of the fear which had possessed him at the start. 'All the same, I think we might as well have waited for the dawn.'

'I don't suppose thar's much risk er a collision up hyar,' said Ephraim quaintly. 'I 'magine we've got the sky pretty much ter ourselves. But ye won't hev long ter wait fer dawn on a June night; and meantime, ef we watch the valve we'll hev no trouble.'

'That brings us down?' said Lucius.

'Ezacly. It's all jest ez easy ez fallin' off 'n a log, this yer balloonin'. When we want ter git up, ye chuck out a bag of ballast, and when ye want ter come down, ye pull the valve cord and let out a smart lump of gas. That's about the lot of it.'

'When we get back to Staunton,' advised Lucius, 'you ought to turn professional.'

'Professional what?' inquired Ephraim, who was busy setting things to rights in the car by the light of the lantern.

'Why, professional—what d' ye call him? The man who goes up in balloons.'

'Airy-nort!' shouted Ephraim joyously. 'By time! Luce, thet's a perfectly grand idee. So I will. I'll turn airy-nort and take folks up and down fer five dollars the trip. Luce, I'm obleeged ter ye fer thet idee. I p'intedly am.'

'If it helps you to get back your pile, I shall be very glad,' said Lucius rather sadly. 'I'm sure I'll be very willing to act as conductor, and rush around and get passengers for you.'

'Shucks!' observed Ephraim. 'Who's thinkin' of the pile?'

'I am,' said Lucius, 'and shall never cease to think of it until I have made it up to you in some way. I really do believe that aeronaut notion is a good one.'

'It is thet,' affirmed Ephraim with conviction, 'and I'll fix it up too; you see ef I don't.'

'I suppose you know that you are still holding the

valve cord,' said Lucius. 'How are we to get up
again if you let out all the gas?'

'By time! I forgot,' exclaimed Ephraim, releasing
the cord. 'I 'low thar's more in this yer airy-nortin'
than I thort thar war. We're abont steady now,' he
went on, throwing out some more paper in the stream
of lamplight; 'but of co'se I dunno whar we air; fer
I han't no notion how fast or how slow old Blue Bag
kin travel.'

'Well, there's not much wind,' said Lucius, 'so I
don't suppose we have gone very far. It would be
rather a joke if we found ourselves standing still over
Staunton, wouldn't it?'

'It would thet!' grinned Ephraim, 'or, better still,
ef we went hoverin' over the Yanks jest ez they war
gittin' their breakfasts.'

'By the way, where do you expect to get to?'
inquired Lucius. 'I suppose you thought it all out
before we started?'

'Waal, I kinder did, ez fur ez might be,' replied
Ephraim, 'though sutt'nly it war like enuff ter
wanderin' blindfold through a wood; but I knew jest
ez well ez everybody else thet old Stonewall war
gobblin' up the Yanks somewhar in the valley, and I
'lowed we wouldn't git much beyond Winchester
'thout lightin' on his trail.'

'Winchester! All that long way off!'

'Oh, come. It ain't so very fur ez all thet comes to,
and besides, ye air carried free, gratis, and fur nuthin'.
'Tisn't ez ef ye war asked ter walk.'

'That's all very well; but supposing the wind
changes, or has changed, and blows us to goodness
knows where. What are you going to do then?

Will there be enough gas left to bring us back again?'

'Oh! I reckon yes,' answered Ephraim rather uncomfortably, for this was a point which he had left unconsidered. 'But it don't matter much after all. It wouldn't be such a trial ez all thet ter do it on foot!'

'I shouldn't mind,' assented Lucius. 'I suppose we could find our way, and as to food—why, Grizzly, did you bring any with you? I never remembered it.'

'Thet's all right,' said Ephraim, relieved at the turn given to the conversation; 'ye'll find plenty in this bag—bread and meat and milk—and ef ye're hungry, why, ye'd better pitch in.'

'I don't mind if I do,' laughed Lucius, 'though, to be sure, it is rather early for breakfast. Oh, Grizzly,' he went on, munching the viands, 'I was in a horrible fright when we first started. I was in two minds about stepping out of the car, when old Blue Bag, as you seem to have named the balloon, shot up to the length of the rope, and then of course I was done for.'

'Ye war,' chuckled Ephraim, following suit with the provisions; 'but now ye see it's jest the nicest kind er travellin' ever invented. I 'low I warn't quite sure myself how it would be when fust we started, but I wouldn't ask nuthin' better than this. Wait till mornin' comes and we'll show our flag.'

'Flag!' echoed Lucius. 'Have you brought a flag?'

'Rayther!' said Ephraim; 'a proper one, too—stars and bars and all. I didn't want our boys ter fire on us ye know, sposin' we came too close to the ground.'

'But the Yanks will fire on us if they see the flag,' argued Lucius.

'By time! I never thort er thet,' confessed Ephraim with humility. His reasoning was not infrequently like that of Sir Isaac Newton with regard to his cat and her kitten. 'Waal, never mind, we'll do without the flag. And ez ter shootin',' he muttered under his breath, 'ef it comes ter thet, I reckon we kin stand a siege.'

Lucius did not hear this remark, and in response to his request for its repetition, Grizzly merely asserted that it didn't matter.

Providence was kind to the two lads in their ignorance, and for a couple of hours they floated peacefully along, sublimely unconscious of the dangers to which they were exposed, and chatting, with boyish disregard of the awfulness of the theme, over their chances of witnessing the most horrible sight in nature—men struggling together in bloody strife, like savage beasts of prey.

Then suddenly a red light flared up in the east, and Ephraim exclaimed cheerfully: 'Thar comes the mornin'. We'll soon larn our wharabouts now.'

But, even as he said the words, the fires of day were extinguished, a wet veil enveloped the balloon, which heeled over as a blast of bitter cold wind rushed shrieking through the cordage. A long, jagged stream of blinding light rent the cloud-bank into which they had entered, while, almost simultaneously, a stunning thunder roll reverberated all around them.

'Oh!' shrieked Lucius, burying his face in his hands. 'How awful! Let us go down. Quick! quick! The balloon will burst.'

'We can't!' gasped Ephraim, also temporarily out of his senses with fright. 'I've lost my grip of the valve cord.'

It was true. Not expecting such a contretemps, he had neglected to secure the valve cord, which at the first lurch of the balloon had swung through the cordage, and now dangled out of reach and invisible in the darkness.

Meanwhile the thunder roared and crackled, and the lightning blazed about them, and the balloon, driven this way and that by contrary currents of wind, swung from side to side, staggering back to the perpendicular; while the frail car, falling with each lurch and recovery to the utmost limit of the binding ropes, shook and whirled and bumped its miserable occupants till they were actually sick with terror and physical discomfort.

'Oh! oh!' moaned Lucius. 'I shall die! Oh! why did I ever come? I shall be killed! Oh! if it were only not so very dark!'

Suddenly there was a shout from Ephraim. Lucius knew in a dim unconscious way that he had risen to his feet and was leaning over the car during a temporary lull in the mad gyrations of the balloon, and in a few moments more old Blue Bag, bursting grandly through the storm, soared peacefully amid tranquil skies into the broad light of day.

'By time!' ejaculated Ephraim, wiping the sweat from his face, which was deadly pale. 'Thet war on'y jest in time. Thet war none too soon. What an or'nery skunk I must hev been ter fergit it.'

'What did you do?' chattered Lucius, still in deadly terror.

'Why, hove out a big lump er ballast, er co'se,'
returned Ephraim, who was fast getting his quivering
nerves under control again. 'And I do hope it'll fall
plump on one er them pesky Yanks and knock the
nat'al stuffin' out er him.—Don't ye take on so, Luce.
I 'low it war awful while et lasted—awful; but we 're
all right now. Old Blue Bag don't set me back again,
I tell ye.'

Lucius cast one despairing look upwards.

'Right!' he groaned. 'Can't you see that we 're
going up and up, and we 'll never come down again
until the balloon has been shivered into atoms. You 've
lost the cord.'

Ephraim followed the glance. Matters were certainly about as bad as they could be. The valve cord,
tangled in the rigging of the balloon, lay twisted
far up on the side of the latter, absolutely out of
reach.

'Umph!' grunted Ephraim. 'Waal, it 's a mercy
thar 's more ways than one. I'll make a hole in her
side.'

He pulled out his clasp-knife, and with a sigh for
the dire necessity of it, prepared to stab the child
of his invention. But, as he stood at the edge of
the car, his fingers, numbed with cold and wet,
lost grip of the knife in their efforts to open the
strong blade, and with a silence more eloquent than
the loudest crash, it slipped down into the cloud
depths below.

A cry of horror broke from Lucius as what seemed
to him their only means of salvation disappeared, but
Ephraim shouted loudly : 'Lend us yourn, quick ! It 's
gettin' ez cold ez a iceberg. Smart, sonny !'

'I haven't got it,' whimpered Lucius. 'I put it out to bring, but I forgot it. Oh! oh! oh! I shall be killed! I shall be killed!' He flung himself upon the floor of the car, grovelling abjectly in the desolation of his spirit.

Another nature might have upbraided Lucius and reminded him that the danger was at least equal for both of them, and that his was not the only life at stake. Not so the old Grizzly. He stooped down, and patting the cowering boy on the shoulder, said in strong, tender voice, in which lurked no perceptible note of anxiety: 'What, Luce! 'Tain't your par's son ter be kyar'in' on like thet. Stand up now—thar's a lamb—and be ready ter ketch hold on thet cord ez I sling her in.'

'What are you going to do?' Lucius would have said, but the words froze upon his lips, and with eyes that bulged with terror he watched his intrepid friend, who had kicked off his boots, and with an ashen face, but steely eyes and hard-set lips, climbed upon the rim of the car and grasped the mass of cordage above his head.

For a moment Lucius felt inclined to faint, but by a violent effort he collected his scattered wits, and shaking like an aspen leaf, leaned with outstretched hand against the side of the car.

Truly it was a fearful sight. As Ephraim, his feet twined among the cordage, slowly mounted towards the network, the balloon, drawn by his weight, careened over, so that he hung sideways—above him the illimitable blue—below, thousands of feet below him, the earth he has so rashly left. Lucius shut his eyes, and his brain reeled with the horror of the thing; but brave old Grizzly never faltered, never hesitated, only mounted inch by inch to where the valve cord rested on the bellying curve of the balloon.

At last he reached it, and freeing it swiftly, sent it inwards with a turn of the wrist. As one in a dream, Lucius saw it waving towards him, opened and shut his hand mechanically, caught it, and pulled with all his might.

'Hold on!' roared Ephraim, scrambling once more into the car. 'Don't ye lug like thet. Ye'll hev the whole gimbang ter bits, and we'll go whirlin' down quicker 'n we came up.'

He gently took the cord from Luce's trembling hand and made it fast. 'Thar,' he said, 'I reckon we've about exhausted the possibilities fer a spell. We'll take a rest, now, thank ye.—Hello!' For as he turned, Lucius flung his arms about him.

'Oh, you dear, brave old Grizzly,' sobbed the over-wrought boy. 'You've saved my life. Oh! How could you go up there in that dreadful place?'

The colour rushed back to Ephraim's face in a great wave, and while he satisfied himself by a look that the balloon was falling, he fondled and soothed the boy by his side as a mother might have done.

'Thar now, Luce; thar now,' he said tenderly, 'don't take on no more. Shucks! It warn't nuthin', now it's over. We're going down now. Steady, bub, steady; we're jist gittin' ter thet bank of storm-clouds. Thar'—drawing Lucius close to him, as the boy shivered with apprehension—'now we're through that lot, and none the worse er it. Look, Luce, look—thar's old Mother Earth. Bullee! Reckon ye'll prefer to stay down wanst ye git thar.'

Ephraim, his feet twined among the cordage, slowly mounted towards the network.

'Oh, yes,' sobbed Lucius. 'We'll get home somehow, but not in this awful balloon.'

Old Blue Bag was now rapidly nearing the earth, and had the boys had the heart to consider it, a wonderful panorama lay stretched out below them. But earth in their regard held but one joy just then—it was a resting-place, a sure haven of safety, and for its beauties they had no eye. With one hand on the valve cord, and holding a bag of ballast in the other, Ephraim regulated their descent. The grapnel was out, and as the balloon slowly sank, dragged through the tops of the trees in a thick wood. Now they were past this, and floating over open spaces again. The grapnel swept along the ground, caught under the bole of a fallen tree—and they were safe.

'Whoop!' screeched Ephraim, flinging out a rope. 'I reckon we've got thar. Over ye go, Luce.'

Lucius did not wait to be told twice. He simply flung himself upon the rope, and scrambling down, sank in a confused heap upon the ground. Ephraim followed quickly, saw that the balloon was fast and secure, and was just bending anxiously over his companion, when a sudden sound caused him to look up.

From all directions men in blue uniforms, and guns with bayonets fixed in their hands, were running towards them.

'Gloryful gracious!' murmured Ephraim, straightening up. 'Ef thet ain't the peskiest kind er luck. We've been and tumbled right inter a nest er Yanks!'

CHAPTER V.

A FIRE-EATING COLONEL.

'SURRENDER! You're our prisoner!' cried several of the soldiers, running up and presenting their bayonets at Ephraim's chest.

'Waal, I ain't denyin' it,' said Ephraim coolly. 'Reckon I kin master thet fact 'thout ye drivin' it inter me with them nasty spikes. Take 'em away.'

The men laughed, and most of them dropped the points of their weapons; but an officer, who just then came up, demanded roughly: 'Who are you? How and why do you come here?'

Ephraim considered the speaker earnestly before replying, and in that moment took his measure accurately. 'He's a hard un,' thought Grizzly. 'He'll make things hum fer us ef he gits his way.' Aloud he said, pointing to the balloon: 'Ye see how we came; and ez fer why we came, it war because we couldn't help it.'

'None of your insolence,' said the officer threateningly. 'What do you mean by you couldn't help it?'

'Jest what I sez,' returned Ephraim, 'and I hadn't no idee of bein' insolent nuther. Ye don't 'magine we

came fer the pleasure er bein' took prisoner.—I won't
rile him willin',' he added within himself.

'Will we haul down this yer balloon, cunnel, and
see if she carries anything?' asked a sergeant at this
stage.

The colonel nodded. 'Now then, you fellow,' he
said to Ephraim in a bullying tone, 'tell me instantly
what brought you here?'

'The balloon,' replied Ephraim without a pause.

'Don't humbug me,' foamed the colonel ; 'I see your
dodge plainly enough. You are trying to gain time in
order to invent a lie of some sort. But I'd have you
know I'm master here, and I'll have the truth out of
you before I'm done with you.'

'Ez fur ez that goes,' began Ephraim, when a voice
at his elbow said in clear, distinct tones : 'It is you who
are insolent. Southern gentlemen do not lie.'

Ephraim started. He had taken all the colonel's
remarks as addressed to himself, supposing that Lucius
was still lying on the ground behind him. But, unknown to his friend, the younger boy had risen on the
approach of the colonel, and taken his stand at Grizzly's
side. To give way when surrounded by dangers of
such a novel and unimagined order as those from
which he had just escaped was one thing; but with
his feet once more on *terra firma*, Luce's courage
returned, and, if he felt any uneasiness at the pre-
dicament they were in, he certainly did not intend to
betray it before the enemies he had been taught to
despise as well as to detest. Therefore, in a very
emphatic manner he delivered himself of the remark
just quoted.

Ephraim turned and looked at Lucius. The boy

E

was standing in an easy attitude, a slight flush upon
his cheeks, and a defiant light in his eyes. All trace
of his recent emotion was gone; and as he stood firmly
planted—his shoulders squared, his well-knit, youthful
figure gracefully poised—his whole bearing formed
such a contrast to that of the red-faced, swaggering
bully whom he faced, that Ephraim could not repress
a cry of admiration.

The poor Grizzly had suffered a good deal in the last
half-hour. The fright of Lucius in the balloon he
could understand, for he had been thoroughly frightened
himself; but the utter collapse of his hero was beyond
him. Not only had he known Lucius heretofore as a
sturdy, manly boy, but he had always set him upon a
pinnacle above every one else in the world, and worshipped him as a superior being, endowed with every
grace and virtue under the sun. Therefore, when
mastering his own fears, he had boldly faced a terrible
danger and overcome it by his presence of mind, the
abject, grovelling cowardice of Lucius had come upon
him with a painful shock. He had caught a glimpse
of the feet of his idol, and, lo! they were of clay. But
he covered them reverently up, humiliated rather than
proud that the accident of opportunity should have
lifted him so high, and loyally making all manner of
excuses for his comrade's conduct. All the same, he
had felt very miserable over it; but now, when he
heard the ringing scornful voice, and noted how fear-
lessly Lucius faced the colonel, all his pain fled, his
doubts were swallowed up, and a great wave of joy
flooded his honest heart. He had been right after all
—his hero was his hero still, and gold from crown to
heel.

'Whoop!' he shouted in his delight. 'Air ye thar, Luce? I didn't see ez ye riz up; but I might hev known ye wouldn't be behind when ye orter be in front. Thet's the way ter talk ter him.—A Southern gentleman don't lie, mister; thet's what he said. By time! ho! ho! ho!'

'Silence, you dog?' vociferated the enraged Federal, his dark face aflame with passion, while at the same time he menaced Ephraim with his revolver. 'I'll blow your brains out if you say another word.'

'Ez ter thet,' retorted Ephraim, his new-born joy overcoming his prudence, 'I han't been doin' the high trapeze a thousand miles up in the sky ter be skeert the moment I come down by a pesky, bunkum Yank, sech ez I jedge ye ter be.'

The colonel ground his teeth with rage, but before he could reply, Lucius pushed Ephraim unceremoniously to one side.

'Shut up, Grizzly,' he said; 'I'll do the talking.— I'll tell you the truth, if you care to listen to it,' he added to the colonel.

'Tell it then, and be quick about it,' said the latter, casting a furious glance at Ephraim. 'And talk more civilly than that low hound there, or it will be the worse for you.'

Ephraim opened his mouth, but Lucius silenced him with a look, and answered quietly:

'We left Staunton early this morning in our balloon. We only intended to have some fun; but we were nearly killed up there'—he pointed to the sky—'and were glad enough to descend anywhere. We had no idea but what we were close home. Certainly, if we'd thought your army was anywhere around, we wouldn't have been fools enough to drop right into the middle of it. That's all.'

The Federal colonel looked darkly at him.

'That's all, is it?' he sneered. 'A likely story. I'll see for myself.' He turned and walked to the balloon, round which the sergeant and half a dozen men were grouped, having hauled it down and secured it firmly to the log. 'What have you found here, sergeant?' he demanded.

The sergeant saluted, and pointed silently to a small heap of articles which had been taken out of the car and laid upon the ground. There were some bread and meat, a bottle of milk and another of water, a telescope, a revolver and a box of cartridges, a small gun—the same which Ephraim had been engaged in making when the war broke out—two bags with powder and shot, and, most compromising of all, the tiny rebel flag with its stars and bars, within the folds of which was concealed a drawing block fitted with a lead pencil.

Lucius stared in astonishment as his eyes fell upon this collection, of the existence of which—save for the flag—he had till then been unaware; for at first the darkness had concealed them from him, and afterwards, when day dawned, his terror had been too great and absorbing to allow him to notice anything. Mutely questioning, he looked at Ephraim, who, vaguely conscious of coming trouble, muttered hastily : 'It's all right, Luce. I put 'em thar. I'll tell him wanst I git the chance.'

'Be quiet,' answered Lucius in the same low tone. 'Let me speak.'

'Stop that whispering,' cried the colonel, coming

back. 'You came out for fun, I think you said,' he went on with an ugly grin on his face, 'in a balloon, too, and in time of war. May I ask, then, to what use you intended to put this armament—and this?' He held up the sketching block.

Lucius was silent, not knowing, indeed, what to answer, for the full significance of the last article had not yet dawned upon him.

'A Southern gentleman does not lie,' mimicked the colonel, a baleful light in his eyes. 'You do well to be silent, you couple of rascally spies.'

Lucius started violently. 'What!' he ejaculated in profound astonishment. 'Spies!'

'Ah!' said the colonel, 'I thought I should corner you.—Search them,' he added to the sergeant.

Nothing but a few odds and ends such as any boy might carry were found upon Lucius, but from Ephraim's pocket was drawn a piece of paper on which he had scribbled a *précis* of the news which had reached Staunton during the last three weeks, and also a road map of the valley, which he had brought with him in order that they might have some indication of their whereabouts if they were forced to descend in an out-of-the-way place.

'Ha!' exclaimed the colonel, when these were brought to light. 'A precious pair of jokers.—Now, will you persist in your denial, my fine young Southern —*gentleman?*' He laid a sneering emphasis upon the last word.

'I haven't denied anything yet,' returned Lucius. 'I 've never had the chance. I tell you we are a couple of boys out for a spree, and that 's all.'

'You 'll find it a precious unpleasant spree before I

get through with you,' said the colonel. 'You may be a boy,' he added dubiously, as though the fact were not self-evident; 'but I'd like to know what you call *him.*' He glanced malevolently at Ephraim.

'He's only nineteen,' answered Lucius, earnestly wishing that Grizzly had followed his oft-repeated advice, and razed the compromising indications of manhood from his face.

'What!' scoffed the colonel. 'Nineteen do you call him, with a monkey face like that?'

'Shave him, then, and you'll see,' answered Lucius, at which remark the soldiers roared, though the boy was perfectly serious.

'Silence!' commanded the colonel, going on to observe caustically: 'Since when have the rebels—I beg your pardon; I have no doubt that a Southern gentleman would prefer that I should speak of Confederates—since when, then, have the Confederates employed boys to ascertain the movements of the National troops?'

The insolence of his tone fired Luce's blood, and he answered scornfully: 'I do not know. Perhaps if you had not been so busy running away from them for the last three weeks, you might have been able to discover for yourself.'

Now, a more unfortunate remark Lucius could not just then have made; for it so happened that in the series of retrograde movements in which the Federals had lately been indulging in consequence of Jackson's smashing flank attacks, the colonel had taken a somewhat too prominent part. Indeed in the last melée, while gallantly leading his men out of action—very far ahead of them—he had somehow become separated from his command, and when the balloon descended, had been making his way back to the Federal lines along with a number of stragglers, whom he had picked up *en route.* So now, when Lucius, amid the suppressed laughter of the men, made his ill-timed observation, the doughty warrior's feelings overflowed, and his fury knew no bounds.

'I'll teach you to insult your betters, you rebel scum,' he shouted. 'I heard of a balloon having been lost from our lines on the Potomac. That's it, I'll take my oath. You've stolen it for your poverty-stricken, rascally, rebel friends. That's what you've done.'

'We didn't,' protested Lucius, edging in a word. 'He made it.' He indicated Ephraim.

'Did he?' stormed the colonel. 'Where did he learn to make balloons, the hairy-faced baboon? Anyhow, if you did or if you didn't steal it, I've proof enough of your object, and I'll show you how to dance upon nothing. Cut a couple of ropes from that balloon and string these cubs up to a tree!' he shouted to the men.

Lucius paled swiftly, but the colour rushed back again into his face at once, and he stood with folded arms, scornfully fronting the colonel. Ephraim, however, took a step forward.

'Ye dassn't do it, ye dirty fire-eater,' he cried. 'Ye dassn't do it, 'thout 'n a trial or nuthin'. Take us ter the ginrul, boys; he'll hear what we've got ter say.'

'String them up, I say,' roared the colonel, more incensed than ever at this defiance. 'String them up, and be sharp about it. I'll let you know,' he ground out at Lucius, 'how the gentlemen of the North treat the gentlemen of the South when they catch them acting as pestilential spies.'

'I should think it's precious little you know of gentlemen anywhere,' Lucius answered boldly back. 'I've seen a good many Northerners, and they are brave men, if they are fighting an unjust war. But what you were before they let you put on a uniform, I don't know; though it wouldn't be hard to guess from the look of you. Why, your men are ashamed of you.'

Two of the men moved slowly towards the balloon. The boy's courage appealed to them. They were soldiers, and brave soldiers too, though they were smitten with a panic now and then as brave soldiers have been before and since. They were willing enough to fight, but not to soil their hands with such a horrid deed as this. Therefore they moved slowly and reluctantly, hoping for a reversal of the order. But Ephraim changed his tone.

'See hyar,' he said submissively, 'I didn't orter hev spoke ez I did. I beg your pardon. Jest ye hear me a moment.'

But the colonel would hear nothing. He was beside himself with wrath, and could not listen to reason. The men had stopped when Ephraim began to speak, and now their commander turned furiously upon them.

'Why don't you obey orders?' he shouted at them. 'I'll have you shot for mutiny if you stand gaping there much longer. Up with them, I say.'

'Cunnel!' shrieked Ephraim in an agony of unselfish fear. 'Cunnel, don't do it. As ye're a Christian man, don't do it. Ye may string me up, and willin'. I'm a outrageous rebel. I'm a spy. I'm whatever you like. I came ter make observations. I'm a spy, I tell ye. Hang me up. But don't you tech Luce. He ain't done nuthin'. He on'y came because I told him I wuz goin' fer a trip. He knows nuthin'—he's done nuthin'. Let him go! Let him go!'

'Pah!' ejaculated the colonel. 'Do you suppose I don't see your game? You can't take me in with your heroics, you filthy cur, you.' And he spurned Ephraim with his foot.

A mist swam before Luce's eyes. His blood boiled over, and, regardless of the consequences, he rushed forward.

'You lie!' he shouted. 'It is for me he wants to die. This is the second time to-day. Take that!' and before the astonished colonel could comprehend or step aside, the infuriated boy struck him twice sharply in the face.

A look as though he were possessed came into the colonel's eyes, and his fingers closed nervously upon his revolver; but ere he could use it, if indeed it were his intention to do so, Ephraim stooped suddenly, and catching him round the legs, flung him sprawling on his back. Then, with a wild yell of 'Run! Luce, run!' he rushed for the shelter of the woods.

After him dashed Lucius, hard upon his heels, as the colonel, foaming and spluttering, staggered to his feet and discharged his revolver at random.

'Follow them!' he roared. And the men, alarmed at what might be the consequences to themselves if they refused, hastened in pursuit. But they had no heart for the game, and once out of sight among the trees, halted or scattered, and presently the fugitives, doubling like hares in and out of the dark boles, heard the noise of following footsteps die away, and sank, panting and exhausted, on the mossy carpet beneath an aged oak.

CHAPTER VI.

A FREE BREAKFAST.

'BY time!' gasped Ephraim, struggling to recover his breath. 'Thet war a narrow squeak. Hi! Luce, how ye plugged him.' He chuckled gleefully.

Lucius only nodded. He was too short of wind to attempt to speak.

'If I'd on'y had my gun, I'd hev gin him ez good ez he gin me and better,' went on Ephraim. 'D'ye reckon he war in 'arnest, Luce, with his talk about hangin', or war it on'y jest ter skeer us 'cause we riled him?'

'Just—as—well—got—away—think he—meant it,' panted Lucius, still breathless.

'Ah! waal, maybe he did. Sorter knocks out one's belief in one's feller-critters, though, runnin' up agin a pestiferous calamity like that cunnel. Howsumever, we got the bulge on him, we did. My! Luce, ye air a man right down ter yer boots!'

'I'm a miserable coward, that's what I am,' said Lucius passionately. 'After the way I behaved in the balloon, I wonder you would do anything for me.' He shuddered, though, as he spoke, at the frightful reminiscence.

'Ez ter thet,' returned Ephraim, 'nobody could say a word agin ye fer bein' sot back. 'Twar an onusual kind er stomachful fer a young man jest out fer a picnic.'

'That's all very well,' lamented Lucius, 'but I disgraced myself. You know I did.'

'Shucks!' remarked Ephraim. 'Look at what ye did jest now. But say,' he went on, wishful to close the discussion, ' we can't stay here after what that redfaced old lump er mischief said.'

'What did he say?' inquired Lucius. 'I was so busy getting away that I'm afraid I was rude enough not to pay any attention.'

'Same here,' grinned Ephraim; 'but I heard him 'tween whiles. "Foller them up," he yells ter the soldiers. "Ye'll drive 'em straight inter our lines."'

'What did he mean by that?' asked Lucius. 'I should have thought we were within the Yankee lines when we were taken prisoners.'

'Waal, we kinder war, and we kinder warn't,' said Ephraim. 'This is the way I put it up,' he went on to explain with considerable shrewdness. 'I 'magine thar must hev been a fight somewhar around hyar, and the cunnel thar, whatever his name is, has lit out er harm's way. He started off ter make his way back ter the camp, gatherin' up men ez he went along, and unfortnitly fer us, he happened ter cross the clearin' et the precise moment we came down in it.' Which, as the reader knows, is just what had happened.

'Well, he'll have a fine story to tell when he does get back to camp,' laughed Lucius.

'Won't he?' laughed Ephraim back. 'Ye may resk your last dime he won't make no small thing of it. My! I wish we could be thar ter hear him.'

'Oh, thank you,' said Lucius hilariously. 'I've had enough of him for one day. I shall be quite content to read his speech in the papers.'

'Ho! ho! ho!' guffawed Ephraim. 'Ain't ye jest ticklish, Luce!'

They were both so overjoyed at their escape from the double danger of the morning that they had no room left for further apprehension. But presently Ephraim was recalled to a sense of the gravity of the situation by the distant notes of a bugle.

'Hear thet!' he exclaimed. 'Thet tells ye. Say, Luce, it won't do fer us to set still hyar. Don't ye know this kentry's full er Yanks. It's bound ter be. We must try and make our way ter old Stonewall's lines.'

'Where are they, I wonder,' said Lucius.

'I wish I knew. Fact is, I'd no idee we could hev come so fer. I thort we must be close home.' He called it *hum*.

'So did I,' agreed Lucius. 'Old Blue Bag, as you call that horrible balloon, must have travelled far and fast.'

'I wish we war in her now,' said Ephraim disconsolately.

'Oh! no, no, no,' exclaimed Lucius vehemently. 'I'd rather be hanged a hundred times than go through that horrible experience again.'

'Waal, ye wouldn't feel the ninety-nine, after ye'd got comfortably done with the first,' said Ephraim with one of his quiet grins. 'But it don't foller, because we got into one rumpus up in the clouds, thet we'd immediately git inter another. We wouldn't go so high for one thing.'

'No, no,' I tell you,' cried Lucius, almost as terrified at the prospect as he had been at the reality. 'I wouldn't get into the awful thing again to save my life.'

Ephraim looked at him silently for a moment. Then he said with a little sigh: 'Waal, Luce, I reckon ye won't be put ter it ter make the choice, fer by this time I should say old Blue Bag has either been busted by thet pesky cunnel, or took inter camp by the men.'

'Oh!' said Lucius regretfully, 'I am real mean, Grizzly, after all the trouble you took to make it.'

'Waal, waal, I ain't keerin,' answered Ephraim hastily. 'It's gone now, and thar's an end er it. Ye'll oblige me, Luce, if ye don't say no more about it.— Hark!' as the bugle sounded once more. 'Thet tells us we'd better quit.'

'I wonder what it means,' pondered Lucius, rising to his feet.

'What, thet call?' answered Ephraim. 'Breakfast, I 'magine. I know *I* feel it must be somewhar about that time. Got yer watch?'

'No,' replied Lucius; 'I forgot that, like everything else, in my hurry to leave home.'

He thought for a minute and added: 'Say, Grizzly, how are we to know but what that bugle is being blown in our own lines somewhere? It's as likely as not.'

'Thar's suthin' in what ye say,' answered Ephraim. 'We sutt'nly don't know whether old Stonewall is ahead of us, or behind, or to the right or to the left.

We don't know nuthin', and we can't see nuthin' fer
this pesky wood shuttin' out the sky. Ef we could
see the sun, we might git an idee of the lay of the
land. We'll move on, anyway.'

'In what direction then?'

'It don't matter. All roads is alike sence we don't
know the right one. We'll move towards the music.
On'y we must feel our way cautious.'

'And keep a sharp eye for the colonel,' observed
Lucius.

'By time! yes. I wouldn't give much fer our chances
ef he gripped holt on us now after that smack in the
face ye gin him. Ef he warn't in 'arnest before, he
will be ef ever he ketches us agen.'

'He owes you one as well, Grizzly, for the tumble
you gave him,' laughed Lucius.

'I reckon,' answered Ephraim. 'But then he war
down on me right from the beginnin', 'cause he got it
inter his thick head I meant ter be impident ter him.'

They walked along for half an hour or so, entirely
ignorant of their direction, until at last the trees
began to thin out, and it was evident that they were
approaching either the edge of the wood or another
clearing. Past experience had taught them caution,
and they were wise enough not to break cover until
they had very carefully surveyed their surroundings.
It was as well. Stealing from tree to tree and tread-
ing as softly as they could, they at length reached a
point where they could see into the open.

What a sight! Grand, impressive, but just then
particularly alarming to our two boys, for right in
front of them, upon a small hillock, frowned eight
black-muzzled cannon, while a lane which led from a

handsome house to a mill beside the stream was packed with Federal troops. Camp-fires were blazing and crackling cheerily in the open, and the grateful odour of coffee was wafted to the noses of the hungry boys. Ephraim signalled silently with his hand, and as quietly as they had come, the two glided back into the friendly shelter of the deep woods. 'By time!' whispered Ephraim, when they had reached a safe point, as they thought, 'thet was a mighty nasty sight. Ef we 'd walked inter the open, we 'd hev been goners shore enuff.'

'It looked as if they were expecting something,' whispered Lucius back.

'It 's maybe old Stonewall they 're waitin' fer,' said Ephraim. 'Shucks! ef we git between their firin', we 'll be a heap wusser off 'n we war in Blue Bag.'

'That 's not possible,' affirmed Lucius, with another shudder. The impression left upon him was evidently not likely to fade in a hurry.

'My land, Luce!' exclaimed Ephraim, who had been thinking so deeply that he failed to hear his companion's remark, 'I tell ye we 're in a pretty mess.'

'Why, what 's wrong now?' asked Lucius.

'I 'll tell ye. Thar 's the Yankee army, or a right smart slice of it, way aback yander, frontin' the wood. Now it ain't likely that if they 're on the lookout for old Stonewall—and I reckon they air—thet they 'd leave this wood unguarded jest for him to pop right out on 'em and give 'em howdy while they war drinkin' their coffee. Is it, now?'

'No, it isn't,' admitted Lucius. 'Well?'

'Waal, ye may be ez shore ez ye air standin' whar ye air that the wood is full er their pickets; likely enough the last line er 'em is almost techin' noses with Stonewall's men. Anyway, we 've got 'em all round us, and between us and our own boys, wharever they may be. Ye kin make yer mind easy on thet. And it 's a mercy we han't come plump on some er 'em before now.'

'Then we 're about done for,' said Lucius. 'It 's only a question of time before we light on some of them if we keep on walking.'

'Hold on, sonny,' returned Ephraim cheerfully. 'It ain't so bad ez thet yit. It 's pretty tough, this situation is, I 'll allow; but we ain't goin' ter Fortress Monroe 'thout a worry ter git back ter Staunton. Ye see,' he went on, 'they 're bound to be pretty thick in the wood; but et the same time they can't be everywhar. We 'll keep on going cautious, and maybe we 'll out-flank 'em yit. Come on!'

'I wish we had a couple of pots of their coffee,' sighed Lucius. 'My! didn't it smell good?'

'We 'll forage ez we go along,' said Ephraim. 'Ye never know what ye 'll find ef ye keep on looking.'

The truth of this bit of philosophy presently became unpleasantly manifest, for after they had wandered on for a quarter of an hour, Lucius suddenly pulled up short with a smothered exclamation of disgust.

'What is it?' muttered Ephraim. 'D'ye see any one?'

For answer Lucius pointed with his right hand, averting his face, which was very pale. Ephraim followed the guiding finger. 'By time!' he exclaimed, 'they 've got it shore enuff.'

A few paces away and close together were the dead bodies of two Federal soldiers, lying on their backs with white, upturned faces, and sightless eyes that stared fixed up into the dense foliage that swept above them.

'Pore critters!' said Ephraim sympathetically, all feeling but that of humanity banished for the moment from his breast. 'Thar's somebody lookin' for them ez will be sorry they don't come home. Thar must hev been a rumpus round hyar lately, Luce.'

'I don't see any more,' answered Lucius, looking round; 'and there are no signs of a struggle anywhere about.'

'Why, thet's so,' admitted Ephraim, also surveying the ground. 'Waal then, how do they come ter be lyin' thar?—I'll tell ye, Luce, most likely thar war a fight yesterday, and they got wounded. Then they sot out ter fetch up ter their own lines agen, and death follered 'em up and overtook 'em before they could git thar. See hyar,' he continued, kneeling down by the fallen men, 'this one has a hole in the right side er his coat. He must hev bled ter death inside. And the other one hez got it in the leg. See, his trousers is all over blood, and he's tied his handkerchief round the place ter try and stop the bleedin'. The wonder is thet he war able to walk at all. Maybe he crawled. Pore critters! pore critters!'

'How can you bear to touch them?' said Lucius faintly. 'They look dreadful.'

'Ah!' returned Ephraim sententiously, 'it's a pictur er the war thet didn't strike us afore we set out, or maybe we wouldn't hev been in such a hurry to come. Ye kin see now, Luce,' he finished grimly, 'what we'd hev looked like ef the cunnel hed got his way.'

'Don't!' exclaimed Lucius. 'Come on. Let us get

F

out of this. We can't do them any good by staring at
them.'

'Thet's so,' acquiesced Ephraim, rising to his feet.—
'By time! thet's a good idee,' he suddenly ejaculated.
'I tell ye what it is, Luce. Ye air right when ye say
we can't do them no good, pore men; but I reckon it
won't do 'em enny harm nuther, ef we make use of
'em fer our own benefit.'

'Why, what do you mean?' inquired Lucius, bewildered. 'How can we make use of them?'

'See their clothes?' answered Ephraim. 'Ef we
git inside 'em, it'll be ez good ez a free pass ter us
anywhar about the Yankee lines. Come now, Luce,'
as the boy made a gesture of horror, 'this ain't no
time fer bein' squeamish. We're in a muss, and
we're bound to git out of it the best way we kin.
Besides, it can't hurt them, remember.'

'It's too awful!' gasped Lucius. 'It's robbing
the dead.'

'It ain't nuthin' of the kind,' retorted Ephraim.
'It's on'y their coats and trousers we want, and their
caps. I reckon Uncle Sam paid fer thet lot. And
we'll cover 'em up with our own. Come now, Luce,
do be reasonable.'

He knelt down again and with no irreverent touch
began to remove the outer garments from one of the
fallen men. 'This one's not much taller than ye air
yourself, Luce,' he said, throwing the coat and trousers
towards the reluctant Lucius. 'Ye kin take this lot.
The other man's about my height. Not so lanky,
maybe; but it'll do, I reckon. Ah! now, Luce, make
up yer mind and put 'em on. We han't got so much
time ez all thet.'

He threw off his own clothes and assumed the uniform he had chosen, and in a moment or two Lucius, bowing to the stronger will, did likewise.

'Feel in the pockets, Luce,' suggested Ephraim. 'Ef thar's ennything they set store by, I reckon we don't want to take it away from 'em.' But search revealed nothing. The dead Federals had evidently been both poor and friendless. Probably they had enlisted as substitutes, or as bounty men, no one caring where they went to or what became of them. Arms and accoutrements they had none, for these had been flung away for lightness' sake when they started on their last sad march. Quietly and carefully Ephraim laid the clothes they had discarded over the corpses, and then, turning to Lucius, who still remained distressfully silent, took him by the arm and led him away from the dismal spot.

'I wish we'd got their guns,' said the Grizzly, a few moments later. 'I'd hev felt safer thet way; but I reckon they throwed 'em off somewhar. No matter, we've found so much already thet we may run up against some in good time.'

'I hope we shall not run up against any more dead men,' said Lucius dismally.

'I'm with ye thar,' answered Ephraim. ''Tain't the purtiest sight in the world, I'll allow.—My! Luce, ye do look a spruce young soldier, I tell ye.'

'Do I?' said Lucius, smiling faintly. 'I'm afraid I don't feel very like one just now. That poor man was taller than you thought, Grizzly. The coat is all right, but the trousers are dreadfully long.'

'Roll 'em up a bit, then,' advised the Grizzly. 'Set

your cap a leetle more ter wan side. Thar, now ye'll do. Say, ain't we a pair er fust-class invaders when all's said and done?'

'You seem to have forgotten one thing,' said Lucius lightly, for he was beginning to accommodate himself to circumstances.

'And what might that be, bub?'

'Why, though no doubt we shall be all right if we meet any Federals so long as we have these uniforms on, yet, suppose we run against our own men, where shall we be then?'

'Safe, I reckon,' answered Ephraim promptly. 'I guess in thet case we'll be took prisoners, and if we're not, why, we'll give ourselves up ter the fust Confederate we set eyes on, and arsk him ter be obligin' enuff ter arrest us.'

'But supposing they shoot before they ask?' went on Lucius.

'I'll be durned ef I suppose ennything er the kind,' retorted Ephraim. 'I'll wait till it happens and then tell ye both what I think of it.—Thar's wan thing, though, Luce,' he added. 'Ye look all right in wan way, smart and spry and all thet; but ye're too young by a long sight.'

'I can't help that,' giggled Lucius, 'unless you'll lend me a bit of your beard.'

'I would and willin',' answered Ephraim seriously, 'ef it would stick on.—Hi! I've got a notion. Hold up a minnit, Luce. Ye mustn't mind ef I spoil yer beauty a bit.'

He grubbed up a handful of loose soil as he spoke, and catching hold of the astonished Lucius, rubbed it well into his face and neck.

'What's that for?' cried Lucius indignantly, starting back.

'Reckon thet's taken some er the bloom off'n ye,' grinned Ephraim. 'Hold on! I han't finished with ye yet. Plague take it, I wish I hadn't lost my knife. By time! hyar's one in the corner er this yer coat pocket. What a good thing! I never felt it before. Now, lend us yer handkercher.'

'Why,' said Lucius, handing him the required article, 'whatever are you going to do?'

'I'll show ye afore ye kin turn round,' replied the Grizzly, and opening the clasp-knife, deliberately cut his finger.

'Grizzly!' cried Lucius. 'Are you gone mad?'

'Not me,' retorted Ephraim coolly. 'Never felt more level-headed in all my life, thank ye. See thet now.'

He let the blood from his finger drip upon Luce's handkerchief until the latter was thoroughly spotted with the bright red stains.

'Now then, up she goes,' he cried; and plucking off Luce's cap, with a deft turn he bound the blood-soaked handkerchief about the boy's brow. 'Thar,' he chuckled, as he replaced the cap, and stepped backwards to survey his handiwork. 'Ye'll do now, I should say. Why, don't ye know, thet puts three or four years onter ye at once. Not ter speak er it givin' ye a look ez ef ye'd come through some tar'ble hard fightin'. We kin move along now 'thout worryin' ourselves, Luce, fer thar ain't a Yank ez is likely ter stop us, 'ceptin', ef course, ef we're seen tryin' ter pass the pickets.'

'You're a genius, Grizzly, as I've said before,' remarked Lucius. 'But I wish you hadn't cut your finger like that.'

'Pooh! 'tain't nuthin',' answered Ephraim, vigorously sucking the wounded member. 'I tell ye what it is, Luce, ef we don't git suthin' ter eat pretty soon, I'll hev ter begin on my boots. I'm thet low, ye can't imagine.'

'Can't I?' replied Lucius. 'Ever since I got that whiff of coffee in my nostrils, I've been sighing for some. Seriously, though, we must get food somewhere. We can't go on walking all day upon nothing.'

'The cunnel 'lowed he war goin' ter teach us ter dance upon nuthin',' said Ephraim, chuckling at the reminiscence. 'The very fust Yank I come across, I'm goin' up ter him to arsk him fer a bite er suthin'.'

'And suppose he hasn't got anything?'

'Oh! drap yer supposin', Luce. I tell ye it's a sartinty. But 'sposin' he han't, since ye will be always 'sposin', then I'll eat him ez he stands, and make no bones about it.'

'Supposing it's the colonel,' laughed Lucius.

'Aw, yah! No, I wouldn't tech his pesky carcass with a forty-foot pole with an iron spike on the end er it.'

'I'd give something to know whereabouts we are,' said Lucius. 'How do we know we are in the valley at all?'

'Pho!' answered Ephraim, 'I 'low I never thought er it in thet light. Er co'se we mought hev been blown across the Blue Ridge during the night; but I reckon not. I should say we're in the valley right enuff, somewhar 'twixt Staunton and Winchester.'

'That's a wide range.'

'Waal, I know thet; but it's the best I kin do fer ye till we git outer this wood and strike up agin some spot that'll serve us as a landmark.—Hello! Hyar we come ter the edge er the wood agen. Hist! now. Let's go cautious.'

Had they but known it, they were not a quarter of a mile from the spot where they had observed the Federal cannon planted, for they had simply been wandering round and round among the trees, and before long would probably have found themselves back again in view of the Federal camp. They had simply changed their direction slightly without ever getting very far from the open country, and now they halted to hold a short council of war.

'I tell ye what it is,' began Ephraim. 'Thar's no sense in our moochin' round through the woods like this, never beginnin' anywhar, and always endin' up nowhar. We'll go now and take a squint inter the open, and ef the kentry seems cl'ar, we'll march along the edge of the woods instead of through 'em. That'll be a lump better, and et the fust sign er danger we kin slip back among the trees.'

'That sounds a good idea,' agreed Lucius.

'Well, come and let us survey the ground right hyar.'

They advanced together, cautiously still, but more boldly than before, for their disguises gave them confidence, and they were not now so concerned at the prospect of meeting a stray Federal or two, provided they could keep clear of the pickets.

'Thar's not a soul in sight, Luce,' said Ephraim, peering through the trees.—'Hello! I see a house.'

'Where?' asked Lucius, edging up to him.

'Thar, a hundred yards or so away ter the left. That is, ef ye call it a house, fer I reckon it's on'y a log cabin.'

The cabin, for such it really was, to which Ephraim drew his comrade's attention, stood folded in, as it were, between two out-jutting arms of the wood. The long arm, the actual trend of the wood in the same line as the boys, swept so close to the back of the house as to almost touch it. Certainly not more than ten paces separated the one from the other. The second arm, formed by a spur of the wood springing off almost at right angles to the main forest, bounded a clearing in front and at the far side of the house. Looked at from the boys' point of view, the back of the house with a solitary window was in full view, one side partly visible, while the front and far side were quite out of their line of sight.

'Thar don't seem no one ter stop us,' said Ephraim, after they had studied the position for a few minutes. 'I vote we go up ter thet cabin, and ef the owner's ter hum, we kin arsk him fer some breakfast.'

'I like the notion,' answered Lucius, smacking his lips. 'I suppose we may take it for granted that it isn't a Yankee who inhabits the house.'

'In the valley! I should smile!' remarked Ephraim with fine scorn. 'Anyway we'll be all right, fer ef by any accident it is a bunkum Yank thet lives thar, our uniforms will fetch him. He can't help hisself when it comes to feedin' a wounded comrade.' He glanced at the handkerchief on Luce's head and grinned. 'But thar,' he went on, 'what'd a Yank be doin' farmin' in the valley? I guess it'll be all squar. Come and let's see.'

They re-entered the wood and worked their way along, keeping well within the trees until they came opposite to the back of the cabin. The window, or rather hole in the wall which did duty for such, was destitute of glass, and the shutter which served to close it swung idly on creaking hinges in the light morning breeze.

'Smell that!' said Ephraim, sniffing the air. 'The old man, whoever he is, has got hot coffee fer breakfast. This ain't no fat thing, I reckon. Oh, no!' He rubbed his hands together gleefully.

'On you go, then,' urged Lucius. 'Only go easy. We don't want to put our heads into a hornet's nest.'

They left the cover of the woods, and crossing the narrow strip of ground, approached the window and looked into the cabin.

It was a one-roomed affair, built entirely of logs, with no flooring and no ceiling. Only under the roof three or four strong rafters ran from end to end, and across these at one end were laid half a dozen stout planks or slabs, forming a makeshift loft. The remainder of the roof space was vacant and unboarded. Not quite opposite to the window was the door, which was closed, and in the middle of the solitary chamber stood—oh! gracious and appetite-inspiring sight!—a rough-hewn table, covered with all manner of delicacies. A pot of steaming coffee was flanked by three or four tin cups full of milk, and a fine cut of ham stood royally among tinned meats of sorts, broken biscuits, and last, but not least, a jar of jam. And all this spread of dainties stood unheeded. Apparently there was no one to enjoy it.

'By time!' whispered Ephraim. 'Did ever ye see

the like? The old man is goin' ter hev a good time fer once, I 'magine. Step right in, Luce. We won't wait till he comes in. I'm sartin he'd like us to make ourselves at home.'

'Hush!' whispered Lucius back warningly. 'I am sure I hear some one.'

'Keep still, then, till I go and reckoniter,' breathed Ephraim. 'I won't be a minnit.'

He stole away round the hut, and presently returned, his face purple, and the sleeve of his tunic stuffed into his mouth to prevent the inward laughter which convulsed him from finding outward expression. 'By time!' he chuckled softly, as soon as he had regained his self-command. 'Sech a joke! Lay low, Luce. Say nuthin'; but laugh!'

'Why, what is it?' whispered Lucius. 'What did you see?'

'Ye'd never begin ter believe it,' responded Ephraim in the same soft undertone. 'Who d'ye think thet breakfast's fer? Why, fer the Yankee gin'ruls theyselves. There's a knot of 'em way yander in the clearin' 'sputin' 'bout suthin'; and there's a sentry marchin' up and down before the door as stiff as a ramrod. By time! it's lucky they didn't think of guardin' the window.'

'It was the sentry I heard,' said Lucius.

'I reckon. No matter. In with ye, bub. We'll help 'em through with some er thet ham and them crackers, and be off again before ye kin say knife.'

Lucius needed no second invitation, and followed closely by Ephraim, climbed noiselessly through the window. Without loss of time they drank off the mugs of milk, leaving the coffee untasted, because it was so very hot, and delays were dangerous. Then, while Lucius stuffed his pockets full of crackers, Ephraim employed his clasp-knife to better purpose than cutting his own fingers by slicing off a goodly wedge of the ham.

'Ready, Luce?' the Grizzly whispered, his face beaming with delight at the humour of the thing. ''Twon't do ter wait fer our hosts. There'd be a leetle too much ter pay.'

Lucius nodded. He had just absorbed an enormous mouthful of jam, and was consequently unable to speak. But he sneaked to the window after Ephraim.

'Bring the jam along,' whispered the latter. 'It'll go fine with the crackers.'

He thrust his head out of the window, preparatory to climbing out, but instantly drew it in again with a low exclamation of intense disgust.

'What is it?' asked Lucius, who naturally could not see.

'Thar's a whole posse of soldiers jest ter the right at the edge er the woods,' replied Ephraim. 'They're settin' on the ground, so I reckon they mean ter stay. We're trapped, Luce, and thet's a fact. Ef it warn't fer thet pesky sentry outside the door with his gun and all, we'd make a dash fer it, and never mind the gin'ruls. Ez it is, we're done. No matter; we'll jest hev ter brazen it out the best way we kin. They'll take us fer two of their own men, and they can't shoot us fer keepin' ourselves from starvin'.'

'Why not get up there and hide? It's as dark as night,' suggested Lucius, who in looking round the hut had discovered the improvised loft mentioned above.

'Git up whar?' inquired Ephraim, who had not noticed it. 'By time! The very place. Up with ye, Luce. They 're comin' up. Hear their talk.'

Lucius replaced the jam upon the table, and making a leap from the ground, caught hold of one of the rafters and swung himself up on to the planking. Ephraim only waited to scatter a few crackers by the window and fling a couple more outside, and then he too sprang up and joined his comrade.

'What did you do that for?' asked Lucius.

'Ye 'll see when they come in. Mum 's the word! Hyar they air.'

They retreated to the farthest extremity of the planking, against the gable of the hut, where they threw themselves down at full length ; for, as Grizzly remarked, they might have to stay there for some time, and it would not do to run the risk of becoming cramped.

Their faces were towards the open space where the table was set, and themselves completely hidden, not only by their position but by the surrounding gloom, they could see clearly all over the room, except immediately underneath them.

Scarcely had they taken their positions when the door swung open, and with a loud clatter of voices and jingling of swords, three Federal officers entered the hut.

CHAPTER VII.

'HA!' exclaimed the foremost of the three officers, who wore the uniform of a general, 'I don't know about you, gentlemen, but I am quite ready for my breakfast.— Eh! What! Who? The dickens!—Here, sergeant! Orderly-sergeant Cox!'

'Sir!' answered the orderly-sergeant, dashing into the hut at the loud, imperative summons.

'What is the meaning of this?' demanded General Shields, for it was he. 'What is the meaning of it, sir?' he thundered, as Sergeant Cox simply stared at him without attempting to reply.

'Meaning, sir? Meaning of what, sir?' stammered the bewildered orderly at last.

'Of this,' vociferated the general, pointing to the table. 'Look at that ham! Look at those crackers! Observe the jam! Where is the milk?'

'Ham, sir! Yes, sir. Jam, sir! No, sir. Milk— crackers, sir,' stuttered the unfortunate Cox, ruefully regarding the denuded table, the lacerated ham, and the empty mugs, which but a few moments before he had himself seen filled with rich creamy milk.

A loud snort burst from Lucius, who, between the angry face of the general and the utter amazement of the orderly, found the situation too much for him, and would simply have suffocated had not this timely explosion of mirth suddenly relieved him. Fortunately the sound was swallowed up in the shout of laughter which, at the same moment, broke from the other two officers, in the midst of which Ephraim found time to whisper hurriedly :

'It's too funny, Luce. But hold up. Don't ye do that agen, or we're ruined shore and certain.'

'Ha! ha! ha!' roared one of the officers, a stout, good-humoured-looking brigadier. 'Evidently a foraging party has been beforehand with us. By George! general, it's a mercy they left us so much as a single cracker. You had better have taken my advice and had breakfast outside, notwithstanding the tendency of the bugs to drop uninvited into the coffee. Ha! ha!'

The angry look died out of General Shields's eyes, the wrinkles at the root of his nose smoothened out again, and after a momentary struggle he gave way and joined heartily in the laughter of his subordinates. 'Well, well, it can't be helped now,' he said—'it is the fortune of war ; but if I can lay hands on the rascal who has played us this trick, I'll—I'll feed him on jam till he's so sick of it, he won't be in a hurry to plunder his general again.' He broke into fresh laughter, till, remembering the presence of the orderly, he restrained himself, and inquired sharply, 'What are you doing there?'

Orderly-sergeant Cox, who, now that his terror and confusion had been sent to the right-about by the hilarity of the officers, would have given a good deal to be able to express his own feelings in the same way, saluted silently, swung on his heel, and made for the door.

'Stop!' ordered the general, and Cox swung round again, managing by a violent effort to dismiss the grin which he had allowed to overspread his features the moment he had turned his back.

'Any news of Colonel Spriggs?' asked General Shields.

'Can't say, sir.'

'Very good. My compliments to him, when he returns, if he returns, and I wish to see him at once.'

'Here, sir?'

'Anywhere. Wherever I happen to be. I can be found, I suppose.'

'Very well, sir,' and with another salute Orderly-sergeant Cox withdrew.

'I believe that beggar knows more of this than he cares to say,' observed General Shields, mournfully regarding the remains of the ham.

'Oh, not he,' laughed the fat brigadier; 'I never saw a fellow look so utterly flabbergasted. No, no, general, your thieves have come and gone through this window. See, here are some of the spoils dropped both inside and out.'

Ephraim nudged Lucius gently, as much as to say: 'Now you see my object in scattering the crackers there. It was to distract attention from our hiding-place.' And Lucius answered by a responsive nudge, which signified comprehension.

'There are the thieves, or I am much mistaken,' continued the brigadier, as his eye fell on the soldiers who were resting on their arms at the edge of the wood. 'But I imagine it would be hopeless to try and get an admission out of them.'

'Better make the best of what is left,' said General Shields. 'Fall to, gentlemen. It is half-past six now, and news from the bridge should soon reach us.'

Only half-past six! The boys heard this announcement with surprise. True, they had dropped from the clouds very shortly after daybreak; but the long light of the summer morning, and the crowding of so many events into a short space, had confused their sense of time, and they had imagined it to be much later.

The day had begun early for more than Lucius and Ephraim. Movements were afoot which were destined to bring about very important results, and the news from the bridge, which the Federal general so calmly anticipated, was likely, when it arrived, to disturb his equilibrium a good deal more than the loss of his breakfast.

For the last four and thirty days, Stonewall Jackson had been making matters very lively for the northern invaders. He was considerably outnumbered, but with such consummate skill did he handle his forces, that he was able to attack and beat the Federal generals in detail, one after another; nor, chase him up and down as they would, could they ever succeed in effecting a combination of their entire armies against him. Indeed, the rapidity of Jackson's movements astounded the Federals, for scarcely did they receive reliable news of him in one place than he was upon them in another, and considering the number and vigour of their marvellous forced marches, it is no wonder that his brigades proudly christened themselves 'Stonewall Jackson's Foot Cavalry.'

After defeating Milroy, Jackson had rushed through
the valley to Winchester, where he fell upon General
Banks so fiercely and suddenly that the latter was
driven in the wildest confusion clear across the
Potomac. The dashing Confederate leader then
retreated up the valley by the great turnpike,
hotly pursued by Frémont, who could not, however,
succeed in bringing him to bay. Shields, meanwhile,
had moved up the south-eastern bank of the Shenandoah, and, by co-operation with him, Frémont
thought at last to crush the daring rebel. But by
a master-stroke Jackson burned the bridge at the
mouth of Elk Run Valley, over which Shields would
have led his troops—for owing to heavy rains the
Shenandoah was not fordable—and took up his position at Port Republic, a little village situated on the
south fork of the river. Shields, therefore, advanced
to Lewiston, the farm of a General Lewis, and there
awaited instructions from Frémont, who was but a few
miles off at Harrisonburg. But he might as well have
been a thousand miles away, for between the two
generals rolled the impassable Shenandoah, and the
building of bridges in face of an enemy so vigilant
and daring as Stonewall Jackson was a proposition
that could not be seriously considered. Nevertheless,
communication had been somehow effected, and it so
happened that, on the very night that Ephraim and
Lucius left Staunton in the balloon, the Federal
generals had arranged a combined attack upon the
restless Jackson for the next day. Frémont was to
advance from Harrisonburg to Cross Keys and engage
the Confederate left under Ewell, while at the same
moment Shields, by a successful dash across the bridge

G

at Port Republic, was to carry the little town and
crumple up the rebel right. But Jackson's cool head
and war-trained mind had foreseen this combination,
and his own plans had been formed to keep Shields
just where he was on the south-eastern bank of the
river until Frémont had been disposed of. When
therefore the boys took refuge in the loft, and the
Federal officers turned their attention to their dese-
crated breakfast, Frémont and Ewell were already
confronting one another at Cross Keys, while Shields's
cavalry were on their way to rush the bridge at
Port Republic and clear the road for the passage of
the infantry and artillery. For some time the officers
devoted themselves exclusively to their breakfast, but
at last General Shields broke the silence by observing, 'I think we shall fix Jackson this bout.'

'If the bridge at Port Republic can be carried,'
agreed the brigadier cautiously.

'If !' repeated Shields with some irritation. 'There
is no *if* about it, sir. It must be carried. It cannot
fail to be. The whole attention of the enemy will be
by this time centred on their left to repulse Frémont's
demonstration at Cross Keys. By ten o'clock my head-
quarters will be at Port Republic.'

The brigadier did not answer, but he thought his
own thoughts. He was not above learning a lesson,
even from an enemy, and his experience of Stonewall
Jackson as a leader and strategist led him to believe
that this confident, even boastful tone was not justified
in the face of recent happenings in the valley. However, he was silent in the presence of his commanding
officer.

'Jackson will not expect an attack on the bridge,'

went on Shields, enclosing a slice of ham between two
biscuits. 'He will know nothing of the movement
until he finds himself driven out of Port Republic, and
then it will be too late.—By the way,' he broke off,
'that reconnaissance yesterday was shamefully mud-
dled.'

'It was,' agreed the brigadier; 'and if you will
excuse my saying so, I thought it rather an error of
judgment to entrust it to Colonel Spriggs. You
remember his appearance at Bull Run.'

'His disappearance, you mean,' corrected General
Shields with a grim smile. 'Well, perhaps it was;
but I couldn't well help myself.'

'I am at a loss to know why we are bothered with
such a fellow,' put in the third officer, a staff colonel.

'Yes, heartily confound all these political generals
and colonels,' said Shields. 'If those meddling carpet
warriors would only mind their own business, and
leave us to manage ours in the field, instead of inces-
santly pulling the ropes, we should have another story
to tell. This fellow Spriggs and others like him are
pitched into colonelcies and even higher commands by
their friends the politicians, while the real soldiers go
begging for a place, or, rather than do nothing, serve
their country unostentatiously in the ranks.'

'He has good stuff in his regiment, too,' said the
brigadier. 'The "Trailing Terrors," or whatever
ridiculous name he calls them by, are stark fighters
when they get a chance, or are properly led.'

'Which they never will be, so long as Spriggs is in
command of them,' answered Shields testily. 'I've
made the most urgent representations about the
fellow, and no notice has been taken. I daren't relieve

him of his command on my own responsibility, though
I am supposed to be at the head of this army.' He
laughed rather bitterly.

'Such a fellow is a disgrace to us all,' remarked the
brigadier emphatically. 'A bully, a fire-eater, and
a '——

'A dirty coward,' finished Shields for him. 'You
may as well say it at once. I agree with you. He *is*
a disgrace to us—he and a few more like him—a dis-
credit to the whole North. The actions of the ruffianly
crew of whom he is a most admirable example do more
to inflame the South against us than anything else.
Confound them!' he fumed; 'it is beyond their comprehension that even war may be waged in a gentle-
manly fashion.'

'You 've got to start with a gentleman, though, you
must remember,' laughed the brigadier.

'I know,' said Shields discontentedly. 'Oh, hang
him! I wish I were well rid of him. He is reported
missing since last night, and it may be that some
obliging rebel has done what I have not the power to
do—relieved him of his command by a timely and
well-aimed bullet.'

'Not while there was a tree between him and
Johnny Reb,' chuckled the brigadier. 'I am afraid
you must not look forward to any such easy solution
of your difficulties with him.'

'Pah!' ejaculated General Shields in deep disgust.
'I '——

The sentence was never finished, for at that moment
the door was flung open, and Orderly-sergeant Cox,
advancing into the hut and saluting, announced:

'Colonel Spriggs!'

Closely following on the orderly's heels came the subject of the above instructive conversation, and it was with something like a thrill of dismay that the watchers in the loft recognised in him the red-faced tyrant from whose clutches they had so recently escaped. Ephraim gave Luce's arm a warning squeeze, and if they had been quiet before, they lay doubly still now.

General Shields returned the colonel's salute with exceeding stiffness and the scantiest courtesy. 'You were reported missing, sir,' he observed drily. 'I congratulate you on your reappearance after the fight.' At which the brigadier put up his hand to his mouth to conceal a smile.

Colonel Spriggs, however, did not appear to perceive the sarcasm. 'Yes, general,' he replied, 'it was pretty warm work while it lasted. The Rebs got us in a tight place, and I fear that a considerable number of my poor lads have stayed behind on the field. But no matter, sir. The "Trailing Terrors," with Josiah B. Spriggs ahead, will go on till the last man is annihilated.'

'I wish you might be annihilated to start with,' thought General Shields within himself. Aloud he said: 'Your reconnaissance was a complete failure, colonel.'

'It was, sir,' acknowledged the colonel. 'I admit it. But it was not my fault. I made the most superhuman efforts to induce the men to advance in the face of the most withering musketry fire it has ever been my lot to stand up to. But they refused.'

'I thought you said they would follow you anywhere,' remarked General Shields caustically.

'Oh! Ah! yes, certainly; so I did,' answered Spriggs, a little flustered. 'But the circumstances were exceptional. All that men could do they did. I myself'——

'I see,' interrupted the general. 'How many men do you suppose you lost?'

'Company D was pretty well cut to pieces, and of the rest—but really at present I cannot give you accurate information. In leading a charge through the woods I was struck by a spent ball, which yet had sufficient force to stun me. My men passed over me as I lay, and when I came to myself I was alone. What came of that charge I cannot tell you; but, doubtless, the men, deprived of their leader, and convinced already of the desperate nature of the enterprise, would naturally fall back.'

'No doubt,' acquiesced General Shields; 'and, no doubt also, your failure to rejoin your regiment completed the disaster, while at the same time it gave rise to the report that you had been killed.—And may I be forgiven for devoutly wishing you had been,' he added mentally.

'My failure to rejoin my regiment was due to the fact that I could not find it, sir,' answered the colonel with some heat, for thick-skinned as he was, he could not fail at last to detect the undertone of contempt in the general's voice. 'Am I to understand, sir, that you imply that I have in any way failed in my duty?'

'I imply nothing, colonel,' replied General Shields. 'I may be permitted to say this, though, that I wish most earnestly that your "Trailing Terrors," as I understand you call your men, would now and again trail in the direction of the enemy instead of so persistently keeping their backs turned to them.'

'General,' began Spriggs, but General Shields held up his hand.

'And I am not to be taken as implying,' he went on, 'that your men are any less courageous than others under my command. Bad soldiers, properly led, may win a battle. Good soldiers, improperly led, will very usually lose one.'

At this stinging speech Colonel Spriggs's red, bloated face became purple. Here was an implication with a vengeance, and there was but one inference to be drawn from it. Moreover, Spriggs dared not attempt to reply, for he knew well enough that General Shields detested him, and only waited for the opportunity of direct and irrefragable proof of his cowardice to make short work of him. Therefore he swallowed his wrath and merely mumbled something about having done his best. But he registered a vow in his heart that four and twenty hours should not pass without a letter from him to his friends the politicians, in which General Shield's name should figure with a very black mark indeed against it.

'I do not doubt that you do your best, sir,' returned the general; 'I do not doubt it at all.'

The irony of the tone was sharp almost to fierceness, and Colonel Spriggs judged it wiser to give the conversation a rapid turn. It was with something like humility that he remarked:

'I have a report to make, general, concerning an incident that occurred as I was making my way back to the lines this morning.'

'Proceed, sir,' said the general stiffly.

'I had fallen in with some of our fellows,' began the colonel, 'not my own men, and we were just casting about for some means to provide ourselves with some breakfast—which I may tell you we did not succeed in getting,' he added, casting a longing look at the table.

'Help yourself, sir,' said General Shields with cold courtesy. Spriggs did not require any urging, but rapidly made an attack upon the remains of the feast, talking as he ate.

'We had approached one edge of a clearing on the other side of these woods,' resumed Spriggs, 'when an exclamation from one of the men called my attention to a singular, I may say, a phenomenal sight. It was nothing less than a balloon, descending into the clearing.'

'A balloon!' echoed the three officers.

'Yes, gentlemen, a balloon. It instantly became clear to me that this was a device of the enemy for the purpose of reconnoitring the position of the national forces, and I thanked my stars that I was on the spot with a handful of brave men to stop their treasonable devices.'

The brigadier's hand again went up to his mouth, and General Shields inquired in a dry voice: 'Am I to understand, colonel, that what you saw was a species of air galley, filled with desperate rebels?'

'Ah! no,' replied the colonel, considerably taken aback; 'I told you it was a balloon. Its occupants were two in number.'

'Two!' interjected General Shields. 'You and your brave handful would make short work of them, eh?'

'We did, sir,' answered Spriggs with a ferocious

grin. 'No sooner had they landed than I rushed up to them, and after a determined struggle, during which I was once thrown to the ground, succeeded in overpowering them.'

At this extraordinary farrago of truth and lies, the two boys interchanged nudges.

'The ruffians were armed to the teeth,' went on Spriggs, 'and in the balloon car we found a perfect armament. They had evidently meant mischief. I had them searched, and on the person of one of them were found plans of our positions, and papers loaded with accurate statistics of the number and disposition of our forces.'

Ephraim's mouth pursed up as though he were about to whistle, so great was his amazement; and as the colonel paused to take a drink of coffee, General Shields said interrogatively: 'You doubtless have those papers with you now?'

'Ah! no,' answered Spriggs in some confusion. 'I destroyed them at once, lest by any inadvertence they should fall into the hands of the enemy.'

'You did wrong, sir,' said General Shields with asperity. 'Those papers should have been brought to camp and handed to the provost-marshal. Well, go on with your story.'

'It is finished in a word,' resumed Spriggs. 'I regret to say that owing to the extreme carelessness of the men, the two prisoners took to their heels and escaped into the woods, while I was absorbed in the contents of the papers.'

General Shields gave vent to an exclamation of impatience. This man tried him almost beyond his powers of endurance.

'Of course I sent the men in pursuit of the spies,' said the colonel, concluding his surprising statement. 'They did not belong to my regiment, and they did not reappear; so I finally made my way to the camp to report the circumstances to you.'

General Shields thought for a moment. Then he said brusquely: 'Thank you. I do not think there is any more to be said. If you have finished your breakfast, you will oblige me by joining the remains of your command, which you will find some two miles to the rear of Lewiston.'

Spriggs rose and saluted. 'General,' he said, 'I do not like to admit myself beaten. The woods are full of our men, and it is well-nigh impossible that those two spies should have passed our pickets. With your permission I will take half a company and thoroughly beat the woods. As likely as not I shall run them down.'

'Certainly, colonel, you have my full permission,' answered General Shields with great alacrity. 'You have probably heard,' he added, with curling lip, 'that an advance on Port Republic is just now in progress. But I will not allow a little thing like that to interfere with your laudable desire to volunteer for a dangerous service.'

Colonel Spriggs bit his lip, and down went another black mark against General Shields. But his desire for revenge, and a chance to exhibit his petty tyranny, assisted him to accept the snub in silence, and he simply replied: 'I am obliged to you, sir. I will start as soon as possible.'

'By the way, what did you do with the balloon?' inquired Shields.

'Left it where it was,' answered the colonel. 'I could not very well do otherwise.'

'Hm!' said Shields. 'Well, I'll see about it later. Good-morning, sir.'

Spriggs saluted again, but at the door he turned. 'I suppose, general,' he inquired, 'that if I come up with those two spies, you give me full discretionary powers?'

General Shields, who was already deep in thought, heard the question without grasping its significance, and muttered absently, 'Yes, oh yes, of course,' whereupon Spriggs immediately left the hut.

Three or four minutes later, the general, coming out of his reverie, and having still the sound of the question in his ears, exclaimed suddenly: 'Discretionary powers! What do you mean by that?'

'It is very evident,' answered the brigadier. 'And you have given him full permission to hang the two fellows out of hand.'

'Confound the man!' muttered the general, walking quickly to the door. But Spriggs was already out of sight. 'Well,' he said, returning, 'it does not matter much, for after all they are spies, and it is a hundred to one that he never finds them.'

To the two listeners in the loft it mattered a good deal, but unfortunately their position made protest out of the question.

'The sight of that red-faced bully always sets my right foot tingling, so great is my desire to kick him,' went on the general, irritably.

'His incompetence is on a par with his cowardice. Imagine now his allowing those two men to escape.'

'His anxiety to retake them was very genuine,' said

the brigadier. 'It seems to me,' he commented shrewdly,
'that there is a personal motive underlying his zeal,
though what, or why, it is difficult to say.—What are
you staring at, general?' he broke off. 'Why, good
gracious!'

Alas and alas! From the loft was proceeding a
most singular shower. Plop! Plop! Plop! Plop!
one after another in regular succession, a cascade of
biscuits descended from the planking to the floor, each
as it fell shivering into fragments after the fashion of
the renowned Humpty Dumpty. No wonder that the
general stared.

'Ha! ha! ha! ho! ho! ho!' roared the jovial brigadier. 'I never thought of that. That is where your
breakfast vanished to, general. And where the crackers
are, there also is the ham, I'll bet a trifle.'

'Come out of that, whoever you are!' ordered the
general sternly. 'Come out of that at once.'

This denouement was due to the unfortunate Lucius,
who, in wriggling into a more comfortable position,
had burst open the front of his tunic, in which a
quantity of biscuits had been bestowed. As the first
of these touched the floor, Ephraim grasped his comrade
by the back of the neck and pinned him down as in a
vice. Then as the general's loud command rang out,
he put his mouth close to Luce's ear, and just breathed
into it: 'Lie low, Luce, lie low. I see a way out er
this muss. Don't move now for the life of ye, whatever
ye see me do.'

'Come out of that, I say,' repeated the general.
'Do you want me to come and fetch you?'

This being the very last thing that Ephraim desired,
he slowly uncoiled his long length, and swinging upon

the rafter, dropped to the floor, where he stood the very picture of sheepishness, his mouth wide open, and a most comical expression—half-humorous, half-terrified appeal in his big gray eyes. But he took care to leave the piece of ham behind him.

The fat brigadier retreated to the wall of the hut, and laughed till the tears ran down his cheeks.

'Well, if this doesn't beat everything I ever saw or heard of!' he gasped. 'What will you do with him, general? Shall I take him to the provost-marshal for a round dozen, or will you have him shot right away? For my part, I think he deserves the rest of the break-fast for his impudence.'

'Silence!' said the general severely, though his eyes twinkled.—'What were you doing there?' he demanded of Ephraim.

The Grizzly drew himself up and saluted. 'I beg yewr parding, ginrul,' he answered in a weak, whining tone; 'I war jest parsing the windy, and when I looked in and see that right down, first-clarse spread, I tell yew I jest felt I had ter hev some.'

Lucius quivered with amazement. The Grizzly was coming out in a new line. The soft Southern voice with its clipped syllables was gone, and in its place was the slow drawl and marked nasal twang of the New Englander. The very expression of the face was changed, though this Lucius could not see. The natural shrewdness was gone out of it, and only good-humoured, dull vacancy reigned in its stead.

'Upon my word, you are a nice young man,' said the general, smiling in spite of himself at Ephraim's ridiculous appearance. 'What do you mean, sir, by making free with my breakfast? Don't you know I could have you court-martialed and shot for this?'

'Oh lordy, lordy! don't you do that, ginrul,' whined Ephraim, seemingly in a paroxysm of terror. 'I'll never dew it again. Yew don't know how hungry I war. Lemme off, ginrul! Lemme off!' He clasped his hands supplicatingly.

The brigadier exploded again, and Shields, with a good-natured laugh, said: 'Well, we'll consider what is to be done with you. Who are you, and to what regiment do you belong?'

'Number twenty, Company D, the "Trailing Terrors,"' drawled Ephraim.

'What! You are one of Spriggs's "Trailing Terrors," are you? By Jove! you look it. Why did you not come out just now when your commanding officer was here?'

'Bekase he war telling lies!' boldly answered Ephraim to the supreme astonishment of Lucius; 'and I never could abide lies.'

'Lies!' echoed General Shields. 'What do you mean, sir? Are you aware that you are speaking of your superior officer?'

'I know that, ginrul,' replied Ephraim, adding with a subdued grin: 'I ain't saying nuthing worse about him than I've heard this morning. All the same, he war telling lies about that balloon. I war thar, so I guess I should know.'

'You were there!' repeated General Shields. 'I understood the colonel to say that none of his men were on hand.'

'Upon my word, you are a nice young man,' said the general.

'Waal, I war thar, whether he saw me or not,' insisted Ephraim.

'Well, what happened?' asked the general, interested.

'Part of what he said, a good deal he didn't say, and a heap less than he did say,' returned Ephraim oracularly. 'The balloon came down right enuff, and thar war two folk in it. They got out and were surrounded instanter. They never raised a finger tew resist. How could they when there war ba'nets agin their chests, and they war nuthing but a couple of boys.'

'Boys!' exclaimed the general in a tone of incredulity. 'What could boys be doing sailing about in a balloon?'

'I guess that's their business,' answered Ephraim. 'Anyhow, thar they war, and what they said and what they stuck tew war that they had made a balloon, and jest came out fer a bit of a spree.'

'But the arms and the plans?' interrogated the general.

'Waal, I allow they had a leetle gun and a pepperbox; but who wouldn't these days?' said Ephraim. 'And as tew the plans, they warn't nuthing but a road map of the valley and a small bit of paper with the news of the war so far as it's got. I saw that, so I know.'

'But what about the struggle?' put in the brigadier.

'I'm coming tew that. Ye see, the kernel he questioned the two boys, he did. One of them war about nineteen and the other sixteen, I should say, or thar-abouts. Fact is, they told him so; but he could git nuthing out of 'em but that they war jest out fer a spree. The leetle one up and told him straight, says

H

he: "Southern gentlemen don't lie." That's what he
said.'

The officers all smiled. 'Well?' said the general as
Ephraim paused.

'Waal, sir, he wouldn't begin tew believe 'em, and
because he couldn't find out nuthing agin 'em, he says:
"Cut a couple of ropes from that balloon and string
these cubs up tew the nighest tree." That's what he
said.'

'What!' vociferated the general. 'Do you mean to
tell me he gave orders for them to be hanged?'

'Jest that,' nodded Ephraim; 'and they war nuthing
but boys, I let yew know. Waal, the men didn't like
the job, and thar war some hanging back instead of
hanging up; and the kernel he got madder than ever,
and when the older boy up and arsked him ter let 'em
orf, he up and kicked him.'

'The brute!' interjected the general, and Ephraim
went on:

'With that the leetler boy got mad, and he runs up
tew the kernel and ketches him one, two, right in the
face, and before he could turn, the other boy grabbed
him round the legs and laid him on his back; and
before yew could say "Abe Lincoln," the two of 'em war
off tew the woods.'

'Bravo!' exclaimed the brigadier. 'I am glad of it.
Were they followed?'

'They war,' replied Ephraim; 'but I guess the men
didn't want tew ketch them, for they got clean off.'

'That is a very different story,' commented General
Shields, when Ephraim had brought his narrative to a
close. 'Still, there are some things to be explained.
The presence of the balloon is itself suspicious, and it

is incredible that they should have made it themselves.'

'That's what they said, anyhow,' remarked Ephraim.

'Quite so; I understand that,' said the general. 'I
suppose,' he added after a pause, 'you would have no
objection to repeat your story if brought face to face
with Colonel Spriggs?'

'Nary a objection,' replied Ephraim with alacrity;
'if ye fetch him back, I'll say it all over agen.' For,
seeing the general's mood, and having heard his avowed
detestation of Spriggs, he began to wish that he had
thrown himself upon the former's generosity to start
with. However, he thought within himself that
there would be no difficulty about that when the time
came.

General Shields scribbled a few lines in his pocket-
book and tore out the leaf: 'Colonel Spriggs, if you
come up with the two men who escaped from the
balloon this morning,' he read out to his officers, 'you
will detain them as prisoners and bring them before
me, without taking further action.'

'I'll send that on to him in the first instance,' he
said, signing the paper.—'Orderly!' But there was
no answer. Cox had, for the time being, disappeared.

'Confound the fellow!' said the general. 'What does
he mean by going out of call?—No matter,' he continued to Ephraim, 'you can take the note yourself.
Your regiment—what is left of it—is a couple of miles
in rear of Lewiston. It will not be in action to-day.
—Well, why don't you go?' as Ephraim took the note,
but made no effort to depart.

'Ef ye please, ginrul,' replied the Grizzly with his
most sheepish air, 'I'd be obleeged tew ye, if ye'd let

me take the ham. I guess you won't want it now, and I left it up thar.' He pointed to the roof.

General Shields burst out laughing. 'Well, you are a "Terror," indeed,' he said. 'Take your ham, by all means. I don't want it, as you say.'

Ephraim instantly swung himself up on the rafter, and while making a great clattering among the planks, as though looking for his ham, contrived to whisper: 'Lie low, Luce. I'll come back fer ye, wanst they go away. We're close ter our own lines.' Then he dropped down again, and with his precious burden hugged close to his breast, saluted awkwardly and turned to the door.

'Stay!' cried the general. 'Before you go, perhaps you can give me your version of yesterday's skirmish, in which the "Trailing Terrors" were so knocked about.'

'Waal, I didn't see much of it,' drawled Ephraim with perfect truth. 'Ye onderstand'——

What he would have said was interrupted by a loud clatter of hoofs outside. A horse was pulled up short, and a courier, hot and perspiring, rushed into the hut.

'General!' he panted. 'The advance has begun. The cavalry are forward, as well as the two batteries. The cavalry have reached the fords without serious opposition.'

'Orderly!' shouted General Shields, scribbling again in his pocket-book.

'Sir,' answered Cox, stepping inside.

'Send that note to General Tyler.—My horse outside?'

'Yes, sir.'

'Good! Come, gentlemen. If all goes well, we shall sup with Frémont to-night. If not, we have a strong position at Lewiston, and there we will await the attack which is sure to be made to-morrow, if we fail in our plans to-day. Come!'

Without another word to or thought of Ephraim, he dashed out of the hut.

CHAPTER VIII.

A PAIR OF RELUCTANT RECRUITS.

EPHRAIM followed the officers to the door of the hut and looked out. For five minutes he maintained this position without moving or speaking; then he turned inwards again, and with his usual quiet grin on his face, hailed: 'Ye kin git down now, Luce. I reckon the coast is cl'ar.'

Lucius swung down to the floor and burst out laughing. 'How well you managed that, Grizzly!' he said. 'Do you know, at one time I thought that you were going to make a clean breast of it, and tell the general that we had been in the balloon.'

'I 'low I had some thorts er it,' answered Ephraim; 'fer he seemed dead sot agin the cunnel himself; but ye never know what 'll happen. After all, they war all Yanks in hyar, and though the ginrul seemed inclined ter be perfeckly fair and squar 'bout them two escaped balloonists, ye carn't tell how his complexshun might hev changed ef wanst he knew he 'd got his claws onter 'em.'

'That 's so,' agreed Lucius. 'It was best to be on the safe side. And you told him the simple truth.'

"'Ceptin' 'bout the "Trailin' Terrors,"' chuckled Ephraim. 'Ye see thet came inter my hed and sorter slipped out before I could stop it. I 'low I war rather sot back when he purposed ter put me up agin the cunnel; and ef it hed come ter thet, I'd hev owned up at once. But it's jest ez well,' he went on, 'fer ef the ginrul hed known who we war, he'd hev been bound ter rope us in fer a while, till he'd got the rights er the story, and thar's no tellin' when we'd hev got home.'

'We're not there yet,' said Lucius dubiously.

'I know thet, sonny; but we're on the way; fer now we know whar we air, and we won't be long in gettin' out er this, I tell ye.'

'Where are we?' asked Lucius. 'Somewhere about Port Republic, I gathered from what was said.'

'Right, bub. We're on'y 'bout three miles from thar, and that's whar old Stonewall is, holdin' the bridge. But the road and the woods between this and thar is choke-full er Yanks; so, ez ye rightly remark, we ain't thar yit. On our right is the Shenandoah, ez full er water ez an egg is er meat, and on our left is the Blue Ridge, so we carn't do nuthin' but go straight on.'

'We can't go by the turnpike either,' said Lucius, 'for I fancy there would be a pretty to do if two Federal soldiers were caught walking in the direction of the enemy.'

'Thet's so,' returned Ephraim. 'We must keep ter the woods and make the best of it. It won't do ter git lost in 'em agen, though, and come wanderin' back upon Lewiston. We must hold close by this edge.'

'Where is Lewiston?' inquired Lucius. 'It's a name I don't know.'

'I reckon it's thet fine big house way back thar, what we saw when we fust came out er the woods, or nearly—whar the Yankee cannon wuz planted. And I tell ye what it is. Ef old Stonewall whips Frémont to-day—and I reckon he will—thar's goin' ter be the biggest kick-up thar ter-morrer you ever heard on. Shields expects it, that's cl'ar; fer didn't ye hear him say he'd wait the attack thar?'

'I did,' answered Lucius; 'but if the bridge is carried, it may make a difference.'

'Shucks!' exclaimed Ephraim with contempt. 'I reckon ef the Yanks hes actually got across, they'll be glad enough to git back agin. Why, old Stonewall, he's thar himself.'

Such was the confidence that this general inspired that it never occurred to Ephraim or to any one else in the valley to doubt that where Jackson was, there also would the victory be.

'Well, then, what do you propose to do?' asked Lucius.

'Waal,' replied Ephraim, 'ez they war so onmannerly ez to plump in upon us before we could git well started with our breakfast, and ez we hev the whole day ter git thar, I p'intedly advise thet we fortify our stummicks fust thing we do.'

'Right!' cried Lucius. 'I'm with you there.' And with much laughter the two boys fell to work upon the provisions, and made a hearty meal.

'I feel better now,' said the Grizzly, wiping his mouth a few minutes later. 'Come along and let us take a squint at what's goin' on outside.'

They peeped, the one through the window, and the other through the door, and no one being in sight, issued from the latter into the open.

'This hyar is mighty pleasant,' remarked Ephraim, like the epicure, serenely full, and enjoying the warm June sunshine; 'but I s'pose we'd better make fer the woods in case any wan comes along.'

'I think so,' agreed Lucius. 'There's no use running unnecessary risks.—Quick, Grizzly, quick! Here come some soldiers.'

'Run, Luce, fer all ye're wuth!' cried Ephraim, setting the example. 'Maybe we've not been seen.'

It was a foolish proceeding, for they had been seen before they took flight, and had they remained perfectly still, they would have had a better chance of escaping unfavourable observation. As it was, their hasty action condemned them. Around the short arm of the wood, described above, swept a column of infantry, and as soon as the officer in command saw, as he supposed, two Federal soldiers in full flight, he very naturally roared out 'Halt!' at the top of his voice. Ephraim and Lucius, however, paid no attention to this courteous invitation, but continued their race towards the friendly shelter at top speed.

But they were soon brought up standing. 'If you don't stop,' shouted the officer, 'I'll fire on you. Halt!' And thus adjured, the fugitives unwillingly checked their flight and stood still.

'Never mind, Luce,' muttered Ephraim; 'we kin bluff 'em, I reckon.'

'Why didn't you stop when I ordered you?' demanded the officer roughly as he came up.

The boys were silent. To give the true reason

was not at all to their taste, and no other seemed just then to fit the circumstances. However, the officer went on without waiting for a reply to his first question :

'Where were you running to ?'

'Makin' fer our lines, major,' replied Ephraim, recognising the officer's rank.

'So. What is your regiment ?'

'The "Trailing Terrors."'

The major laughed. 'As usual,' he said, 'with their backs the wrong way. Fall in here, both of you.'

'Oh, I say, major,' whined Ephraim, 'our regiment's three miles back of Lewiston.'

'Is it ?' answered the major. 'I know. Well, I'll start you three miles in front of Lewiston, and show you a little fighting for a change.'

'General Shields told us the "Terrors" warn't ter be in action ter-day,' protested Ephraim, still hanging back.

'Rubbish ! None of your cock-and-bull stories for me. Fall in !'

'But my comrade's wounded,' declared Ephraim desperately. 'How kin he fight ?'

The major was a good-humoured man, but he began to lose patience. 'What do you mean, sir, by arguing with me ?' he cried, striking Ephraim with the flat of his sword. 'Do you suppose I don't know a couple of confounded skulkers when I see them ? There's nothing wrong with your comrade's legs, I should say. I'm not going to stand here all day. Fall in !'

'But we han't got no guns,' whimpered Ephraim as a last resource.

'Fall in!' roared the major.—'Sergeant Pierce, draft these two cowardly skulkers into the middle of the column, so that they can't run away; and keep your eye on them during the action. If they try to bolt, cut them down.—Column, forward!'

The sergeant thrust Ephraim and Lucius into the ranks, and the column moved forward at the double to atone for the short delay.

To exchange ideas on this unpleasant development was impossible; but Ephraim glanced at Lucius as they trotted along, as much as to say: 'We are in for it this time, and, for the life of me, I don't see how we are going to get out of it.' The column was marching two deep, and the sergeant kept abreast the file formed by the two boys. Presently, as the men fell by order into the quick step once more, Ephraim addressed the grizzled warrior in plaintive accents.

'See hyar, sergeant,' he said; 'it ain't thet we don't want ter fight. We feel powerful like fightin' ef we git the chance; but how air we goin' ter do it 'thout nary a gun or a ba'net?'

'You'll git 'em before long,' answered the sergeant. 'You bet.'

'Whar air we gwine ter?' next inquired Ephraim.

'Oh, shet yer head,' retorted the sergeant. 'You'll know when ye git thar. Yew two "Trailing Terrors" is going ter hev one day's gunning this time, I tell yew.'

Ephraim glanced again at Lucius. The boy's head was erect, and his face was flushed; but though his eyes glittered with excitement, he met his comrade's look boldly and confidently as he marched along with easy swinging step. He certainly had not the appearance of one who was afraid.

Grizzly heaved a breath of relief. Despite his loyalty, his thoughts would recur to that scene in the balloon; but now, though full of fears for his friend's safety, the old pride in him revived in full force, and he knew that, whatever desperate move their dangerous position might necessitate, he would be able to count upon Luce's cool and hearty co-operation. His feelings insisted upon expression, and slily grasping Luce's arm, he gave it a fervent squeeze. In return, the boy smiled up at him.

'I dunno what's goin' ter happen,' thought Grizzly; 'but I 'low it 'll be funny ef they kin persuade Luce and me ter shoot our own friends. By time! Luce war sot on seein' a battle, and I reckon he's goin' ter hev his way this time, same ez always. On'y, things hes got twisted upside down most outrageous. And it's all along er me, too.' A sharp pang of generous self-reproach shot through him; but the current of his reflections was rudely turned aside by the loud, abrupt command:

'Column, halt!'

The blue ranks stood fast, awaiting the next order.

It rang out, followed by others in rapid succession. 'Form line on the leading company! Remaining companies four paces on the right backwards—wheel! Quick march! Number one, eyes right—dress! Eyes front! Number two, halt — dress! Eyes front! Form line! Quick march! Number one, number two, number four, right—wheel! Halt—dress up! Eyes front! Steady!' And so the column moved into line.

Lucius was the front man of his file, Ephraim the rear, and when the rush and hurry of the movement were past, and they had opportunity for observation, their eyes rested upon a strange and unfamiliar scene.

They had reached Port Republic, the streets of which were swarming with Federal cavalry, the advance of Shields's army, who had dashed into the village by the fords of the South Fork; while a couple of field-pieces rumbled along to take up an advantageous position. Right in front, over the rolling Shenandoah ran the long wooden bridge, so much coveted by the Federal commander as the key to Jackson's position, and one of the field-pieces had nearly reached the end which abutted on the village. On the heights upon the opposite side of the river could be seen Confederate horsemen and the pickets who had been driven in, fleeing for their lives upon their supports. From the other end of the village came the crackling rattle of musketry, telling that a stand of some sort was being made, though what or where they could not see. Only, overhead the bullets sang with angry, venomous *wheep!* And Lucius, unaccustomed to the fearsome sound, felt his head duck of its own accord, so close did the fatal singing seem to his ear.

The boys' hearts sank within them. To their inexperienced eyes it looked as if old Stonewall must be caught at last. The terrible field-piece had reached the head of the bridge, unlimbered, and now commanded the narrow way. And other approach there was none. The second cannon, planted below them in the village, already roared its angry defiance and

hurled its iron messengers of death upon the wooded
heights, where the enemy was supposed to be.

Flash! A bright streak of light far up on the
heights. A curling wreath of smoke. Then boom!
A shell hurtled through the air, shrieked for an
instant like a fury in their ears, then bang! crash!
it exploded in front of the line, hurling frightful
jagged fragments right, left, front, rear—in all directions.

An involuntary moan burst from Lucius. The
file next him and Ephraim on their right had gone
down, and the two men who had composed it lay a
blood-stained heap upon the ground, all semblance of
humanity gone, and only a few twitchings of the
shattered limbs to tell that the wretched atom of
life left in them was hastening fast away.

'Hold up, Luce!' whispered Ephraim, all his thoughts
upon his friend, though he felt sick with the horror
of the ghastly sight.

Lucius nodded to the heights in front of him. He
could not turn round. His tongue had slipped forward
between his teeth, and he bit it till the blood flowed
into his mouth. A vague wonder possessed him as
to where the salt taste came from—came and passed
through his brain like lightning. Then his head went
up again and he stood still—so still that he excited
the admiration of his left-hand man, who muttered,
'Ye stood that well!' Whereas, as a matter of fact,
Lucius was simply stiffened into immobility. Then
something seemed to give way in his brain. The
swift thought crossed him, 'It's soon over, anyway;'
the tension of his limbs relaxed, and all fear fled. He
had received his baptism of fire, and his heart grew

strong within him. Another puff of smoke from the battery on the heights. Another screaming shell. And Lucius found himself idly wondering where it would fall, and careless where it fell.

'How odd,' he thought within himself, 'that I should feel so cool now in this unknown, terrible situation, while in the balloon '—— Fatal recollection! The dreadful memory fell upon him like a bolt, and his knees shook under him so violently that he nearly fell to the ground.

His neighbour looked curiously at him, unprepared for the sudden change, while from Ephraim came again the warning whisper, 'Hold up, Luce!'

Recovering himself, Lucius turned and laughed in Ephraim's face. 'I was thinking of Blue Bag just then,' he muttered.

Utterly taken aback by this singular statement, Ephraim weakly ejaculated, 'Oh!' and finding nothing more to say, relapsed into silence.

Sergeant Pierce stepped through the broken file to the front, and stooping down, picked up the rifles from the road and removed the belts with their ammunition pouches from the two dead men.

'Hyar, yew two "Terrors,"' he said, 'ketch hold on these. Yew can't say yew haven't got anything to fight with now. I thought it wouldn't be long before yew war provided.' Lucius received the rifle and belt with a little giggle which he could not entirely suppress. He was feeling strangely light and cheerful. Tragedy was turning to comedy. He was wearing the clothes of one dead man; why should he not receive the arms of another? He longed to speak, to say something—anything. He had the greatest difficulty in repressing a hilarious shout of 'Hi! Grizzly, isn't it a joke—two young Rebs asked to shoot their own men?' His feelings found vent at last in the admonitory remark to Pierce, 'Mind you keep your eye on us, sergeant.'

The air was full of flying missiles, but Lucius no longer ducked his head. He seemed not to hear them. The sergeant looked down at him from his superior height and grinned. 'I guess we misjudged yew,' he said. 'Yew're'—— He stopped suddenly. The pupils of his eyes, still fixed upon Lucius, dilated; the upper lip, drawn up by the action of the genial smile, drooped down upon the lower in a pout. For an instant his sturdy frame kept its position, martial and erect to the last, and then without a word or a groan he fell dead, shot through the heart.

Lucius looked at him and did not blench, but his neighbour growled discontentedly, 'This air gitting too hot, I guess. Ain't we never tew git the word to fire?' Then that man, too, fell suddenly dead. It was, as he had said, getting remarkably hot. All at once on the crest of the heights three more batteries appeared, the black-muzzled cannon grinning down upon the village. But the guns were silent, though the cannoneers stood beside them, ready to teach them their one deadly monosyllable. They were waiting for something. What was it? Ah! here it comes.

Down the hill, marching by the flank in a strong, steady gray line, came a regiment, and as they caught sight of the bridge, the supreme point of advantage, the men, carried away by enthusiasm, roared out the Rebel yell, and rushed towards it at double quick.

Alongside them, directing every movement, rode their general, erect upon his horse, calm and serene as though his troops were passing him in review order. To be led by him! To go in under the eye of Stonewall Jackson! Ah! there was not a man there but would have died where he was rather than face about and flee. There was not a regiment upon the hill that did not envy the 37th Virginia, marching to take the bridge.

Ephraim bent forward and grasped Lucius by the arm. 'By time! Luce,' he hissed into his comrade's ear, 'it's old Stonewall himself! Lie low, fer goodness' sake.' For he feared lest a shout of joy from Luce should betray them to the Federals for what they were.

On came the 37th, and now all down the long Federal line ran the one word 'Ready!' and the gunners at the bridge sprang to the gun.

Then Jackson was seen to stop, and from his lips rang out a sharp, stern word of command. The boys could not hear what he said, but they watched his every movement with blazing eyes. Standing in his stirrups, Stonewall waved his sword towards the bridge, and cried in ringing tones: 'Fire one round upon those people at the bridge. Then charge and give them the bayonet! Fire!'

He dropped the reins upon his horse's neck, and all the light of battle dying out of his face, raised his hands and eyes to heaven in mute supplication.

Down the hill swept the 37th, and without pausing to wheel into line, fired one volley and charged. Before that withering fire the gunners melted away from the gun like snow in the sun, and with a yell that set

I

the old hills ringing, the Virginians rushed across the bridge.

'Fire!' roared the Federal commander, and one thin sputtering volley rattled from the ranks where Luce and Ephraim stood. But ere they could reload, from every cannon on the height burst forth an iron hail, from the streets in rear of them came crashing deadly volleys, from the bridge in front of them the Virginians poured upwards, mad, vengeful, resistless. That flashing line of steel, that terrible ear-piercing yell—they were more than mortal man could stand. The gun by the bridge was taken, the gun in the streets was deserted. It was hopeless to wait, for their supports had not come up. Panic seized the Federal infantry, and as the cold steel gleamed in their eyes, they broke and fled.

CHAPTER IX.

WHEN the stampede before the onrush of the Virginians occurred, Ephraim and Lucius would have been heartily glad to bolt in the opposite direction—namely, towards their friends; but two circumstances precluded the possibility of such a course. The one, that without any consultation on the subject, they both recognised the danger they ran of being shot down or bayoneted by the men of the 37th, if they ventured to run towards them, dressed as they were in Federal uniforms. For in the fury of that charge but little opportunity was likely to arise for either offering or receiving explanations. Another and even more potent reason was that, however their inclinations might have prompted them to such a step, it was absolutely impossible for them to carry it out, for the rush of the Federal troops behind them swept them forward with such an irresistible impulse that they had no choice but to take to their heels in the direction of Lewiston. And this they did with a hearty good-will which the roar of cannon and rattle of musketry behind them kept very fully alive.

The retreat was not conducted in what is called good order. It was a regular *sauve qui peut*, and it was not until the fugitives ran into the fresh troops coming up to their support that a stand was made and something like a rally effected. But even these were of no avail, and the advance was promptly checked by the well-directed shot from the Confederate batteries, which were now all in position upon the opposite heights across the river; and the supporting columns, shattered by the murderous discharge, wavered, recoiled, broke, and in their turn bolted back to the shelter of the woods near Lewiston. As they fled, the Confederates limbered up and pursued them, keeping, of course, to the north side of the river, till at last the discomfiture of the Federals was complete; and Shields, recognising the futility of any further attempt upon a position so well defended, and which he could only attack at such absolute disadvantage to himself, was compelled to remain quiet all day, actually within sound of the cannonade which told of the struggle in which Frémont was engaged alone at Cross Keys.

When the second repulse and consequent flight took place, Ephraim and Lucius followed the example of most of their comrades by compulsion, and sought the shelter of the woods, where they were at least safer from the cannonade than in the open. Looking up the valley from Lewiston towards Port Republic, a bird's-eye view would have revealed three marked topographical features, roughly speaking, parallel to one another. On the right was the Shenandoah River;

next to this, and to the left of it, open country and
cultivated fields; and farther still to the left, the dense
forest, three miles wide, which extended to the base of
the Blue Ridge.   When forced to descend in the
balloon, the boys had entered the wood on the side
next the mountain, and their flight from the colonel
and subsequent wanderings had carried them clear
across it to the side facing the river, where they had
fallen in with the little hut in the clearing, which was
really a woodsman's cabin on the Lewiston estate.
They were now, therefore, still on the same side as
the hut, but a mile or so above it.

'I tell ye what it is, Luce,' said Ephraim in his
companion's car, as they hurried along, 'we air goin'
too fast.   We'll be in the Yankee camp at this rate
before many minnits is over.   Let's hang back a bit.'

They did so, gradually slackening their pace, and
allowing the stream of fugitives to roll past them, till
at last being, so far as they could see, alone, they sat
down under a tree to take breath.

For a moment they looked at one another in silence.
Then Ephraim said with a good deal of emotion in his
voice: 'I am the most or'nery fool in a town whar
there's a good few er the sort.   I thort ter let ye hev
a piece er funnin', and now I've nearly been the death
er ye twice, and gracious knows what'll happen yit
before we git through with this one-horse adventure.'

'I don't call it a one-horse adventure,' replied Lucius.
'A whole team would be more like it.   I imagine this
is what you might call a pretty crowded day.   Eh,
Grizzly?'

'Waal, I 'low it is so fur,' admitted Ephraim with
the ghost of a smile.   'Same time, I dunno what I'd

hev done ter myself ef ennythin' had gone wrong with
ye in thet rumpus jest now. I'd never hev got over
it or fergiv myself. By time! ter see them two pore
men go down like thet alongside us all in a moment.
It might jest ez well hev been you.' He blew his nose
loudly, and furtively knuckled his eyes.

'But it wasn't, you see,' returned Lucius cheerfully.
'A miss is as good as a mile, Grizzly. And I wish
you wouldn't blame yourself, for I came with you of
my own free will.'

'Ye didn't bargain fer all this, though,' said Ephraim
mournfully. 'Ye didn't 'magine ye were ter be stuck
up ez a target fer our own boys.—By gracious!' he
added with animation, forgetting his troubles in the
glorious recollection, 'didn't they give the Yanks
howdy in fine style? See 'em comin' across thet bridge!
Didn't they jest nat'ally tear along?'

'They did,' answered Lucius with glistening eyes.
'It was splendid.—So we've seen a battle after all,' he
went on, with a low laugh of satisfaction.

'Ah!' replied Ephraim. 'And ye warn't sittin' on
the ring fence nuther.'

'No,' chuckled Lucius, 'and thet bull er Holmes's is
powerful servigerous.' He laughed out again.

'Garn away! What air ye givin' me?' said Ephraim.
'But I 'low, Luce, ter see ye standin' thar in the ranks
like a bit er rock, it war marvellous.'

'I can tell you I felt badly enough at first, when
those two men were killed alongside us,' said Lucius.
'I might have been a thousand miles underground for
all the power I had to move. I was simply stiffened
where I stood. Then it all seemed to go away and
leave me, and I felt quite cool. How did you feel?'

'Pretty bad,' admitted Ephraim. 'But I war so taken up with thinkin' about you thet it soon went orf.' He made this remark in the most matter-of-fact way, not in the least to draw attention to his own unselfishness, but as if it were the most natural thing in the world that Lucius should be his first concern.

'Well, I'm afraid that I was thinking of myself,' said Lucius; 'but after the first burst I only grew more and more interested in the fight.'

'Oh yes,' exclaimed Ephraim, struck by a sudden recollection. 'What made ye turn round and say thet about old Blue Bag?'

The fire went out of Luce's eyes; the glow faded from his cheeks and left them pale. Again the memory of those awful moments in the air overcame him. His voice was unsteady as he answered: 'I don't know what set me thinking of it; but all of a sudden the thought crossed me, and I felt as if I should die. I never shall forget it. I never can forget it as long as I live.'

He shuddered violently. He was not exaggerating. The impression made upon him by his adventures in the air had been supreme. It had taken fast hold of some corner of his brain in a manner which perhaps the doctors could explain, and whenever imagination or memory called it forth, it threatened to unman him.

Ephraim considered him curiously. He could not understand the almost simultaneous exhibition of such opposite states of mind. However, he had wit enough to let the subject drop, and only answered: 'Waal, we won't talk about thet any more; I guess it's over now. See hyar, Luce, I think our best plan will be to make

fer thet little cabin agen and lie low thar till evenin',
when we kin make a break fer our lines.'

'I don't think that we ought to venture into that
loft a second time,' said Lucius. 'If the general
caught us there again and recognised you, there would
be trouble.'

'Thar would, shore enuff,' agreed Ephraim; 'but ye
misonderstand me, Luce. I didn't mean to hide in
the loft, but ter walk right inter the cabin, lie down
and take a snooze till it gits dark enuff ter be orf.
Ef any one comes in we kin jest walk out agin. We
kin always say we're makin' fer our lines.'

'I see,' said Lucius. 'Very well. Besides, it doesn't
follow that the general will return. But are you
sure that you can find your way there?'

'Why wouldn't we?' returned Ephraim. 'It's on
this side er the wood, and not so far away et thet.
Come on.'

They hugged the edge of the wood, and after walking for twenty minutes or so, again reached the clearing in which the log cabin stood. No one was in
sight; but still, instead of approaching it from the
open side, they preferred to skirt the wood a little
further and reconnoitre through the window in case
of accidents.

At last they stood opposite to the window, and here
Ephraim pulled Lucius back.

'You stay hyar, Luce,' he said. 'I'll go forward
and see ef the coast is cl'ar.'

'Not at all,' answered Lucius; 'you're always doing
that sort of thing. I'll go for a change.'

'No, lemme go,' protested Ephraim. 'What's the
use er runnin' yerself inter danger 'thout any reason?'

'The danger is the same for you as for me,' retorted Lucius. 'I tell you I am going.'

'Then we'll both go,' said Ephraim decidedly, and accordingly they went.

Cautiously approaching the window, they peeped in and surveyed the cabin. To their great relief it was empty; but before Lucius knew what he was about, Ephraim stole quietly round the hut and surveyed the open space.

'It's all cl'ar, Luce,' he said in a tone of satisfaction. 'I don't see nary a Yank. They're not fur orf, though, fer the camp is jest beyond the woods thar.'

'Then shall we go in here?' asked Lucius. 'You think that is the best thing to do?'

'I reckon,' returned Ephraim laconically, and slipped in through the window by way of illustration. 'By time!' he exclaimed when he was fairly in, 'thar's been some one in hyar sence we made tracks out er it.'

'How do you know?' inquired Lucius, scrambling in to join him.

'Why, all the food is gone,' sighed Ephraim, pointing to the table with a sigh. 'I war looking forward ter a fresh supply er them crackers after all this runnin' around.'

'I've got plenty here,' said Lucius, slapping his pockets; 'and you've got the ham.'

'It won't do ter gobble up thet jest yet, Luce,' explained cautious Ephraim. 'Ye kin hev jest wan slice ef ye're sharp set, but we must keep some fer ter-night in case we run dry.'

'No, I'm not very hungry,' answered Lucius; 'but

I've turned most unaccountably sleepy all of a sudden.'

'Nuthin' onaccountable about thet,' said Ephraim, 'seein' ye never went ter bed at all last night, and hev been up all ter-day. Lie down in the corner and take a snooze. I'll look after things.'

'Why,' asked Lucius, surprised, 'aren't you sleepy, too? You said you were just now.'

'Ez ter thet,' responded Ephraim, 'I kin hold old man Nod orf a bit yit, I reckon. It'll maybe suit better ef we don't go ter sleep at the same time.'

'I see,' said Lucius with a huge yawn. 'Well then, you lie down, and I'll take the first watch.'

'Shucks!' ejaculated Ephraim. 'What does it matter? Ye air half over already. Go ter sleep. I'll git my allowance by-and-by.'

'But,' began Lucius drowsily, 'you always do everything. I—I—don't see—why'——. He mumbled on for a second or two, nodded heavily, started into semi-wakefulness, nodded again, and rolled over fast asleep.

Ephraim looked down at him with an expression in which tenderness for his friend and self-reproach were blended. 'Pore Luce,' he murmured, 'ye air jest nat'ally tuckered out. I wish I hadn't been sech a or'nery fool with my notions. I'd give suthin' ter see ye back agen safe and sound in the old home et Staunton. Pray God I'll git ye thar yit, though.

He stole to the door, and going outside, planted himself with his back against the logs of the cabin, so that he could command a view of all approaches by the front or sides. For he rightly judged that only skulkers would be likely to enter by the window, and for them he did not care.

'"Carry me back to old Virginny,"' he hummed softly to himself, as he glanced up and down; up to where he knew the Federal camp lay concealed behind the bend of the woods; down to where, though he could not see them either, he knew that the Confederates were still standing to arms, expecting a fresh attack on the part of Shields, and wondering why it never came. But Shields was too astute. It was as if he had heard the remark made by Jackson to his chief of staff, when the latter expressed the opinion that Shields would make a more determined attack on the bridge at Port Republic before the day was out. 'Not he,' said Stonewall, waving his hand towards the heights. 'I should tear him to pieces. Look at my artillery.'

Boom! boom! boom! came the sound of the heavy guns at Cross Keys, and Ephraim's face brightened as he pictured the struggle, in which he made not the slightest doubt Frémont was getting very much the worst of it.

'Old Stonewall will be hyar ter-morrer,' he thought, 'and then thar 'll be big doin's.'

Boom! boom! The monotony of the sound, fraught with no matter what deadly meaning, began to weary him. He straightened up and walked slowly up and down in front of the cabin. He was fearfully tired, and the desire for sleep threatened to overcome him even as he walked. But he shook it angrily off, pinching himself into wakefulness, until at last the desire fled from him.

The hours wore on to mid-day, mid-day passed to

afternoon, afternoon dragged towards evening, and still he kept his self-imposed vigil, pacing up and pacing down, leaning against the wall of the cabin, or occasionally stepping discreetly inside, when a messenger or a patrol hurried by, or when blare of bugle or roll of drum in the Federal camp beyond the trees seemed to indicate a movement in the direction of the bridge.

It never occurred to him to wake Lucius, who still lay wrapped in profound slumber, only every now and then he stole in to look at him as though to satisfy himself that the boy was safe, and then out again to his sentry go.

About four o'clock he had just stepped outside after one of these little visits, which consoled him a good deal for the trouble he was taking, for even to look at Lucius was always a delight to Ephraim —he had just stepped outside, when his watchful eye, turned in the direction of the Federal camp, observed two persons coming round the bend of the woods.

One he instantly recognised as General Shields; but with the features of the other, who was in civilian dress, he was unfamiliar. Like a flash Ephraim was back again in the cabin, peering round the corner of the door at the advancing couple. 'I wonder ef he 's comin' in hyar,' he thought. 'I should say not, but it 's better to be on the safe side these days. I hate ter wake Luce; but I reckon it 'll have ter be done.'

He sped to Luce's side, and bending over him, shook him strongly. The boy stirred, moaned uneasily, but did not open his eyes. Ephraim rushed to the door and back again.

'Wake up, Luce!' he called, shaking him more

violently than ever. 'Wake up! The ginrul's outside, and ef he comes in and ketches me hyar, thar'll be trouble, ez ye said. Wake up!'

This time Lucius opened his eyes, but only to close them instantly, and fall once more heavily asleep.

'By time!' muttered Ephraim, glancing at the window, the desperate thought occurring to him that the best thing to do would be to heave Lucius straight out, as the most effectual way of awakening him. Then he shook his head. 'No,' he said to himself, 'thet'll not do. He might yelp, and then we would be spotted shore and certain. Whar air they now?' He took another squint from his vantage point. The general and his companion were approaching, sauntering slowly along, deep in earnest conversation.

Once again Ephraim repeated the shaking process, and this time with such good effect that Lucius sat up, rubbed his eyes, stared at the Grizzly in a bewildered fashion for an instant, and concluded by asking where he was.

'Wake up!' returned Ephraim. 'Ye'll soon know. Through the window, quick! Ah!' as voices were plainly heard outside, 'it's too late. We must just face it out. Maybe they won't come in.'

His next glance relieved his apprehensions. Evidently the unwelcome visitors did not intend to enter. They were walking wide of the hut, not looking at it, and in a moment or two would have passed it by. Ephraim made a warning sign to the now wide-awake Lucius, as fragments of the conversation floated to them.

'So you see,' General Shields was saying, 'it is of the highest importance that what we could not do for

him to-day, General Frémont should do for us to-
morrow. Whatever be the result of to-day's fight at
Cross Keys, he must effect a junction with me to-
morrow, and to that end those despatches, detailing my
plans, must be in his hands to-night. I know it is
difficult; but do you not think '——— The rest of the
sentence was lost in the distance, as the two passed on.

'Shall we get through the window now?' asked
Lucius, as the voices died away.

'I reckon not,' returned Ephraim; 'they might
see us from the other side. Better stay whar we air
till they air out er sight. They 're not thinkin' er us
jest now.'

'What were they talking about?' inquired Lucius,
who, having been further from the door, had not heard
the conversation so perfectly.

'I dunno rightly; but it 's suthin' about gittin' word
over ter Frémont about ter-morrer's fight. Sh! Hyar
they come back again. Now, lemme do the talkin' ef
they come in.'

This time it was the voice of the civilian that reached
them. 'I 've done it before in the boat, general,' he
was saying, 'and I don't know what is to hinder me
doing it again.'

'Well, I don't want to confuse you with suggestions,'
said General Shields in reply. 'You know your own
business too well for that. You are sure the boat is
there?'

'It was there two hours ago, snug under the bank.
I don't see why it shouldn't be there now.'

'You know our new word, of course?'

'Oh yes; and theirs too, unless it has been changed
since this morning.'

They came to a halt opposite the door of the cabin, behind the door of which Ephraim instantly flattened himself, while Lucius stood stiffly erect in a corner.

The general began to laugh. 'If you can take a dip down, and learn anything of Jackson's intentions before you return, you admirable civilian, I shall be all the more pleased,' he said. Then noting the look of surprise on his companion's face, he added hastily: 'I was laughing at the recollection of a ridiculous incident which happened in there this morning. I'll tell you as we go along.' And taking the civilian by the arm, he continued his walk in the direction of the camp.

Ephraim stole a cautious glance round the post of the door. 'By time!' he grinned, when they were out of earshot. 'Ef he'd come in and suspected we'd heard thet pretty bit of news, I reckon he'd hev larft the wrong side of his mouth.'

'Tell me, what does it mean?' asked Lucius eagerly.

'I reckon it means thet the admire-able civilian, as the ginrul called him, is a pesky spy,' replied Ephraim.

'As Colonel Spriggs said you and I were,' laughed Lucius.

'Ezackly! On'y this yer's the real article, wharas we war on'y imitashuns. Anyway, this is the way I put it up. The civilian thar—who most likely ain't a civilian at all—hes got a pocketful er despatches fer Ginrul Frémont. Likewise, he hes got a boat somewhar over thar under the river bank. Likewise, he perposes to row across above our pickets and hand 'em ter Frémont. Likewise, his intention is, the orn'ery skunk, ter take a stroll down ter Stonewall's camp, and find out all he kin. Likewise'——

'Likewise,' interrupted Lucius, 'you've got an idea

into your head that those despatches would be better in General Jackson's hands than in General Frémont's, and you are wondering if we couldn't somehow manage to get hold of them.'

Grizzly made a step forward and caught Lucius by the hand. 'Right ye air, Luce!' he cried, beaming upon his friend. 'Ye hev struck it. Thet war my idee, on'y I don't ezackly see how it's gwine ter be done.' He paused to put on his considering cap.

'I'd like to have a try for it,' said Lucius with a grimace. 'You see, I've been thinking a good deal what an awful row there'll be when I get home—that is, if I ever do get home; but if we could show that we'd done some real service to them, why, they wouldn't have so much to say,' he finished, having become rather mixed in his pronouns. 'Why shouldn't we make for the river and head him off, Grizzly?' he continued, after a pause. 'We've got guns and ammunition now. I believe we could do it.'

'Ef we on'y knew ezackly when he'd start, and how fur away his boat is,' said Ephraim dubiously.

'Well,' said Lucius, who had gone to the door, 'there is a civilian walking towards the river now. See, he has just come round the bend of the woods from the camp. Of course, I don't know whether it's your admirable civilian or not, for I didn't see him, but'——

'By time! It's him, shore enuff,' broke in the Grizzly excitedly. 'Now, Luce, ef we're goin' ter do ennythin', we must do it sharp and quick. We carn't foller straight in his tracks, thet much is cl'ar. He's got a start, and we must allow him a leetle more. What we got ter do is, to go down the woods a space, and then make a bee-line fer the river. We kin steal up the bank through the belt er trees thet fringes it, and ef we carn't head him orf, maybe we kin stop him before he gits across.' He tapped his rifle significantly.

They set off running as hard as they could through the trees for a hundred yards or more, and then Ephraim stopped to spy out the land.

'He's goin' very slow, Luce,' he said. 'I reckon we shall head him off if we kin git thar 'thout bein' stopped. Now, bub, across the first field fer all ye're wuth.'

Three wide fields intervened between them and the river, and the risk that they would be seen was very great. They were forced to incur it, though ; and, besides, they hoped that their blue uniforms would divert suspicion from them if any one should catch sight of them. However, they crossed the first and second fields in safety, and concealed themselves in a ditch while making a survey of the third. The man was out of sight now, but it was only the conformation of the country which concealed him. As a matter of fact, the boys were nearer the river than he was.

'Thar's one thing, though,' said Ephraim, as they sat in the ditch. 'Thet belt er wood by the river is bound ter be full er Yankee pickets. We han't got the countersign. What's ter be done ef we air stopped ?'

'Let's go on until we are stopped,' urged Lucius the bold.

Ephraim shook his head. 'No,' he said ; 'that'll not do. We should on'y be turned back agen.' He thought deeply for a moment, the blue vein coming out in the middle of his forehead, as it always did when his mind was concentrated. All at once he slapped his hand upon his thigh. 'By time! I've got it!' he exclaimed, and burst out laughing.

'What have you thought of?' asked Lucius eagerly.

The Grizzly made him a rapid communication, the effect of which upon Lucius was to cause him to throw himself flat upon the bank of the ditch and roll about with delight.

'Come on!' cried the Grizzly. 'Now mind ye do ezackly ez I do, and when ye run, keep a sharp eye fer the boat.'

They set off again at a quick pace, until they had cleared the field and entered the broad belt of trees which fringed the water. Here they slowed down, and made a bee-line, so far as they could, for the river. In five minutes or less they heard the splash of the swollen current against the bank, and turning their faces sharply down stream, moved on for two or three minutes more, making all the noise they could.

'Halt! Who comes there?'

No sooner did the sharp challenge ring out than, as if at a signal for which they had been waiting, the two boys burst into wild, panic-stricken yells: 'The Rebs! the Rebs! They're on us! The pickets are driven in!' Shouting which they charged madly down upon the sentry who had challenged them. Seeing, as he supposed, two Federal sentries in full flight, the man never doubted for a moment that the alarm was genuine, and discharging his rifle in the air, set off as hard as his legs could carry him through the belt of trees towards the fields, beyond which lay the camp.

And now all along the river bank the cry was taken up, 'The Rebs! the Rebs!' and everywhere could be heard the sound of feet crashing through the undergrowth, as the pickets bolted in upon their supports.

Bursting with laughter, Ephraim and Lucius watched the disappearance of the man immediately in their front; but the sharp call of a bugle and the noise of the long roll upon the drums, as the Federal regiments sprang to arms in anticipation of the threatened attack, warned them that there was no time to lose, and they continued their race down the bank.

'There's the boat!' panted Lucius, after a few minutes. 'I see her nose just peeping out.'

'Down in the underbrush, then!' said Ephraim sharply, 'and don't git up unless I call ye, or ye see thar's need.'

'What are you going to do?' asked Lucius, obeying the order.

'Give 'em a taste of their own sauce, I reckon! Hush! Hyar he comes. Lie low!'

He flung himself in front of Lucius, with his rifle at the port, and waited.

Hurrying footsteps drew nearer. Some one was coming on at express speed.

Ephraim gripped his rifle tight, and set his teeth.

Swish! The bushes parted, and the civilian stood before him.

'Halt!' shouted the Grizzly, bringing his bayoneted rifle down to the charge. 'Halt! Who comes thar?'

CHAPTER X.

HOW THAT DESPATCH WAS INTERCEPTED.

'HALT! Who comes thar?' repeated Ephraim, as the civilian paused, regarding him with an expression of supreme astonishment.

There was reason for the stranger's amazement. He had moored his boat well above the chain of sentries—a good quarter of a mile, indeed—for no attack could be expected from the river, and naturally none could come from the north below Lewiston, and therefore only the sentries whom Ephraim and Lucius had scared had been posted in the former place, and none at all in the latter.

Consequently the civilian was puzzled. His first thought was, that he had struck a point too low down for his boat; his second, that he remembered every detail of the appearance of the spot, and that he could not possibly be mistaken. However, when, for the third time, the peremptory challenge sounded in his ears, he put as good a face as he could upon the matter, and answered distinctly and with confidence, 'Friend!'

'Advance, friend, and give the countersign,' ordered Ephraim, to the huge delight of Lucius, with whom he had many a time and oft rehearsed just such a scene in the workshop, little imagining it would ever be carried out in actual practice. The stranger advanced till the point of Ephraim's bayonet was within six inches of his chest.

'Halt!' cried Ephraim once more. 'That's close enough. Now stand and give the countersign.'

The civilian hesitated an instant. He could not tell where the suggestion came from, but somehow the thought flashed into his brain that all was not as it should be. 'Potomac,' he answered steadily.

Ephraim saw the momentary hesitation, and read it aright. His own danger made him alert. 'Go back the way you came,' he said, keeping his rifle at the charge. 'That ain't the word.'

It was a bold move, but it told; and the Grizzly, to his own relief, noticed the expression of mingled surprise and satisfaction on the stranger's face.

'Shenandoah,' said the civilian. 'Will that suit you?'

'That's better,' answered Ephraim, but without shouldering arms. 'Why did you give me the wrong one fust?'

'I—I was thinking of yesterday,' replied the stranger rather confusedly.

'Ah!' retorted Ephraim drily. 'Waal, I'm put hyar tew think on to-day. What d'ye want?'

'What do I want, you fool?' replied the man angrily. 'Why, I want to pass, of course. Shoulder arms.'

'Who air yew orderin' about?' snapped Ephraim.

'And yew keep a civil tongue in yewr head, mister. Don't yew be so ready tew call names.'

'Well, I didn't mean that,' said the stranger, wishful to conciliate him. 'I was anxious to pass, that is all. I am sorry. Let me pass, please, for I am in a hurry.'

'Hurry or no hurry,' returned Ephraim stolidly, 'ye don't pass hyar. Go back, or I'll run ye through.'

He looked so fierce as he said it, that the stranger actually did recoil a pace or two. But he recovered himself instantly, and said smoothly:

'Look here, my good friend, what is your objection to letting me pass? I gave you the word.'

'But yew gave me the wrong one to start with,' answered Ephraim, glowering at him.

The stranger bit his lip. He saw he had made a mistake, and, in endeavouring to explain it, he appeared to offend the sentry still further.

'I said it in jest—to try you—to see if you were a smart fellow,' he said, with a little laugh.

'Oh, did yew?' Ephraim frowned upon him. 'Waal, yew'll find I'm smart enuff fer the like of yew, I guess. Quit now. I ain't got no time or inclernashun fer more fooling.'

'Nor I, either,' answered the civilian haughtily. 'So let me pass at once—or'——

'Or what?'

'Or I'll report you.'

'Yew'll report me!' sneered Ephraim, advancing upon the man until the ugly-looking bayonet just touched his coat. 'I tell yew, ef yew ain't out of that afore I count ten, thar won't be much left of yew to report. Quit, I say.'

The civilian made another backward step. 'Look

here, sentry,' he said, 'this is getting beyond a joke. I tell you, I have important business, and I must pass. I've given you the word, and that gives me the right. Come, now,' he wheedled; 'don't be obstinate.'

'And I've the right, and, what's more, it's my duty tew stop any one I consider a suspishus character, word or no word,' replied Ephraim. 'Yew come here, a soldier dressed up ez a civilian; yew gimme fust the wrong word, and then the right word; and then yew try tew git round me tew let yew pass. I say yew shan't pass.'

The man started during Ephraim's speech. 'How do you know that I am a soldier?' he asked.

'By the set of yewr shoulders and yewr walk,' replied Ephraim. 'Any one could see ez much ez that.'

'Then, perhaps, you know who I am as well?'

'No, I don't; but I guess I have a fairly good notion what yew air ez well.'

'And what may that be?'

'A spy,' answered Ephraim gloomily. 'I don't know but what I orter run yew through whar yew stand ef I done right. But I'll give yew one more chance. Quit, or take the consequences.'

'Look here,' said the man suddenly. 'I know you are only doing your duty according to your lights; but if you knew everything, you'd find you were rather exceeding it. I tell you what, I am all right. There's nothing wrong about me. I don't want a fuss, or to lose time. Here are ten dollars for your trouble. Now stand aside.'

'Thet's enough!' replied Ephraim. 'Thet about sizes yew, I should say. Now, I'll not only not let yew pass, but I'll detain yew hyar till the rounds comes along.   Yew're my prisoner.'

The man looked this way and that, flushing and paling with rage. 'You time-honoured thickhead!' he cried at last. 'I'll tell you who I am, and then maybe you'll alter your mind.   I'm Captain Hopkins of the "—— Massachusetts."'

'Ho!' drawled Ephraim.   'Fust yew're a civilian, and then yew're a soldier, and naow yew're a capting. Waal, I han't altered my mind. I guess ef yew kin bluff, why, so kin I.'

'Very much better than the captain can,' thought Lucius in his hiding-place.

'Let me pass, or take the consequences,' cried the captain, and quick as thought he drew a revolver and presented it at Ephraim.

Like lightning the glancing bayonet swept upwards, met the dull blue tube with a clank, and away went the captain's weapon ten feet into the air behind Ephraim, splash into the river.

'Yew see,' drawled Ephraim.   'I guess I didn't come down in the last shower of green mud.'

'Confound you!' said the captain, laughing in spite of his evident vexation. 'You are too smart. I see that I shall have to tell you everything.   Pay attention to what I say now, and hold your tongue about it when you get back to camp.—By the way,' he broke off, 'why didn't you run in with the rest of them just now, when there was that scare?'

'Ef I war to go runnin' fer the camp every time thar war a skeer ter-day, I'd never be done,' answered Ephraim. 'My post is hyar, and hyar I mean tew stay.   What's this yew want tew tell me?'

'Simply this,' replied the captain. 'Mind now, hold your tongue. I am the bearer of despatches from General Shields to General Frémont.'

Ephraim's face was a study. He shouldered arms at once, and gasped out: 'What! Then why in thunder didn't yew say so before?'

'For very good reasons,' smiled the captain. 'Come, now, I've put off time enough already. My boat is waiting there, and '——

Down came Ephraim's rifle to the charge again. 'Boat!' he echoed. 'Yew hev a boat?'

'Certainly,' said the captain. 'You didn't suppose I was going to walk across the river, did you?'

'Back with yew!' cried Ephraim, feinting to lunge. 'Good land! yew nearly fooled me, Mister Secesh. So yew thort yew war going tew git in yewr boat ez easy ez that, and jine yewr friends the Rebs.'

'Frankly,' said the captain, 'your idea of duty is an extreme one; but I suppose, in these days of slipshod soldiers, you ought to be commended for it. Look here,' he unbuttoned his coat, 'I'll show you the despatch, and may be that will convince you.' He pulled out a large envelope, sealed, and addressed to General Frémont. 'There,' he said. 'Now, are you satisfied?'

With a sudden, unexpected movement, Ephraim snatched the packet, cast it to the ground, and set his foot upon it. 'Keep off!' he cried, as the captain made a rush to recover his precious document. 'Another step, and yew're a dead man. Yew must think me green, ef yew 'magine I couldn't see through that game. Why, any one could write Frémont's name outside an envelope. I'll bet a trifle thar's things in that yew wouldn't keer fer Frémont tew see, all the same.'

'Give me my letter!' shouted the enraged officer.

'It's my letter now, and yew're my prisoner. I'll give it and yew up tergether when the grand rounds come.'

Captain Hopkins changed his tone again. 'I never knew such a fellow as you,' he said. 'You mean well; but you have no idea what an amount of valuable time you are wasting. I swear to you I am not a rebel spy, but what I told you—the bearer of a despatch to General Frémont. As a last resource, if you will let me go, I will return to the camp, and bring back some one who will identify me. Will that do?'

Ephraim appeared to meditate. Finally he said: 'How am I tew know yew ain't fooling me? I might ez well have a prisoner, naow I've got one.'

'You have only my word for it, of course,' said the captain.

'Oh, waal, I guess I'll trust yew,' answered Ephraim after another pause. 'Off with yew, and come back ez soon ez yew kin git. I'll keep the despatch safe.'

The captain needed no second telling, but turned and ran. Ephraim hailed him when he had gone a little way.

'Well,' demanded the captain, turning round, and fearful of a bullet, by way of a keepsake, from this very officious sentry. 'What is it?'

'Ef yew air reely Captain Hopkins,' said Ephraim— 'and mind, I'm not saying yew ain't—yew won't git me inter trouble fer this. Yew'll tell 'em I only did my dewty.'

'Confound you and your duty!' shouted back the captain, and sped out of sight among the trees.

'Sh! Keep quiet!' said Ephraim warningly, as a curious explosive sound, half snort, half cough, came upwards from the undergrowth. 'Wait till he gits well out er the road, and then ye kin larf. Hold on till I track him down.'

He stole through the belt of trees, and, to his great satisfaction, observed the captain hurrying as fast as he could across the fields. The commotion in the camp, too, had died away, now that it had been ascertained that the alarm had been a false one—like so many more on that eventful day. But Ephraim's common sense told him that it would not be very long before fresh sentries were placed along the river; and, moreover, the outraged bearer of despatches would lose no time in returning, to prove his identity and reclaim his precious letter.

The Grizzly, therefore, made all haste back to Lucius, whom he found sitting up in the brushwood, apparently the picture of distress, for tears were streaming down his cheeks, and deep, labouring sighs escaped his chest.

'What's the matter? What's wrong?' exclaimed Ephraim in real concern. 'What ye cryin' for?'

'Crying!' snorted Lucius. 'Ough! ough! Is he gone? Ough! ough! Oh! ho! ho! ha! ha! ha! I can't help it! Ough! ough! I must laugh if I'm killed for it! Ough! Oh, Grizzly, I never saw anything so funny in my life.'

He went off into fresh paroxysms, while Ephraim, to whom the affair had been serious enough in all conscience, grinned quietly in sympathy.

'Waal, I 'low it might hev sounded funny ter ye, listenin' thar, Luce,' he said. 'Somehow it didn't strike me in thet light et the time. I war so sot on gittin' thet letter.'

'Sounded funny!' echoed Lucius, his laughter exhausted to a helpless giggle. 'It wasn't only that. You *looked* so funny. Oh! oh! oh! if you could only have seen your own faces.'

'I 'low he looked a bit sot back when I got the ba'net agin his chest,' chuckled Ephraim.

'Ah! but your own face,' put in Lucius. 'Don't forget that. And the way you talked to him. My! It was the 'cutest thing in the world. What put it into your head?'

'It come thar ez we war runnin' along,' returned Ephraim; 'an fer the rest, it jest argued itself out ez it went. But come, thar ain't too much time. We must be orf out er this before he gits back.'

'In the boat, of course,' said Lucius, rising.

Ephraim nodded. 'Yas, sir!' he answered with a light laugh. 'And I do think it war mighty nice of 'em ter hev thet boat hyar fer us jest ez we wanted ter git away and all.—In with ye, Luce.'

Lucius scrambled down the bank, and catching hold of the painter of the boat, drew her in to the shore and leaped aboard; while Ephraim, with the all important document in his hand, stood for a moment to consider.

'It won't do to run no risk er losin' this, after all the trouble we've been at ter git it,' he said. 'Whar d'ye reckon I'd better put it?'

'Stow it in your cartridge pouch,' suggested Lucius. 'That will be as safe a place as any other.'

'Right!' said Ephraim, folding the letter up small and placing it in his pouch. 'Haul her in, Luce.'

'What are you going to do?' asked Lucius, bringing the boat's nose again to the bank. 'If we pull out into the river, we shall be seen.'

'Likely, ain't it?' inquired Ephraim cheerfully, as he gathered up the rifles. 'No; we'll head her up stream and glide along the bank till we git below their outposts. Ketch hold er the guns.'

'But they may search along the bank,' demurred Lucius, laying the rifles in the bottom of the boat.

'Nary a doubt er that,' replied Ephraim, stooping to unloose the knot of the painter from the sapling round which it was tied. 'But et first they'll be in sech a confusion thet I 'low they won't be able ter think er everything et once. And the fust idee'll nat'ally be thet we hev gone down stream and then headed fer the opposite side.'

He untied the rope, and jumping down the bank, slung it aboard and scrambled in after it. Instantly the boat swung round, obedient to the current, and with her nose to the north, drifted rapidly down stream.

'Out oars, Luce!' cried Ephraim, fumbling in the bottom of the boat. 'Head her round. By time!'

He stopped suddenly and straightened up. At the same instant Lucius grasped the facts, and they stared at each other with white, scared faces.

There were no oars in the boat!

CHAPTER XI.

FOR a moment Ephraim was, as he would him-self have expressed it, 'sot back,' but he was not one to remain so long, and seizing his rifle, he grasped it by the barrel, and using the butt as a paddle, endeavoured to guide the course of the boat.

'Quick, Luce!' he exclaimed. 'Take yourn, and we'll see what kin be done. The pesky Yank! Of co'se he'd hid the oars somewhar in the bresh, so as nobody could steal his boat. By time! What an or'nery fool I war not ter hev thort er thet before.'

'No; it was I who was the fool,' corrected Lucius, labouring away with his makeshift oar. 'You had quite enough to do with the letter and the rifles. I should have looked to see if everything was right.'

'Waal, thar's a pair of us, then, ef ye will hev it so,' returned Ephraim gloomily. 'Ennyway, it don't matter a corn cob now whose fault it war. The mischief's done. I wouldn't so much keer,' he added, beating the water furiously with his rifle-butt, 'on'y when that clever captain comes back and finds the oars whar he left 'em, he'll nat'ally know we must

be down stream, and they won't be long gittin' on
our trail.'

Twilight was fast settling over the valley; for the
high mountains which surrounded the cup of land
in which this living drama was being enacted, effectually shut out the sun as the day declined, and Lucius
remarked hopefully that it would soon be dark.

'It'll not be so dark ez all thet comes ter on a
June night,' responded Ephraim in a cheerless tone.
'Thar'll be plenty er light fer them ter take pot-
shots et us ez we drift along. Yit it ain't so much
fer thet I'm keerin'. I'm thinkin' er the despatch
and the importance it 'ud be ter old Stonewall ter
git it before mornin'.—I'm afraid we ain't doin' much
good with the guns, Luce.'

The crafty captain had removed not only the oars
but the rowlocks, and consequently they had no support for their extemporised oars, but were obliged to
paddle with them Indian fashion, holding the barrel
high and sweeping the butt through the water on
either side of the boat. But the rounded, highly
polished wood offered little resistance to the rushing
stream, and the current swept them steadily down,
all their efforts to turn the boat's head proving ineffectual.

'We'll make the Potomac at this rate, ef we go on
long enough,' said Ephraim grimly, the sweat pouring
off his face as he strove desperately with his clumsy
implement; 'and then all we hev ter do is ter float
gracefully down and give 'em howdy in Washin'ton
city.' He laughed in the very bitterness of his spirit.

They were swirling along only about twenty yards
from the south bank; but as Ephraim remarked, they

might as well have been a mile away, for by no
possibility could they reach it, and he looked longingly
at the boughs that dipped into the rushing waters,
thinking how different matters would be if only he
could lay hold of them.

Suddenly there was a spurt of flame, followed
instantly by a loud crack. Ephraim's cap soared
into the air, mounted for a moment and then fell
with a dull splash into the river, while its owner,
with a shrill yell, tumbled over into the bottom of
the boat.

As Ephraim fell, his gun slipped from his nerveless
fingers and sank instantly out of sight, and Lucius,
hastily drawing his on board, bent terror-stricken over
his friend.

'Oh, Grizzly!' he cried in piteous tones. 'What
is the matter? Are you shot?'

An inarticulate gurgle from Ephraim was the only
reply.

'Speak to me!' Lucius almost shrieked. 'Oh! oh!
Surely you are not killed. Speak to me, Grizzly!
Speak to me! Oh! oh! Whatever shall I do?'

Thus adjured, Ephraim slowly opened his eyes
and looking up into the anxious face bent over
him, remarked quaintly, though without the least
intention of being humorous: 'Hello, Luce! Is thar
a hole right through my head, or what?'

So great was his relief that Lucius broke into a
joyous laugh. 'Grizzly,' he demanded with mock
severity, 'if you were not shot, what did you mean
by tumbling over; and if you are not killed, what are
you lying in the bottom of the boat for?'

'Ye may say thet, Luce,' returned Ephraim, uncoiling his long length and struggling into a sitting posture. 'It war a mighty close thing, I reckon. Look at thet.'

He lifted his face as he spoke, and Lucius, with an exclamation of dismay, saw that his forehead was blackened with powder, and that one of his eyebrows and part of his front hair were singed off.

'Ye see,' said Ephraim, gingerly touching the raw and tender skin, 'a leetle more and ye'd hev had ter steer yer way home alone. I reckon it's a powerful frightenin' sort er thing, a gun bustin' off et ye when ye least expect it.'

'But what happened?' asked Lucius. 'I wasn't looking. That is, I looked up in time to see your cap go off and the gun slip out of your hand. The next I knew you were on your back.' He gripped Grizzly's hand and added earnestly: 'I'm so glad you weren't killed, old Grizzly.'

'I'm obleeged ter ye,' answered Ephraim, still very white about the lips. 'So am I.' His voice shook a little as he tried to explain the matter to his comrade. 'Ye see,' he went on, 'this is how I put it up. Ez I war splashin' around with the gun-butt in the water, the trigger must hev got caught, or the hammer drawn back by a bolt and let go agen. The next thing I knowed war a rush er blindin' light past my eyes, a wave like the breath er a bit of iron from a blacksmith's furnace on my forehead, and thet's all. I went down et thet, and didn't feel like stoppin' ter arsk questions.'

'Was that the way of it?' said Lucius. 'At first I thought that somebody had fired at you from the bank.'

K

'By time!' exclaimed Ephraim, the colour rushing back into his face, and his nerves steeling again as he heard this. 'I tell ye, bub, that's ezackly what they will be doin' before very long. Why, don't ye know, the sound er that rifle-shot'll bring the Yanks down on us quicker 'n ennything. Luce, we must do suthin'.'

'What are we to do?' asked Lucius helplessly. 'If we could not manage the boat when we had both guns, what shall we do now that we have only one?'

'Waal, then,' inquired Ephraim drily, 'do ye want ter set still hyar while the Yanks make a target er ye? I tell ye I don't feel that way myself.' He made a wry face at the thought of his recent experience.

'I don't either, you may be sure,' answered Lucius. 'But something must be done.—I have it, Grizzly; I have it.'

'What hev ye struck?' queried Ephraim, roused by the hope in his voice.

'Why, of course,' replied Lucius, 'let us swim ashore and leave the ugly old boat to take care of herself.'

'Bullee!' cried Ephraim, unbuckling his cartridge belt and flinging it into the bottom of the boat. 'Bullee! So we will. Let's—— Thar's just one thing agin it, though, Luce,' he broke off dismally.

'What's that?' demanded Lucius, who had already removed his belts and taken off his coat. 'What's against it?'

'Why,' answered Ephraim, looking as shamefaced as if he had been confessing to a grievous sin, 'it ain't much, maybe; but I reckon it's enuff. I can't swim.'

At this plain statement of an unpleasant fact, Lucius looked aghast. 'Why, of course you can't,' he said. 'I'd forgotten that.' Then recovering himself, he added cheerily: 'Well, never mind, Grizzly; I'll do the swimming. You just grab me lightly round the back and kick out well behind, and I'll get you there. 'Tisn't far.'

Ephraim shook his head. 'It isn't ez fur ez all thet, Luce, I 'low,' he said; 'but thar's a tur'ble strong current. Ef I drew ye under by my weight and felt myself drownin', I might ketch hold on ye and drown ye ez well. A man couldn't well know what he war about in sarkumstances like thet, ye see. So I'm obleeged ter ye fer thinkin' er it; but ef it's all the same, I'd ruther not resk it.'

'There's no risk,' urged Lucius. 'All you have to do is to hold on tight.' But Ephraim was obdurate.

'Well, what are we to do, then?' asked Lucius disconsolately. 'Every minute is precious.'

'I know thet,' answered Ephraim, 'and the best thing ter be done is this. Ye swim ashore ez soon ez ye kin. I'll drift on in the boat, and maybe it'll be dark afore they find me, and I may run agin a spit or suthin,' and so git ashore. Thar's no use lettin' 'em cotch the two er us. Now, is thar?' But he looked down as he made the suggestion.

'I don't wonder you are ashamed of yourself to propose such a disgraceful thing,' cried Lucius indignantly. 'To think for a moment that I would leave you in the lurch just on the chance of saving my own skin, after all you've done for me. Oh, Grizzly, what a shame to suppose I would do it!'

'I didn't think ye'd do it, Luce,' mumbled Ephraim, looking a very crestfallen Grizzly indeed. 'On'y I thort'——

'I don't want to hear what you thought,' interrupted

Lucius, who was undressing himself while he talked. 'I've made up my mind what to do, and I'm going to do it. So there.'

'What mought thet be?' inquired Ephraim, eyeing him curiously.

'I'll show you fast enough,' answered Lucius, now stripped to his shirt. 'If you are afraid to trust yourself in the water along with me'——

'Fer fear of drownin' ye, Luce; fer fear of drownin ye,' put in Ephraim deprecatingly.

'Of course. What else? I didn't suppose you were thinking of yourself. I've had teaching enough to know that's not your way. If you're afraid of drowning me, then there's only one thing to be done —I must swim ashore myself and tow the boat after me, with you in it.'

'See hyar,' began Ephraim, but Lucius cut him short.

'Come on, now. Don't waste time in talking. Fasten the painter round me. You can tie a better knot than I can.'

'It'll hurt ye monstrous, Luce,' said Ephraim.

'Nonsense! It will not hurt at all, tied around my shirt; and if it should, what matter? It's better than being shot, I should say. Oh, do be quick! Don't you see this gives the best chance to both of us to get off scot-free? Tie it tight now. Don't be afraid.'

Under this incessant urging, Ephraim fastened the rope round Lucius with fingers that trembled a good deal from excitement and apprehensions for the safety of his young comrade. But at last it was done, and Lucius turned and faced him.

'Now,' he said, 'you can see that the current is very

strong by the rate at which we are travelling. We are not far off the shore; but it may take a long time to get there. I think that I can do it, though; but if not, if I call out to you, or if I should sink, haul me on board again. That's all you have to do, besides helping as much as you can with the butt of my rifle.'

'I wish ye wouldn't, Luce,' implored Ephraim. 'The light is goin' fast, and thar's no rumpus yit, ez fur ez I kin hear. Ef we hev good luck, they'll miss us altogether. But ef they come and pop at ye while ye're in the water'——

'Pooh!' interrupted Lucius, 'I shall be all right. Just you keep a sharp lookout along the bank, and be ready to haul me in if necessary. Good-bye! I'm off!'

He waved his hand, and slipped noiselessly off the gunwale of the boat, feet foremost, into the river.

Meantime a very different scene was being enacted at the Federal camp. Hardly had General Shields informed himself that the scare created by the boys was a false one, and that he had at present nothing to fear from the dreaded and ubiquitous Jackson, than his attention was arrested by the sudden appearance of his 'admirable civilian,' Captain Hopkins, who with disordered dress, flushed features, and breathless from running, rushed unceremoniously into the presence of his commanding officer.

'Captain Hopkins!' exclaimed General Shields in astonishment. 'Back already. Why, you've been gone little more than an hour.' Then as his eye fell upon the captain's untidy dress and general look of tribulation, he added anxiously: 'There is nothing wrong, is there?'

'The despatch!' panted Hopkins. 'I'——

'Don't tell me anything has happened to that,' interrupted Shields vehemently. 'Surely not. Surely not.'

'No,' got out the captain between his struggles for breath; 'only a leather-headed sentry—a question of identity—won't let me pass—send some one back with me.'

'Take time to breathe, sir, and you will be better able to explain yourself,' fumed General Shields, adding inconsistently: 'Go on, sir. Don't keep me waiting all day. Let me hear your news.'

The captain drew a few deep inspirations and felt better. 'General,' he said, 'there is nothing wrong; only a little provoking delay. I found a sentry just about where I had moored my boat, and because I was in civilian dress, he refused to allow me to pass.'

Found a sentry alongside your boat!' repeated General Shields. 'I thought you had moored it well above the line.'

'So I thought myself, sir,' answered Hopkins; 'but evidently I was in error, for there the sentry was.'

'But you had the word,' said Shields in a puzzled voice.

'Of course, sir; but I'm afraid I behaved rather foolishly, for, having an idea that all was not right, I gave the wrong word, and that made the fellow so suspicious of me, that even when I gave him the right word afterwards, he would have none of me.'

'You might have explained your business, then,' suggested the general, 'rather than have incurred this aggravating delay.'

'That is just what I did sir,' protested Hopkins. 'I

even went the length of showing him the despatch, and
when he seized it '———

'What!' vociferated the general. 'Do you mean to
say that the despatch is no longer in your possession?'

'Hear me out, sir,' said Hopkins uncomfortably, for
he felt that at the very best he made a ridiculous
appearance in the affair. 'I merely held the despatch
before his eyes, when he instantly seized it and
declared that it must be a bogus document, and I
myself a rebel spy.'

'Then why did you not recover the document by
force?' demanded the general sternly.

'He had already disarmed me, sir. I was completely
at the mercy of his bayonet.'

'Well, well,' muttered the general irritably. 'Go
on.'

'He was for detaining me until the arrival of the
rounds; but I gave him my word that I was not a
rebel spy, and, with great reluctance, he at last permitted me to depart to obtain evidence of my identity.'

'Retaining the document,' mused General Shields.
'Why did you not appeal to some of the sentries
higher up?'

'You forget, sir, they imagined themselves driven
in, and had all returned to the camp.'

'Then why had this fellow not followed their
example?' inquired General Shields sharply.

'I asked him the same question, sir, and his reply
was that there he had been placed, and there he
meant to stay.'

General Shields reflected. 'I will go with you
myself, captain,' he said at last. 'You have either
been dealing with a very staunch soldier, or a most

accomplished rogue. Pray Heaven you have not been fooled in this business.'

'Oh, I should say not,' answered Hopkins confidently. 'The fellow was staunch, as you say, and a bit pig-headed—indeed you might call it thick-headed —but he was not fooling me.'

'We shall see,' answered the general drily. 'It is an awkward business, very.—Major Wheeler,' he added, turning to a staff officer, who stood close beside him, 'order a corporal and ten men to follow me, fifty paces in the rear.—Now, Captain Hopkins.'

They walked rapidly across the fields, followed by the corporal and his men, and as they neared the river belt the general said: 'You are sure you can go straight to the place?'

'Certain, sir,' was the reply. 'See, here is where I broke cover on my way back. We have only to follow the trail I made as I ran.'

'Humph!' muttered the general as they pushed through the trees. 'It is not a little odd that your pig-headed sentry does not challenge us.—Halt!' he called to the corporal. 'We will go on alone. March forward when I hail you.'

They went on for another twenty paces, and still remained unchallenged, which was not so very odd after all, considering that there was no one there to challenge them.

'It is very singular,' murmured poor Captain Hopkins. 'I can't have mistaken the place.—General! General!' he cried, 'you were right. I have been fooled. The boat is gone!'

General Shields uttered a fierce exclamation. 'I'll be hanged if I didn't think so from the very first,' he

shouted : 'Here, corporal, bring up your men.—You
should not have moved from this spot, sir, when once
you lost possession of those papers,' he thundered at
the unfortunate Hopkins. 'You should have died
rather than let them fall into the hands of the enemy,
and as you once suspected trickery, there is no excuse
for you.'

'That was at first, sir,' stammered Hopkins. 'Afterwards I had every reason to believe that'——

'Silence!' raged Shields. 'Your carelessness has
effected enough already without your offering lame
explanations. Heaven only knows what the consequences of this wretched fiasco will be to us.—
Corporal!'

'Sir,' answered the corporal, saluting.

But before the general could issue his order, whatever it was, Hopkins, who had been groping about in
the undergrowth, shouted excitedly : ' Here are the oars
and the rowlocks, general, just where I hid them. If
the fellow has cut the boat adrift and gone in her, he
can't be far off.'

'Can't he?' sneered Shields. 'And how do you
know, sir, that the rascal had not a boat of his own
under the bank, and simply cut yours adrift to lessen
the chances of pursuit?'

The bitter suggestion appeared to confound Hopkins
for a moment, but he answered humbly : 'Of course,
general, we must allow for possibilities ; but if I may
be permitted to say so, if the fellow had no boat of
his own, and swung out into the stream in mine before
he noticed the absence of oars, the current would
carry him rapidly down stream. He could not land
either on one side or the other.'

'No,' sneered the general again; 'and with a current like that, I think we might as well look for him at Harper's Ferry by this time. Further, you seem to forget, sir, that the man had the use of his hands, and by clinging to the trees alongside the bank, might very well work the boat up stream in the direction of the enemy.—Moreover,' he muttered vexedly to himself, 'we have no proof that he ever left dry land. Such a fellow, in Federal uniform, too, might pass anywhere.—And I'll be bound, sir,' he flashed out at the miserable Hopkins, 'that your carelessness has put him in possession of the countersign. Gad! I shall have him mounting guard outside my quarters to-night if I don't take care. This must be seen to.—What was he like, sir? What was he like? Describe him.'

'He was a tall, loosely made young man, sallow complexioned, and with a quantity of black, curling hair upon his cheeks and chin,' answered Hopkins feebly, utterly taken aback by this new view of the situation.

General Shields started as if he had been stung. 'By George!' he said under his breath. 'If I don't believe that was the identical fellow I spoke with this morning, and who told me that rigmarole about the balloon. Perhaps I have been too hard upon Spriggs. I have been, if my suspicions are correct. And if so, this is a dangerous fellow. We must lay him by the heels without delay.—Corporal!'

'Sir,' said the corporal again.

But once more the general's order was stayed upon his lips, for at that moment a solitary rifle-shot rang out, far down the river. It was that caused by the accidental discharge of Ephraim's gun.

'There he is! there he is!' began Hopkins excitedly;
but the general silenced him with a wave of his hand.

'We have no proof of that, Captain Hopkins,' he
said coldly. 'I do not suppose that if your friend
wishes to escape, he is likely to go gunning on the
Shenandoah. However, we will take measures to
ascertain.—Corporal!'

'Sir,' answered the corporal once more, and this
time he received his order.

'Send five of your men up the river to thoroughly
search the bank. Take the other five with you down
the river in the direction of that shot. Lose no time,
and leave no stone unturned to secure the man whom
Captain Hopkins has just described. You noted the
description?'

'Yes, general.'

'Very good. Be off, then. Remember the fellow is
—or was—in Federal uniform.—Now, Captain Hopkins,
attend to me, if you please. You will return to camp
at once, give Major Wheeler my compliments, and
repeat your description of this man. Then add that
it is my order that he at once send out search parties
in all directions, up the river, down the river, and in
and about the woods, with instructions to bring before
the provost-marshal every stray Federal soldier they
can pick up. We shall recover a lot of stragglers that
way, even if we do not get our man. And—er—one
thing more,' as Hopkins moved away. 'When you
have executed this order, you will'——

'Yes, general?' said Hopkins, quailing under the
former's withering look.

'Report yourself to your colonel as under arrest,
sir,' snapped the general, and turned upon his heel.

Left alone, General Shields made a careful survey of the river and the bank in his immediate vicinity, but finding nothing for his pains, returned without further delay to the camp, where he at once gave orders that the pickets should be doubled along the line next the enemy, and also, as might have been expected, changed the countersign for the night.

The moment Lucius took the water, it became plain to him that he had entered upon no light undertaking, and looking round, he informed the Grizzly of this.

'Say, Grizzly,' he cried, 'this is going to take me all my time. The current is tremendous. Watch out now, and the moment you see that the rope is taut, work your paddle for all you're worth, so as to bring her nose round.'

He drew a deep breath, and turning half over, cleft the water with a powerful side-stroke, in order to bring the greatest possible force to bear on the nose of the boat, and suddenly. It told. She stopped with a shiver, the water churning at her bows, and slowly her nose began to come round. Ephraim worked madly with his rifle-butt, hissing at every splash like a stable-boy grooming a horse.

'She's round!' he cried joyously. 'She's round, Luce! Her nose is ter the bank!'

On hearing this satisfactory piece of intelligence, Lucius turned over on his chest and swam with frog strokes towards the shore. He was wise enough not to attempt this in a bee-line, but moved diagonally, content to progress if it were but an inch at a time, so long as, aided by Ephraim's paddle, he could keep the boat's nose in the right direction. It was for-

tunate for him that he was young and strong, and that
he knew how to husband his strength, for he needed
it all in that chill, swiftly flowing stream.

Presently Ephraim hailed him with encouraging
words: ' Ye 're gittin' thar, Luce. Ye 're gittin' thar.
Air ye tired, bub? Let yerself drift ef ye air. Thar 's
not a sign er any wan on the bank above or below.
My! I wish I could swim, Luce. Ye wouldn't be long
in thar. Keep it up, sonny. Ye 're gittin' us thar.'
And so on, with many soothing, senseless words that
fell gratefully upon the ear of the almost exhausted
Lucius.

The boy lifted his eyes and glanced ahead. The
bank was now but thirty feet away; but at the rate
he was making it, it was not unlikely that ten minutes
more in the water awaited him. He could not bear
to think of it, for already his limbs felt numb, and his
breath began to fail him. He shut his eyes, set
his teeth hard, and struck out blindly. He heard the
plashing of Ephraim's sorry paddle behind him, and
the sound was as the noise of thunder in his ears.
His strokes became feebler and less frequent, his body
swayed more and more to the rush of the current, and
for all that he could do, the rope slackened every now
and then. Still he kept on, beating down that wild
desire to hail Ephraim, who he knew would haul him
in at the first call, and slowly struggling towards the
goal of all their hopes, the shore. Suddenly his heart
gave a great leap, seeming to turn over in his chest and
stop dead. A great roaring filled his ears, his head
seemed to split asunder with the force of the pain that
racked it; a shriek which made but a bubbling in the
water about his mouth burst from his throat; and as

a dead-weight seemed to drag him downwards, he threw his hands above his head.

Something touched them, and he grasped wildly, clawing at the yielding support. Joy! It was a branch. He hung on with all his remaining strength, and in another instant Ephraim had made fast and dragged him into the boat.

For some minutes he lay down there, unable to speak or move, but gradually, as the Grizzly rubbed and chafed him, the power came back to his limbs and the sense to his brain.

'Thet's well!' cried Ephraim, overjoyed. 'Oh, Luce, it made me sick ter see ye so done. By time! ye did thet pull in grand style. Air ye all right now?'

Lucius nodded.

''Cause ef ye air,' went on Ephraim, 'I hev got an idee. Ye see thar, right in front er us, is a cave. It's not very deep. Fact is, it's nuthin' but a hole in the bank, but it'll serve fer a restin'-place till we kin git some notion er what is goin' ter happen. Git up thar. I'll send up the things.'

Standing on the seat of the boat, the hole was just on a level with Luce's chest, and with a little assistance from Ephraim he easily climbed in.

The Grizzly had passed up the clothes, the rifle, and the two belts, when something arrested his attention. He listened intently for a moment, and then clinging to the floor of the hole, gave a backward kick with his feet that sent the boat spinning out into the stream, and sprang in beside Lucius.

Scarcely had he done so, when a loud voice, not far away, shouted exultantly: 'I see him, corporal! There he is!'

CHAPTER XII.

A DUEL IN THE DARK.

S this alarming shout rang in their ears, Lucius, forgetting his fatigue, sprang to the mouth of the hole and made as if he would dive again into the water. But Ephraim held him back.

'Steady, Luce!' he exclaimed. 'Lie low! It's the boat he sees—not us.'

Thus restrained, Lucius withdrew, shivering with cold, to the farthest extremity of the hole, where he proceeded to rub himself down and dress. Ephraim, meanwhile, took his stand at the entrance, and listened intently for any indications of the whereabouts of the enemy.

They were not long in coming, for presently footsteps resounded on the bank above, and a voice eagerly questioned: 'Where? Where did you see him?'

'Well, I didn't exactly see him,' answered the first voice, much to Ephraim's relief; 'but there's the boat, and I guess he won't be far off.'

The corporal strained his eyes after the boat through the gathering darkness. 'I guess it's empty,' he said after a long look. 'However, squad, attention! At one hundred yards, fire a volley! Ready! Present! Fire!'

Bang! crash! splinter! sputter! as some of the balls struck the boat, and the rest fell like hailstones in the water round about her.

Ephraim chuckled softly, and rubbed his hands together in delight. 'We air jest ez well out er thet, Luce,' he whispered. 'I reckon wan or two er them Yanks kin shoot straight.'

'Load!' ordered the corporal above. 'You four,' addressing his men, 'follow that boat along the bank, and see if you can discover any signs of life in her. Fire at discretion.—You, Whitson,' to the man who had first caught sight of the boat, 'stay here and show me where you think that boat came from. It was not in sight two or three minutes ago.'

Whitson pushed through the trees to the verge of the bank. 'It seemed to come out of the bushes just here,' he said, peering over; 'but I don't see anything.'

'You don't suppose the fellow is going to rise right up and look at you, do you?' inquired the corporal with fine scorn, adding: 'Did you hear anything?'

'Not a sound,' admitted Whitson.

'Then it's pretty certain there was no one in her,' said the corporal. 'Most likely she got caught on a snag and turned in here, broke loose, and drifted off again. The general was right—the fellow has either gone up the bank or struck inland. All the same, we'd better search the bank hereabouts.'

But the projecting roof of the hole offered a sure protection to the boys; and though more than once they could distinguish the trampling of the feet of the soldiers above their heads, their hiding-place remained undiscovered, and presently the search was discontinued.

'It's no use,' said the corporal. 'He is not here. Never was, I should say. We're only wasting time. Let us go back to camp.—Hello! What do you suppose that is?'

That was Ephraim's cap, which, supported by its own lightness and the water beneath it, hove in sight, floating gracefully down stream, some forty yards away.

Ephraim saw it at the same moment, and softly whispered to Lucius to come and see the fun.

'It looks like a cap,' answered Whitson, peering through the gloom. 'Blamed if I don't believe it is a cap.'

'With a head inside it?' pursued the corporal, also doing his best to see.

'I can't say. Shall I try and find out?'

The corporal nodded, and Whitson, throwing forward his rifle, fired. The ball struck the water some feet beyond the cap, which still moved unconcernedly along.

'Missed!' cried the corporal, firing his own rifle immediately afterwards. 'That's better. That wiped your eye.'

His bullet had struck the cap slantwise on the crown, turning it over, so that it immediately filled and sank to the bottom.

'My!' whispered Ephraim gleefully. 'It's ez good ez shootin' et bottles et a fair.'

'I guess it was only a cap,' said the corporal, reloading his rifle; 'but we can't be sure. We'll report the

circumstance, anyhow.—Hello! What did you find?'
This to the four men who had returned.

'No one in the boat, corporal,' answered one of
them. 'We followed her down to the bend, and she
ran on a shoal and turned over on her side. We could
see right into her.'

'We'll report that too,' said the corporal with military brevity.—'Fall in! Squad, attention! Shoulder
arms! Slope arms! Quick march!'

'Thet's one more down ter us,' said Ephraim, with
an air of relief, as the noise of footsteps died away in
the distance. 'Thet old boat served our turn well,
after all. They won't worry ter hunt up in this direction any more. Thar's been a fuss, though, Luce. Did
ye hear what he said about the ginrul? My! I reckon
them Yanks will be ez lively ez a Juny-bug ter-night,
looking fer us and all.'

'So lively,' returned Lucius, 'that I think we may
as well give up all hope of placing that packet in
General Jackson's hands. It is enough that we, or
rather you, have prevented it from reaching Frémont.'

'I reckon not,' said Ephraim thoughtfully. 'Shields
is pretty sure ter try and git a message over ter him
now thet this wan's failed.'

'Even so, he may change his plans,' argued Lucius.

'He han't the time,' answered Ephraim with considerable shrewdness. 'Thet is, ef he's on the lookout
fer an attack to-morrer, and I reckon he is. Of co'se,
he may alter 'em hyar and thar, jest ter try and bluff
old Stonewall; but in the main I b'leeve he'll hev ter
abide by 'em.'

'Well, what is it to be, then?' asked Lucius, yawning.
'I'm out for the day, so I may as well take a hand in

the fun. If we're caught with that despatch about us, we're as good as done for. However, I suppose we may try for the sheep now that we've got the lamb.'

'But we ain't goin' ter let them ketch us,' said Ephraim. 'Ye see, we're a heap better off than we war this mornin' or this afternoon, for we know the countersign, and ef with thet we don't manage ter slip past their sentries, it's a wonder. All the same, though,' he went on, 'we may ez well take a couple er hours' rest. I'm about done, I own up ter thet, and I should say thet you wouldn't be the worse fer it.'

'Considering that I had four hours' sleep this afternoon, thanks to you,' answered Lucius, 'I'm not so bad. I could eat something, though; so if you'll produce the ham, we'll lay the table.'

Ephraim laughed, and opening his coat, extracted the wedge of ham which he had carried there since the morning, and which, whatever it might have been at first, did not look very inviting now. However, hunger is the best sauce, and nearly dark as it was, the dishevelled appearance of the ham did not count against it; so between it and the biscuits the two boys made a very hearty meal, chatting merrily all the while, as if they had not a care in the world.

'Now,' said Lucius, when they had finished, 'I feel as fresh as a daisy. You lie down and sleep for the first hour, and I'll keep watch.'

'Air ye shore ye kin hold out?' asked Ephraim, who did indeed feel terribly sleepy.

'Certain. Lie down, old Grizzly. I'll wake you when I think the hour is up.'

Ephraim took off his coat, and making a pillow of it, went to sleep almost instantly, so worn out was he; while Lucius, going to the mouth of the cave, sat down and looked over the river into the night.

It was almost dark, for the sky had clouded over, and every now and then a few drops of rain fell, but the soft light of the summer night prevailed to some extent, and Lucius, who could see the outlines of the steep heights across the river, fell to picturing the battle which had been waged beyond them that day, and wondering which side had gained the victory. He lost himself in his musings for a quarter of an hour, and then fumbled mechanically for his watch. 'I wonder if the hour is up,' he said to himself; 'I'm beginning to feel drowsy now. Oh, I forgot. I left it at home.'

The word gave his thoughts a new turn, and in fancy he saw his mother grieving over his absence, and despairing of ever seeing him again. The idea distressed him, and presently conscience began to add her stings, and strive as he would to excuse his disobedience, his mood grew gloomier and gloomier. 'I hate the dark,' he muttered; 'it always makes me feel so lonesome. Surely the hour must be up.'

As a matter of fact, he had kept watch but for twenty·minutes, but those who have tried it know how slowly the minutes drag themselves along in the dark, when the sense of time is, as it were, abolished, and the attention, with nothing else to attract it, is firmly fixed on the hours, whose wings seem to have been clipped for the occasion. It is the watched pot that never boils.

At last the lonesome feeling overcame Lucius to such an extent that he could bear it no longer; so rising to his feet, he stole softly across the cave and sat down beside the snoring Grizzly, for company, as he expressed it to himself. Sitting there in the deeper darkness, a gentle drowsiness fell upon him. He made one or two not very vigorous efforts to shake it off, and then, yielding to its delicious influence, sank into a refreshing sleep.

Scarcely a moment later, as it seemed to him, he was awakened. A hand was laid upon his shoulder, and another pressed lightly over his mouth.

'Hush, Luce,' whispered Ephraim's voice close to his ear. 'Git up softly. It's time we war out er this. They're huntin' fer us.'

'Where?' whispered Lucius back.

'Thar's a boat comin' down the river. I jest caught sight er the flash of a lantern. They're searchin' the banks. Come, quick!'

They groped about in the dark until they found the rifle and their belts, which they put on, and stole to the mouth of the cave. Far up the river they saw a little twinkling light, which, as they watched it, grew slowly larger. Very slowly, for the search was a careful one, and the hunters were taking their time.

'What a good thing you saw it!' said Lucius in a low voice. 'They might have walked right in upon us if you hadn't. Oh, Grizzly,' he added in a tone of deep self-reproach, 'I went to sleep without waking you!'

'Ye rolled over on me wanst ye war asleep, and thet woke me,' answered Ephraim. 'I let ye snooze ez long ez I dared. Never mind thet now. Let's consider how we're ter git out er this.'

At first sight it appeared to be no easy matter, for the bank shelved away on each side of them, and the overhanging roof of the cave projected so far over the floor that it was impossible to reach it, while to attempt to leap for it in the darkness would infallibly result in a ducking, if nothing worse, in the river.

'Ef we on'y had a light,' muttered Ephraim.

'I have,' said Lucius. 'There are some matches in the pocket of these trousers.'

'Ah, but we dassn't show it,' returned Ephraim. 'We must think out some uther way.'

'Could we not just drop into the stream?' suggested Lucius. 'It's so close to the bank, we could not fail to reach it.'

'We'll do thet if the wust comes ter the wust,' replied Ephraim; 'but not ef thar's enny uther line; fer we might git separated in the dark, and besides, we don't know the depth.'

'Be quick and think of something, then,' said Lucius. 'They are coming nearer.'

Ephraim was lying down at the mouth of the cave, leaning out as far as he could without overbalancing himself, and feeling along the face of the rock in all directions for a ledge. At last he uttered a low grunt of satisfaction.

'What is it?' asked Lucius.

'The face of the rock jest underneath us is rough and projecktin',' answered Ephraim. 'I b'leeve we could work along it. Anyway, I'm goin' ter try. Ketch hold er the gun.'

Lucius felt for the rifle with which Ephraim had been making investigations, and took charge of it, while the Grizzly placed his hands upon the ledge formed by the floor of the cave, and cautiously swung himself over.

With dangling legs he explored the rocky wall until his feet struck the projection he thought he had felt, and resting them there, began to worm his way along. When he had reached the extreme angle of the cave, he stopped, and, clinging with one arm, thrust out the other to continue his explorations. It met the stout bough of a tree overhanging the river. Ephraim pulled with all his might. It held, and he determined to risk it. Letting go his hold of the ledge, he threw all his weight upon the bough, grasping it with his disengaged hand as he swung off into space. The bough bent beneath his weight, and his feet dipped into the river as he hung, but he struggled blindly on, and in another moment felt the firm earth under him as he struck the shelving bank.

'Bullee!' he said, as with an effort he regained his balance.—'Luce! Air ye thar?'

'Yes,' answered Lucius. 'Have you managed it?'

'You bet,' returned Ephraim cheerfully. 'All ye hev ter do is ter hang on ter the ledge and feel with yer feet till you kin git a hold. Then work yerse'f along till ye come ter the end of the hold and grab fer a branch. Hang on ter thet, and ye'll be safe.'

'But the gun,' said Lucius. 'Shall I leave it behind?'

'By time, no!' exclaimed Ephraim. 'It's all we've got, and we don't know when we may want it. Hyar, I'll come back fer it, and ye kin pass it along.'

He felt for the friendly bough, and presuming that he had found it, threw his weight upon it. Instantly it cracked across, and down he went into the water with a great splash. Fortunately he fell close under

the bank, and wildly grasping, caught a clump of
bushes and dragged himself out.

'It's all right, Luce,' he called up to the boy, who
was listening anxiously. 'I must hev caught the
wrong one. I'm on'y wet about the legs.'

'It's all wrong,' replied Lucius under his breath;
'those fellows have heard the splash: I'm sure of
it by the way the lantern is being moved about.'

'Half a breath,' said Ephraim. 'We won't leave
the gun ef we kin help it. I'll hev anuther try.'

He went to work again more cautiously, and this
time got hold of the right bough.

'Send her along, Luce,' he said. 'Careful now.
We don't want her goin' orf like the first wan.'

Lucius cautiously extended the gun, which, after
one or two ineffectual attempts, Ephraim caught and
landed safely. For an active boy like Lucius the
rest was easy, and in a very short time he joined
the Grizzly on the bank.

'Which way now?' inquired Lucius, when once
they had attained the level ground above.

'Oh, up the river,' answered Ephraim. 'We must
keep our faces towards old Stonewall's camp. We're
all right now, I reckon, with these uniforms and
the countersign. It's lucky we've got thet.'

Alas, poor Ephraim! He did not know of General
Shields's order, nor how anxiously his arrival was
expected by every sentry along the line.

'I wonder what time it is,' said Lucius in the low
tones they had learned of necessity to adopt.

'It orter be about nine o'clock,' answered Ephraim;
'but we've no way of knowin'. Thar's a moon, too,
about midnight, I'm sorry ter say; but p'raps the

clouds won't let her through. I'm fond er the moon; but jest this wan night I'd do without her and willin'.'

'It won't be as dark outside this belt of trees as it is here,' said Lucius, as they moved along.

'All the wuss fer us,' said Ephraim; 'fer outside 'em we must go. This belt is shore ter be full er sentries all along the river line. We must work our way down ter them fields we crossed this afternoon, and grub along through the ditch. That'll be—— Hush! Some one's comin'. Lie down.'

He sank noiselessly to the ground among the underbrush as stealthy footsteps were heard approaching. Lucius followed his example, and the two lay side by side, scarcely daring to breathe.

General Shields had left nothing undone to recover his all-important despatch, and the search was being vigorously prosecuted in every direction. A couple of boats had been procured, one being sent up and the other down the river, while, at the same time, land parties patrolled the bank, so that the fugitive, if discovered, would be caught, as it were, between two fires. Such a fate would have been inevitable for the boys, had not the vigilance of the Grizzly averted it, and Lucius blushed in the darkness as a pang of shame shot through him at the thought of the danger to which his self-indulgence in going to sleep upon his post had exposed them. He burned with affection at the recollection of Ephraim's quiet self-abnegation in calmly accepting the inevitable and rising to take a double share of watch, and roundly resolved that when the next time of trial came he should not be found wanting. As it was, their position was precarious enough, for the footsteps drew nearer, and their eyes could catch the gleams of a lantern as it swung to and fro, while up from the river came the soft splashing of oars, dipped gently by careful rowers.

Nearer and nearer came the lantern, and now by its light the anxious watchers could distinguish dimly the outlines of half-a-dozen soldiers, who stealthily followed their guide. Now and again a beam of the lantern light flashed upwards and was reflected back from the fixed bayonets of the party, and an uncomfortable thrill passed through Lucius as he wondered how it would feel to be skewered to the ground like a beetle with a pin stuck through it. He was rather fond of collecting things, and for the first time in his thoughtless existence he realised what must be the feelings of the 'bugs,' as he called them, which he was in the habit of treating so unceremoniously. However, he was quite content to realise it in imagination, and having no desire to experience the sensation in actual fact, kept his place as immovably as a statue thrown to the ground.

The search party was almost abreast of them now, keeping pace with the men in the boat, and the two lanterns, one flashing upwards, and the other downwards, made a pool of light which came uncomfortably close.

Another moment of breathless suspense and the party had passed by and darkness once more swallowed up the trembling watchers.

But they were not out of danger yet, and Ephraim's hand stole out and gripped Luce's shoulder as a soft hail came from the river.

'Above there!'

'Here!' came the muttered reply.

'This should be about where we heard that splash.'

'A little farther on, I think.'

'Forward, then, and keep your eyes open.'

Tramp! tramp! The soft tread was resumed, and Ephraim put his mouth close to Luce's ear.

'They'll find the cave in anuther minnit,' he whispered, 'and when they do, we must move off. Thar's shore ter be a hullaballoo.'

He was right. In a few minutes more another hail arose from the river, this time louder, more imperative, more confident.

'Above there!'

'Here!'

'Halt! Close up towards our light. There's a hole of some sort here. Maybe he is inside.'

Silence for a little space, and then an exultant shout from the bank.

'What have you found?' This from the boat.

'Nothing in the way of a man. But a broken branch and a sloppy mess all around.'

'Hold on till we pull under. If he's in there, we'll soon have him out.'

'Mind you don't get your head blown off.'

This very probable consequence to the first man who should put his head into the mouth of the hole caused a corresponding diminution of enthusiasm, and low mutterings arose from the boat.

'Private Storks, stand up in the boat and flash the lantern into that hole.—You above there, throw the light down as far as possible, and be ready.'

Great alacrity on the part of those on the bank.

Considerable hanging fire on the side of Private Storks.

'Now then, Storks, look sharp. You're not afraid, are you?'

A muttered disclaimer from the reluctant Storks.

'Private Flemming,' in a very angry voice, 'lift up that lantern and show this fellow Storks what a man is made of.'

A noise of scrambling in the boat, the twinkling of the lantern for an instant through the trees. Then bang! and a roar of laughter, followed by a storm of angry execrations. Private Flemming, by way of showing Private Storks how to be brave, had raised the lantern in one hand, his gun in the other, fired into the hole in order to make safety sure, and incontinently tumbled backwards into the boat to the imminent danger of his trusty comrades.

'Confound you!' shouted the officer in charge. 'Who told you to fire. You've given the fellow warning now, if he's not there. Up with you, some one, and see if this fool has been firing at a blank wall or not.'

The laughter above ceased at the angry command of the officer, but long ere it died away, and under cover of the friendly noise, the two boys, wriggling on their stomachs like a couple of great snakes, had put a good fifty yards between themselves and the men on the bank.

'By time!' muttered Ephraim. 'Thet's mighty good fun fer them; but it's jest ez well you and me war out er thar, Luce.'

They rose to their feet, and moving warily, soon passed out of the fringing belt into the open. Then, at Ephraim's direction, they ran as fast as they could, till a multitude of twinkling fires told them that the Federal troops lay close upon their left hand.

'Five minnits fer refreshments,' whispered Ephraim, 'and then the next act 'll begin. See hyar, Luce, it 's all Virginny ter a sour apple thet they 've got a chain er sentries right across from the camp to the river-side. We must dodge 'em. Ef wanst we kin git ter the ditch, we 'll be safe—so fur.'

They stole back just inside the belt of trees, and moved on, a step or two at a time. Sure enough, presently they could hear the measured tread of a sentry as he paced backwards and forwards upon his short beat.

'It won't do to try the countersign just here,' whispered Lucius. 'It 's too close to the camp.'

'No,' answered Ephraim. 'We must crawl past him, one at a time. You go first. Ef he sees ye, thar 's this.' He touched Lucius with the rifle.

Once again Lucius cast himself down flat upon the ground, and progressing by fractions of an inch, approached to within a few feet of the sentry. So close was he as the man passed him, that by stretching out his hand he could have caught him by the leg. But the darkness favoured him, though it was light enough to see ten paces away, and the man walked past unsuspiciously. Before he could turn again, Lucius had writhed beyond his beat and ensconced himself among the trees, where he waited for Ephraim.

The Grizzly had stood with his finger on the trigger, ready to fire if occasion arose; but now judging that

Lucius must be past the human obstruction, he noiselessly lowered the hammer of his gun and prepared
to make the effort on his own account.

It was more difficult for him than for Lucius,
encumbered as he was with his rifle; but Fortune
favours the bold, and in ten minutes' time he found
himself once more beside his comrade. They waited
till the sound of footsteps told them that the sentry's
back was once more turned to them, and then crawled
farther away. In this way they passed a second and
a third sentinel, and at length the end of their labours
presented itself in the shape of the field which they
had crossed in the afternoon. They dared not rise,
however, for fear of being seen, and a final crawl of
nearly a hundred yards had to be accomplished before
they found the safe retreat of the ditch.

'Thet's well,' said Ephraim, contentedly placing his
back against the side of the ditch and thrusting his
long legs out in front of him. By the time we git
ter the end er this, we'll hev got over a right smart
piece er the way.—How d' ye feel, Luce?'

'I'm all right,' answered Lucius. 'Have a cracker?
I've got a few left.'

'We may ez well eat 'em,' said the Grizzly, accepting
his share and beginning to munch; 'fer it's pretty
sartin thet ef we don't breakfast in our own camp
ter-morrer, we will in the Yanks'. Ef we don't reach
Stonewall ter-night, we never will.'

'Come on, then,' urged Lucius. 'Another mile and
a half ought to take us there.'

'Right!' said Ephraim, rising to his feet. 'Wait
a minnit, though.' Something clanked in his hand
as he spoke.

'What's that?' asked Lucius. 'What are you doing?'

'Fixin' my ba'net,' quoth Ephraim. 'Ye never know what'll happen, and it's best ter be ready. We've gone along and come safe through up ter now; but wan er my books says somewhar "the darkest hour's before the dawn," and maybe jest ez we think we're safe the bust'll come.'

Prophetic words, though Ephraim knew it not. The ditch in which they were had been marked by General Shields as a possible means of exit for any one lurking in the fields, and a thorough search of it had been made. This, of course, led to no result, as the boys were far away at the time; but the general's astuteness had not ended there, and a sentry had been placed at the end of the ditch remote from the camp— that is, nearest the Confederate lines, with definite orders to shoot any one issuing out of it if he could not give a good account of himself, and that, even though he wore the Federal uniform.

Sharp orders these, and liable to make any Federal skulker realise that there were other paths beside those of glory which led to the grave. Moreover, there was but slender chance that they would be disregarded, for the sentry chosen for this special duty was a grizzled sergeant, who had smelt powder in the Mexican campaign, and by reason of years of training on the frontier, was up to every dodge of those masters of deceptive strategy, the redskins. Small hope, then, that honest Ephraim, with his simple cunning, would, notwithstanding his victory over the green Captain Hopkins, be able to beat to windward of so astute a warrior as Sergeant Mason.

The darkest hour which Ephraim had hinted at was at hand. And yet not quite the darkest.

The ditch down which the boys were travelling intersected, as has been said, two fields—that on the right, some two hundred yards from the river; that on the left, about four hundred from the wood. These two spaces on a line with Sergeant Mason were destitute of sentries, though four hundred yards behind the sergeant, who stood expectant, but unconscious of the approach of his prey, ran a double line of pickets, right across from river to mountain. These were the outposts, and kept their watch almost cheek by jowl with Jackson's men, not half a mile beyond. Thus the outlet of the ditch had but this solitary defender, but in placing Sergeant Mason there, General Shields had shown his wisdom; and, moreover, the alarm of the sergeant's rifle, should he see fit to discharge it, would within five minutes bring him support from a dozen different points.

Sergeant Mason stood with his rifle resting easily in the hollow of his right arm, more in the attitude of an expert backwoodsman than in that of a sentry on guard, but his keen eyes glanced continually right and left over the dim, yet not absolutely dark, meadows, or straight ahead into the black funnel that intersected them. He had been there three long hours already, and was beginning to feel a little out of temper. And when Sergeant Mason was out of temper, it boded ill for whoever should cross his path at that inauspicious season.

Suddenly the sergeant started slightly. His quick ears, intently strained, had caught a faint sound, as of some one moving in the ditch. His ill-humour

vanished, down came his rifle with its sharp bayonet
to the charge, and he was at once the veteran soldier,
used to war's alarms, and ready for any emergency.

He leaned forward striving to pierce the gloom
of the ditch; but he could see nothing. Only once
again that soft rustling sound, as of the wind gently
blowing over reeds. Then it ceased.

Ceased so suddenly that the sergeant's suspicions
were at once redoubled. Evidently it was not the
wind. But Mason was too old a hand to act rashly,
so he did not challenge, for fear of scaring his game,
but waited patiently for the end.

Again the rustling. This time surely a little louder,
a little nearer. The sergeant's heavy moustache
bristled with anticipation, and his lips parted in a
cruel smile, as he tightly grasped his rifle.

Not a sound he made as he stood there, silent and
stiff as if carved out of ebony. But he had been seen
for all that, and even now the boys, crouching low
in the ditch, were holding a whispered consultation.

'I think thet he hes heard us, Luce,' said Ephraim.
'Listen ter me and do jest ez I tell ye. Crawl out er
the ditch on yer left and make a wide leg ter git
behind him. Ez soon ez ye start, I'll up an' face
him so ez ter cover any noise ye make. Wait fer
me until I git past him—and I will git past him one
way or anuther—and when ye hear me run, foller
ez hard ez ye kin.'

The first part of this well-laid plan was carried out
to the letter; but as to the second—ah! there Ephraim
had reckoned without Sergeant Mason.

Lucius made off as he had been told to do, for after
what he had seen, his faith in Ephraim's strategic

M

powers was absolutely unbounded, and as soon as
he was clear of the ditch, the Grizzly, with much
rustling of his feet and a great outward show of
confidence, advanced towards the outlet of the ditch.

From his superior height upon the slight embank-
ment Sergeant Mason looked down and smiled grimly.
He never suspected the presence of Lucius, wriggling
along to attain a point behind him. His whole mind
was intent on the solitary figure, advancing towards
him.

'Halt!   Who comes there?' he challenged, and
Ephraim brought up standing, halted within six paces
of the bayonet's point.

'Friend!' he answered laconically.

'What's your business?' demanded Mason, wishful
to make sure of his ground and his man.

'Speshul,' returned Ephraim, also feeling his way.

'That so? What mought be the natur of it? I'm
hyar tew find out, yew know.'

'Out after a man wearin' a Federal uniform, and
supposed ter be a rebel spy.   Kin I pass?'

'I guess so.   If yew have the countersign.'

Alas, poor Grizzly, the fighter of redskins is going
to be too much for you! Ephraim advanced a pace
or two.

'Halt!' said the sergeant again.   'Is that yewr idee
of giving the countersign?'

'Shenandoah!' replied Ephraim boldly, and never
before had been so near death as at that minute.

Had Sergeant Mason, smiling grimly behind his
thick moustache, obeyed orders strictly, he would have
fired then and there, for the word was not Shenandoah,
and Ephraim's account of himself had not been good;

but two reasons restrained Mason. If the man turned out to be a brother Federal, he did not wish to have his blood upon his hands, skulker though he might be in view of the morrow's expected fight; and, secondly, if the man were proved to be the rebel spy, Mason considered that a capture would redound more to his credit than an execution.

Therefore Sergeant Mason held his hand, and bringing his rifle up to the port, said briefly: 'Pass, friend!'

On came Ephraim, his shambling gait and loose-jointed frame contrasting ridiculously with the square, well-knit, soldierly figure in front of him; but just as he had set one foot on the bank to leap out of the ditch, being so far at a disadvantage, the sergeant suddenly altered his position, and bringing his rifle to the low guard, said sharply: 'Surrender, my man. You're my prisoner.'

On the lookout for surprises, Ephraim's heart yet seemed to leap into his mouth at this; but he was quick to act. Jumping back from the steel that almost touched his neck, he grasped his own rifle with one hand by the breech and with the other by the barrel, and before the sergeant could realise his intention, rushed madly at him up the bank.

Their bayonets met with a clash; but so furious was the assault, and so utterly unexpected, that even Sergeant Mason, man of iron though he was, gave back before it, and Ephraim springing from the ditch, found himself, so far at least as the ground went, at an equal advantage with his foe.

For an instant they stood fronting each other, their bayonets crossed, and only the space of their rifles between them.

The sergeant breathed hard and drew back the hammer of his gun. 'Surrender!' he said, 'or you're a dead man.'

Ephraim heard the click, and his answer was another rush. Swift as thought he turned his wrist, and by sheer force tossed the barrel of the sergeant's rifle in the air, just as the latter's finger touched the trigger.

Bang! The bullet soared away high over the tops of the trees in the wood, and once more the sergeant recoiled before his impetuous antagonist. He began to wish that he had fired first and made inquiries afterwards.

'Surrender, you fool!' he hissed through his clenched teeth; 'that shot will bring a hundred men down upon you.'

For answer, Ephraim cocked his own rifle and fired. There was a slight fizzle as the cap snapped, but no report. The various uses to which the rifle had been put that day had not improved its quality as a 'shooting-iron,' and the powder was thoroughly wet.

The rifles were the old-fashioned, muzzle-loading pattern. There was no time to reload, and like lightning Ephraim rushed forward to renew the attack.

Then began a battle royal. Sergeant Mason was a strong man, and knew the use of his weapon; but the Grizzly was a living instance of the truth of the saying, that a man who knows nothing of rule will very often puzzle an expert. So it was now, as Ephraim, fired with unaccustomed fury, lunged and thrust, parried and recovered, or swept his bayonet in narrowing circles round his antagonist's head, to the utter mystification of Mason, accustomed to the one, two, three of the regulations.

Clink! clank! rattle! crash! The sharp steel met and parted, parted and met again. The fighters could but just distinguish each other in the gloom, even as they stood now with bayonets locked, breathing hard in anticipation of the next rally.

Clank! The sergeant disengaged, and lunged straight and swiftly out. The bayonet passed under the Grizzly's left arm; but he brushed it aside with a wild swirl of his rifle, and thrust in return so close to the sergeant's heart, that but half an inch further would have settled the question for good and all.

Mason sprang backwards just in time, now hotly pressed by the furious Grizzly. Here was a foeman of a temper he had not bargained for when he made that light arrest.

'Help!' he roared at the top of his voice. 'A spy! a spy! Over hyar by the ditch.'

Clank! clank! clink! clink! Fierce thrust and sudden parry. Another fiery rally. This time the sergeant felt the wind of Ephraim's bayonet past his neck, and a hot spurt of breath upon his face, as the Grizzly, almost overbalanced by his frenzied rush, stumbled forward.

With a mighty effort he recovered his footing. Clink! clank! Down swept Mason's glittering steel. Another lock. A rapid disengagement; and, ere Ephraim could retreat, the long blade lunged straight at his face.

The Grizzly dodged; but the sharp point, driven by the strong, angry arm behind it, found its way through his coat, and ploughed up the muscles of his shoulder. The pain drove him wild, and with a roar of rage he

ran in upon his foe, careless of his own exposure,
and raising his long rifle by the barrel, brought it
smashing down upon the bare, defenceless head.

Under that frightful stroke Sergeant Mason
dropped his weapon, reeled from side to side like a
drunken man, and dropped to earth as one dead.

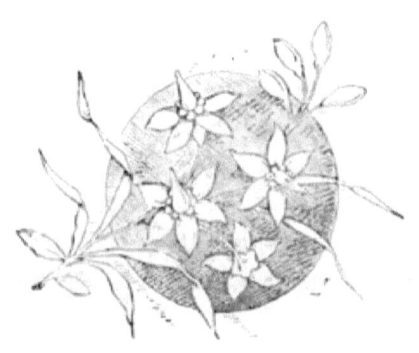

CHAPTER XIII.

HOW THE DESPATCH WAS BROUGHT TO STONEWALL JACKSON.

HILE this frightful battle raged, Lucius stood some little distance off, in an agony of apprehension for the safety of his friend. At the first clank of the meeting steel he had risen to his feet, and strained his eager eyes to see what was about to happen; but, even though he drew a little nearer, he could distinguish nothing clearly. Only in the dusk a pair of tall forms dashed from right to left, or bounded from side to side, meeting, recoiling, and meeting again. But if he could not see, he could hear; and at each jarring clank of the clashing bayonets his heart leaped, and his hair rose on his head, for he could not believe that Ephraim would win the fight. Oh for a gun! he thought, as he ran wildly backwards and forwards, groping along the ground, in the hope that he might come upon some straggler's discarded piece. All at once he heard shouts and the noise of rushing footsteps. From the river bank, from the woods, from the pickets behind him—from every direction—men were hastening to the scene of the conflict. Then that furious cry from the Grizzly, and the dull crash as the sergeant fell under his powerful stroke. Finally silence for a little space around the combatants.

Lucius did not know which had fallen: he could just see that one was down—that was all—and his fears told him that it must be Grizzly. A dull, apathetic feeling stole over him. He did not try to move. He knew that in a few minutes more he must be a prisoner, and he did not care. A mournful voice seemed to chant in his ears, slow and solemn as a dirge, 'The Grizzly is dead! the Grizzly is dead!' And all concern for himself vanished in the presence of this overwhelming sorrow.

Then, as he stood, the sound of the well-known voice thrilled him like an electric shock, jarring his whole frame with the one pregnant monosyllable, 'Run!' And, without stopping to question or to reason, he turned his face and fled. Fled at first madly, unthinkingly, right in the teeth of the advancing enemy. He had no knowledge of Ephraim's whereabouts—whether he was ahead of him or behind him. He was alive—that was just enough then—and on went Lucius like the wind.

When two people are running at top speed in the same line, but from opposite extremes, it stands to reason that, sooner or later, they will meet. And this is exactly what happened now. They met, Lucius and the leading man of the racing sentinels—met with a crash, like two charging footballers—with the result that both went down in a heap upon the ground.

Lucius was the first to recover himself, and the shock seemed to clear his brain, so that he realised sharply what he was doing in thus throwing himself into the arms of his foes. He was a slow thinker as a rule— or, rather, he seldom troubled himself to think at all; but now his plans were formed upon the instant, such a stimulus is necessity.

Tearing himself free from the man upon the ground, he leaped to his feet, and running a few paces, still towards the advancing crowd, wheeled round suddenly, and with a loud shout of 'This way! Over here!' rushed back by the way he had come, only at a much slower pace.

Fortunate it was for him that it was so dark. Guided by his voice, the soldiers hurried after him, surrounded him, noted him running in their midst in the same direction as themselves, and—passed him by.

Still Lucius held on, slowing down at every stride, till the last man of the supports, puffing and blowing, shot ahead of him, and then he turned in his tracks once more, and sped like a deer towards the Confederate lines.

He took a diagonal path, making by instinct for the corner of the wood, which more than once that day had been their means of salvation, and reaching it after a tearing run of nearly a mile, plunged just inside its border and flung himself face downwards to recover his wind.

All at once, as he lay, a sharp pang shot through him. The Grizzly! Where was he? Was he, too, running for his life in the open? Had he reached the wood? Or, bitter thought, had he been captured after all? The bare possibility stung Lucius into action, and he leaped again to his feet, glaring wildly round him in the dark.

What would they do with him if he were taken?

Would they shoot him then and there? Or would they take him back to the camp, and after a mere formality of a trial, hang him like a dog? Lucius strained his ears until they pained him, listening for the fatal shot. But he heard nothing. 'Oh, Grizzly,' he thought bitterly, 'if you are taken, if you are shot, and I have run away and left you to your fate!'

He was hardly fair to himself in his sharp self-upbraiding. To run had been the Grizzly's own command, and he had obeyed implicitly. He began to take a little comfort. Perhaps they had only missed one another in the dark. Perhaps the Grizzly was even now in safety, waiting opportunity to make a dash for the Confederate lines. He would go on. Then again the cruel thought, 'What if he be a captive while I am free?' 'Go on and save yourself, at all events,' whispered self-preservation. 'It is what he himself would have you do.'

'And just because it is what he would have me do,' answered the spirit of manliness in the boy's breast, 'I will not do it. I will go back and find him, if I have to march right into the Federal camp.'

He was almost beside himself with pain and grief, but the one idea took possession of him, and in his brain the words repeated themselves over and over again: 'Go back and find him! Go back and find him!'

'Oh, if I had but a gun!' he sighed, 'I would make somebody pay for this.'

His hands struck against his cartridge belt. 'Pah!' he said in disgust, opening the pouch. 'What is the use of you without a gun?' Then a gasp of astonishment escaped him. His fingers, idly groping in the

pouch, had encountered a piece of folded paper—two
pieces.

For a moment he could not understand it, and then
the meaning flashed across him, and everything became
clear. In the dark of the cave he had picked up and
assumed Ephraim's belt instead of his own. The papers
were General Shields's despatch to General Frémont,
and the written order to Colonel Spriggs regarding the
escaped prisoners.

Luce's first feeling was one of joy that, even if the
Grizzly were taken, at all events nothing compromising
would be found upon him. His second, a wild impulse
to fling away the despatch, and rid himself of its
dangerous companionship. But something restrained
him in the very act, and the thought crossed him:
'The fate of an army may depend upon that paper,
and that army your own. You must carry it to
General Jackson.'

Poor Lucius! He was on the horns of a dreadful
dilemma. If he were caught with that paper upon
him, it would be short shrift, he knew, and few questions asked. Yet if he did not deliver it, the consequences to the Confederates might be fearfully
disastrous. And yet again, if he did attempt to carry
it through, he must turn his back upon his friend,
presuming him to be a prisoner, and after the thoughts
of self-preservation in which he had indulged, how
could he do that without laying himself open to the
charge of grasping an excuse to ensure his own safety
by an attempt to reach the Confederate lines?

He wrung his hands together in the extremity of
his despair. Which was the right thing to do? Who
would help him in this desperate strait?

He leaned against a tree, his head throbbing and his whole mind bewildered in the presence of the most serious problem he had ever had to face. Then once again came to him one of those mysterious, silent promptings, so frequent in the last anguished quarter of an hour. And this time it was as if Ephraim spoke: 'Do yer duty, Luce, and never mind me.'

'I will,' he cried aloud, dashing the tears from his eyes. 'I will. But I'll come back and find you afterwards, Grizzly, if I die for it!'

He braced himself up to consider the best means to carry out his dual resolve. He knew very well that, no matter how many men might have been detached to the aid of the sentry at the ditch, the Federal outposts would still remain in their place, with beyond them the last line of sentinels on the side of Jackson's army. To reach his goal he must first pass this obstacle, and he realised that in the ferment raised by the present crisis, the time for further stratagem had passed, and that his only hope lay in making a rush for it.

A sense of uneasiness was everywhere, and the outposts were especially alert. Not only had the rumour spread of the presence in camp and subsequent escape therefrom of a supposed rebel spy, but there was a pretty well defined feeling that the morrow would not pass without an attack on the part of Jackson, though exactly how or where the blow would be delivered, no man could say. Therefore the outposts kept even stricter watch than usual, ready at the first sign of the advance of the enemy to give the alarm and fall back upon the camp, where, on that night, the Federal soldiers lay on their arms.

The uneasy feeling was justified by what was happening in the Confederate camp. The night had descended upon another Federal repulse. The veteran Ewell had hurled back Frémont at Cross Keys, and driven him from the field after a long and desperate conflict. Then, when the darkness put a stop to the operations, Jackson recalled the troops of Ewell, and leaving a strong rearguard in front of Frémont, returned to Port Republic. Here he hastily constructed a foot-bridge, by means of wagons placed end to end, over the south fork of the Shenandoah, and gave orders that at dawn his infantry were to cross and try conclusions with Shields at Lewiston. He then retired to snatch a few hours of well-earned repose. Shields, meanwhile, had managed to get a second despatch conveyed to Frémont, laying before him a plan of operations which differed little from those set forth in the lost despatch; for as Ephraim had shrewdly surmised, there was but scant time to alter the disposition of an entire army; and, moreover, Shields, sanguine to the last, could not bring himself to believe that, from a camp so strongly guarded, the spy had really been able to make good his escape. He was convinced that if accident did not deliver the bold rebel into his hands during the night, his capture would certainly be accomplished in the morning. That there were two people concerned in this escapade he had never fully realised, and that the despatch had passed from one hand to another, he never even dreamed.

Fully alive to the dangers of the situation, Lucius moved cautiously along, feeling the edge of the wood lest he should lose himself in its gloomy depths, and

every moment drawing nearer to the Federal outposts.
A white glow on the hill-tops warned him that the
moon was rising, and he prayed earnestly that the
clouds which were driving across the sky would form
up and shut behind them the silver light which would
make the difficulties of his perilous advance so much
greater.

Suddenly he pulled up short. Not far away he
heard a sound, a suppressed cough. There it was
again, its owner evidently doing his best to stifle it.
Lucius surmised clearly enough from whom the sound
proceeded. It was one of the communicating sentries
between the outposts and their reserves. He felt
rather than heard that the man was walking in his
direction, and with the painful thought troubling him,
'What if I were to cough or sneeze?' drew close behind
a tree to wait till he had passed by. Standing
there, he heard another sound—the measured tramp
of feet, as if a body of men were stealthily approaching
him. The sentry heard it too, for he halted a few
paces from Lucius and prepared to act.

'Halt!' he challenged in a guarded voice, at the
same time bringing his rifle to the charge. 'Who
comes there?'

'Patrol!' was the reply, also given in an undertone.

'Stand, patrol! Advance one and give the countersign!'

Some one stepped forward to the point of the
sentry's bayonet, and answered in a tone so low as to
be almost a whisper: 'Winchester!'

'So,' thought Lucius, who caught the word, 'the
countersign has been changed. That is how Grizzly

came to be stopped at the ditch. Well, it won't do me any good, for I dare not try it on now.'

'Pass, patrol! All's well!' said the sentry, still keeping his rifle at the charge.

The patrol moved on, the officer in charge turning back to inquire: 'Any sign of the spy?'

'No, sir,' replied the sentry, and Luce's heart thrilled with joy at the word.

Presently the sentry resumed his beat, and Lucius slipped past and continued his heedful advance. The most difficult part of his work lay before him, for the outposts were in strength, and their advanced sentries had also to be negotiated. Still he thought that, once past the outposts, he would be able to show the sentinels a clean pair of heels. But there was one thing on which he had not reckoned, and presently he came upon a sight which took his breath away. A line of light lay right across his path—the bivouac fires of the pickets.

They extended as far as he could see on either hand, and the boy's heart sank within him as he wondered how he should pass across that line of radiant light without being discovered. However, on closer investigation, he saw to his intense relief that, though the fires were not very far apart, yet between each was a dark space, and through one of these he trusted to be able to slip. Moreover, he noted that, while most of the men were lying down, some few were standing up or walking about, and so was led to hope that his upright figure, if observed at all, would not attract attention.

There was no help for it—it had to be done; so drawing a long breath he set his teeth hard, and making carefully for the dark path between two of the fires, advanced with firm and deliberate step.

Some one spoke to him as he came on. He did not hear the question, but he was conscious of returning an answer of some sort, though a moment afterwards he could not have told what he had said.

He reached the coveted path between the two fires, and again a soldier who was reclining by one of them hailed him.

'That yew, Dick?' asked the man. 'Why can't yew keep still? I believe yew're a funk.'

Lucius spared a thought to bless the restless Dick, and strode on.

'Dick,' said the man again, 'did yew hear that?— Why, Dick! Look at him! By'——

For Lucius had passed beyond the line, and casting all idea of further concealment to the winds, leaped forward like a startled hare.

In a moment all was bustle and confusion. The pickets sprang to arms, orders were shouted in rapid succession, and twenty men darted upon the track of the fugitive, while the advance sentries, hearing the commotion, stopped on their beat, eagerly waiting the explanation of the unusual disturbance, which, so far as they were concerned, seemed to come from the wrong quarter.

The very energy of the pursuit saved Lucius; for sentries, pursuers, and pursued were all mixed up in one inextricable tangle in the darkness, and the noise the soldiers made in following him of itself prevented them from getting any clear idea of his whereabouts.

On he dashed. Shots were fired here and there at

random; but if any one was hit it was not Lucius, and in less than five minutes he plumped into the middle of a Confederate picket, under arms, and ready for an affair of outposts, if that were what the noise presaged.

'I surrender! I surrender!' panted Lucius. 'Take me prisoner! Quick!'

'I reckon ef thet's what ye've come fer, ye've got yer way,' said a Confederate soldier gruffly, at the same time seizing him by the arm. 'Air thar enny more er you uns on the road?'

'No,' gasped Lucius; 'there's only me. Take me to the General. Quick! Oh, do be quick!'

'Take ye to the Ginrul! Thet's good! Ho! ho!' The men around broke into loud laughter; but an officer, coming up at that moment, sternly ordered silence, and raising a lantern to look at Lucius, demanded who he was, and what he meant by running into them like that.

'I want to see the General,' repeated Lucius, who just then could think of nothing else to say.

'State your business to me,' said the officer. 'I will be the judge as to whether it is of sufficient importance to justify the granting of your request. Are you a deserter from the enemy? Do you bring news of his movements?'

'No—yes,' replied Lucius hurriedly. 'I mean I am not a deserter, but I bring important news.'

'If you are not a deserter, what do you mean by wearing that uniform? Explain yourself.'

'Captain,' answered Lucius earnestly, 'believe me, I am telling the truth. I found this uniform, and put it on to disguise myself. I have a despatch from General

N

Shields to General Frémont, and I will give it to the General, if you will take me to him.'

'Give it to me,' urged the captain, holding out his hand. Lucius hesitated. If he gave up the despatch and then asked leave to return, the captain would become suspicious of a trick, and perhaps detain him there till the rounds passed by, and so valuable time would be lost. He felt that his only resource lay in an appeal to some one in authority who would grant him the required permission, and the memory of Jackson's face at Staunton on that last Sunday suggested that the appeal should be made to him, and him alone. 'He will understand me,' thought Lucius; 'these other fellows will not.' Aloud he said: 'Captain, I've gone through a good deal—in fact, I've risked my life—to bring that despatch here, and I beseech you to let me give it to the General with my own hands. More depends upon it than you think.'

The captain considered. The earnest pleading moved him. 'Who are you?' he asked at length.

'I belong to Staunton,' answered Lucius. 'My fa—— I have a relative in this army.'

'Who may that be?' inquired the captain, for it was no uncommon thing for different members of a family to be fighting on opposite sides of the line.

'I'd rather not say,' answered Lucius. 'Oh, captain, let me go. I am sure that the General will tell you you have done right if you do.'

'Corporal,' said the captain, after another moment's reflection, 'take this fellow to headquarters. Report the affair to the adjutant, and hear what he has to say.'

Lucius thanked him gratefully, and presently started

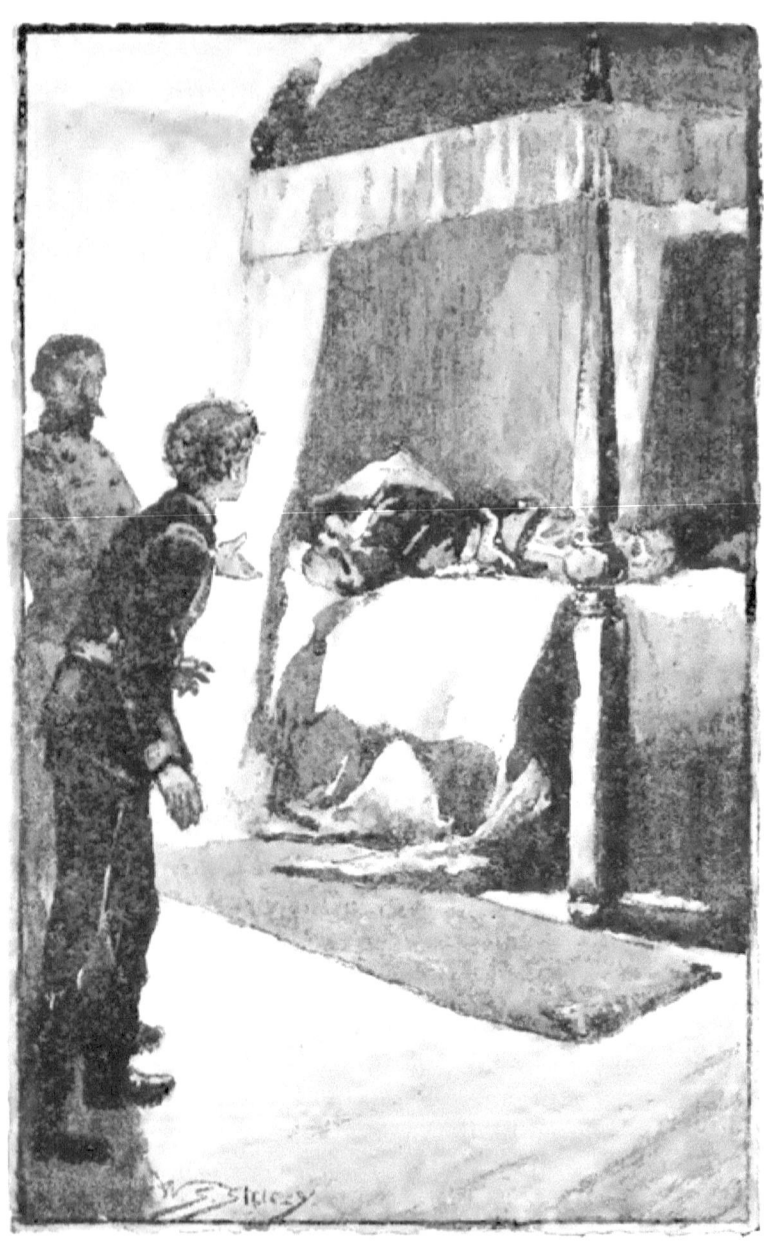

A candle was burning on a table by the window.

for the village between two men, the corporal leading the way.

'Hi!' shouted the captain after him. 'Was there any sign of movement on the part of the enemy when you left?'

'No,' answered Lucius; 'all was quiet. It was me they were after.'

To all the numerous questions of the corporal, as they marched along, he maintained a rigid silence, and at last they reached the house where General Jackson had taken up his quarters for the night.

Leaving Lucius in charge of the two soldiers, the corporal slipped past the sentry and rapped up the adjutant-general, who occupied a room in the same house, and who at once rose and came down-stairs on hearing what was the matter.

To him Lucius repeated his story, winding up with a supplication that he might be allowed to give his message to the General himself.

'Corporal, remain on guard here.—You, fellow, follow me,' said the adjutant.

The corporal saluted, and Lucius, his heart thumping with excitement, followed his guide upstairs.

The adjutant paused at a door and knocked softly. As there was no reply, he turned the handle, and entered the room with Lucius at his heels.

A candle was burning on a table by the window, and by its light Lucius discerned the figure of an officer, fully dressed, even to his sword and jack-boots, lying face downwards across the bed. He stirred uneasily at the noise, turned over, and then sat up, yawning and rubbing his eyes. It was General Jackson.

'Pendleton!' he exclaimed, starting from the bed and standing erect upon the floor. 'You! What is the matter?'

'All is quiet, General; and I would not have ventured to disturb you; but this fellow here avers that he brings important news of the enemy, which he will communicate to no one but you. So far as I can judge, he is telling the truth, so I brought him up.'

'What is your news?' asked Jackson quietly of Lucius.

Lucius glanced at the adjutant. It was possible that if he heard the story he might throw his influence into the scale against a return to the Federal camp. It would be easier, he thought, to manage General Jackson alone. So he answered: 'I would rather speak to you alone, General.'

'Leave us, Pendleton,' said the General.

'But, sir,' protested the adjutant, 'I—he'—— He made a step forward and ran his hands all over Lucius to see if by any chance he carried hidden weapons. Finding none, he saluted and withdrew.

Jackson smiled at his subordinate's excess of caution, and turning to Lucius, addressed him again with: 'Now then, my man, what is your news? Out with it.'

Lucius drew a breath of relief. The General did not recognise him, which was scarcely wonderful, for they had met but once, and then Lucius had presented a very different appearance.

He made no verbal answer, but drawing the soiled and crumpled despatch from his pouch, handed it silently to the General. Equally in silence Jackson received the package, and withdrawing to the table, sat down to examine it. No sooner had he read the superscription than he glanced sharply round at Lucius, but restraining himself, broke open the envelope and began to peruse the contents. He smiled as he read on, for the plans of Shields were so exactly what he had hoped and even prognosticated they would be. He did not look up again, though, until he had finished his scrutiny of the document. Then he rose, and holding the paper in one hand, laid the fore-finger of the other upon it, and fixing his keen blue eyes upon Lucius as if he would read his very heart, asked sharply : ' How did you come by this ?'

Lucius was prepared for the question. While the General had been busied with the despatch, he had been debating with himself how to explain his position. He was sharp enough to know that if once his identity with Lucius Markham were revealed, all hope of being able to rejoin Ephraim would be at an end. His one chance lay in allowing the general to suppose him an ordinary citizen of the valley. He concluded, therefore, that while suppressing his name, his best and wisest course would be to furnish a plain and simple statement of facts. So he answered at once :

' I will tell you, General. Early this morning my companion and myself—both of us live in the valley— were taken prisoners by a number of Federal stragglers. We were roughly handled, but escaped, and concealed ourselves in the wood between this and Lewiston. There we found two dead Federal soldiers, and disguised ourselves in their uniforms. Presently we were seen and forced to march to the attack upon the bridge this morning. When the Yankees ran away, we were obliged to run with them, and once more took refuge in a hut in the wood. While there we overheard a conversation of General Shields with a Federal scout, and determined to try and intercept the despatches he carried. We were successful, and tried to get up the river in the spy's own boat, but as we had no oars, the current carried us down, and we only got ashore after a great deal of trouble. We were getting along all right, when we were challenged. There was a fight in which my companion got the best of the sentry, and then we broke and ran, and lost each other. I had the despatch in my pouch, and came on with it at once. I was nearly caught at the last post.'

Jackson listened in silence to Luce's explanation, and when he had finished, remarked drily: 'That sounds a very plausible story; but how am I to know that it is a true one?'

Lucius flushed through the dirt which encrusted his cheeks. He was about to reply in his usual haughty and imperious style, but remembering his assumed character in time, choked back the words and said instead : 'You have only my word for it, General, of course; but the despatch itself is a proof of what I have told you.'

'Not at all,' was the unexpected retort; 'for even that may not be genuine. The whole thing, including your assumption of the Federal uniform, may be merely a device to impose upon my credulity and lead me into a trap.'

At this Lucius was so completely taken aback that for a moment or two he had nothing to say. Then, as Jackson regarded him with his shrewd, dry smile, he burst out passionately: 'General, we have risked our lives all along the line to bring you that despatch. One of us is, for all I know, a prisoner, or perhaps dead. We could have got away easily enough by simply stopping in our hiding-place if we had not tried to do you this service. If you don't believe me, I can't help it; but I declare upon my honour as a Southerner that I have told you the truth.'

The last words came out with so proud a ring that Stonewall eyed him curiously.

'Who are you?' he demanded by way of reply.

'I live in the valley,' answered Lucius vaguely. 'So does my chum.—Oh, sir, sir,' he broke off wildly, 'do believe me and let me go! They may be killing him even now.'

Jackson started in astonishment, and took a step forward. 'You don't ask me to believe,' he said, 'that you contemplate returning to the Federal lines to look for him?'

'I do, I do!' cried Lucius. 'Why should I not? Twice or thrice already to-day he would have given his life to save mine. How can I desert him now? It would be too base.'

The utter simplicity of the thing carried its own conviction with it. No professional trickster would delude himself into the belief that, coming from the Federal lines, he would be at once allowed to return there on the strength of his own story. The genuine emotion of the young man, as he supposed him to be, went straight to Jackson's warm heart.

'Do not distress yourself, my young friend,' he said kindly; 'I believe you. But as regards your comrade, what do you imagine you can effect by going back?'

'This,' answered Lucius, as the recollection of the hut in the forest came to him like an inspiration: 'if he has not been taken, and has not been able to

break through their line, I know where he will go
to look for me. I will go there. I can find out
that way whether he is dead or a prisoner, or alive
and free.'

'No,' answered Jackson; 'for he might reach our
lines just while you were looking for him. You could
do no good, and for your own sake, if for no other
reason, I cannot allow you to return. I do not suspect
your honesty,' as Lucius made a passionate gesture;
'but it would serve no useful purpose. To-morrow, if
God blesses our arms as He has hitherto done, we
shall sweep Shields from the field, and your comrade,
if he has not managed to escape, may be recovered
in the struggle. At the worst he will be sent north
with other prisoners, and exchanged in due course.'

'Oh, but you are forgetting that he is a civilian,'
urged Lucius, 'and that if they find out that he took
the despatch, they will kill him for it.' His voice
trembled so that he could hardly enunciate the
words.

'They would serve you the same way if they got
hold of you,' answered Jackson.

'But they shall not get hold of me, General,' said
Lucius. 'I know their word, I wear their uniform,
and I know the way. Once I get to the wood I
shall be all right. Besides,' he added cunningly, 'as
soon as I have found out what has become of him,
I will return and give you fresh information about
the troops—all I can collect.'

'My scouts are out already,' answered Jackson, 'and
there is little likelihood that you would be able to
accomplish more than they will with their trained
powers of observation.'

' Have they brought you a despatch like that ?' asked Lucius, with a certain pride in his voice.

' A fair hit,' returned Jackson, smiling. ' No; but I may tell you that the information I have received through them tallies exactly with the contents of the despatch, which is perhaps fortunate for you. So you see that you have but confirmed the knowledge I already possess. In saying that, I do not wish to underrate the value of the service you have performed. If you were a soldier, I should know how to reward you. As it is '——

' General,' broke in Lucius, ' I never thought of reward. Something told me it was my duty, and I tried to do it. But if I have really been of service, give me leave to go back. That is all I ask.—Oh, General, if you knew what friends we are! If you knew what he has done for me! And I stand here talking while perhaps he—— Oh, General, let me go! let me go!' He sprang forwards with clasped hands, his chest heaving, his breath coming and going in quick, short gasps, while great tears, which only pride kept from falling, rose in his eyes.

' You are a devoted friend, young man,' said Jackson, moved by his passionate appeal. ' If I thought you could do any good—— You know the country ?' he broke off.

' Oh yes, yes,' cried Lucius. ' That part of it, at least. Haven't I been running around there all day ?'

' When you broke away from the sentry who stopped you, and took to flight, I suppose you would both be likely to take the same direction ?' queried General Jackson.

' I imagine so,' answered Lucius. ' Why ?'

'Because if your friend succeeded in making our lines, he would most likely enter them at or near the point that you did. Come,' he added kindly; 'to relieve your anxiety, we will go together and make inquiries.'

He caught up his hat, and beckoning Lucius to follow him, strode out of the room.

Outside, the adjutant-general was anxiously awaiting him, and Jackson stopped a moment to whisper a few instructions.

'Tell them to meet me here in three-quarters of an hour,' he concluded.—'Now, young man, come with me.'

They walked on for some distance in silence; but at last Lucius said shyly: 'I beg your pardon, General, but we could hear the firing as we lay in the woods. Would you mind telling me whether you whipped Frémont to-day, or yesterday, for I don't know what the time is?'

'By the blessing of God we were victorious,' answered Jackson devoutly.

'Hurrah!' cried Lucius. 'We were certain you would be. It will be the same to-day, or to-morrow, or whenever it is. Oh, General, when we stood among the Yanks this morning and watched you on the hill when our fellows carried the bridge, we felt we wouldn't mind being killed, so long as our side won. It was glorious!'

'You ought to have been soldiers, you two,' said Jackson, laughing at his enthusiasm; 'but I suppose you prefer your ploughs and harrows. Farmers, aren't you?'

'Oh, well, some one must look after the crops, I

suppose,' answered Lucius evasively, glad of this loophole to escape the inconvenient question of identity.

'Quite so,' admitted the General with a sigh; 'but I fear that before long you will have to beat your ploughshares into swords, for we shall need all the stout hearts and strong arms we can muster in the trouble that is coming upon us.'

'You shan't have to wait long for me,' exclaimed Lucius fervently. 'Once I get home again, nothing shall keep me from joining, and so I'll tell them.'

'Halt! Who comes there?'

It was a sentry on the inner line of pickets who challenged them, and as in answer to the General's question he reported all well, they passed beyond him and hurried towards the outposts.

Here, too, all was quiet. There had been no further scare, and presently they reached the picket in charge of the captain who had forwarded Lucius to head-quarters. He saluted the General, and glancing in some surprise at Lucius, whom he recognised, observed that he hoped he had been right in what he had done.

'Perfectly,' returned Jackson. 'No one else has come in since this young man, I suppose?'

'Only one of our scouts, sir,' replied the captain. 'He is on his way to you now. He reported a scrimmage somewhere between this and Lewiston. He couldn't tell what it was about; but there was a great fuss, and some one, he presumed a prisoner, was being taken to the Federal camp. He was unable to ascertain whether it was one of his brother scouts or not.'

At this doleful communication, Lucius felt his heart leap, and like lightning a plan flashed through his brain. He sprang to Jackson's side, and caught his hand in both his own.

'General,' he cried in piercing tones, 'that must have been my friend. I am sure of it. I will go, if I die for it. Do you remember you spoke to me in Staunton that Sunday? I am Lucius Markham. If I never come back, tell my father it was I who brought in the despatch.' And before the astonished General could move a finger to stop him, he had darted away and sprung beyond the outpost.

'Stop him! Fire on him!' shouted the captain, who was very far from comprehending the meaning of the scene.

'Order arms!' commanded the General loudly, as some of the soldiers levelled their guns at the rapidly disappearing Lucius. 'Let him go. You will never catch him now. No pursuit, captain. Good-night.' He turned away and walked quickly back to his quarters. 'Lucius Markham!' he muttered to himself as he hurried along. 'Well, somehow I thought I knew his face. The plucky little rascal! I remember he was burning to be allowed to join. What with his dirt and his bandages, he looked so much older that it is no wonder I did not recognise him. Who is this friend of his, and what have they been up to between them? Well, well, I can do nothing but pray that no evil may befall him, for his father's sake. He is in the hand of God. I can do nothing—nothing.'

A solitary shot from the direction of the Federal outposts. General Jackson stopped and listened anxiously. Then as all was still, he shook his head sadly, and turning once more upon his heel, went slowly on.

CHAPTER XIV.

GRIZZLY IN THE TOILS.

EPHRAIM was not long in following out his own recommendation to Lucius, but unfortunately, instead of bearing away to the left, he took a straighter line, and before he had gone fifty yards, found himself surrounded by a dozen men, who had approached the scene of conflict with more caution and less noise than their fellow-soldiers. The Grizzly, indeed, was among them before he was aware of their presence, and ere he could attempt to resist or break through the circle, was firmly seized and held fast.

'I guess we've got some one,' said a rough voice. 'Who may yew be, and whar air yew running to?'

Ephraim did not answer at once. His first thoughts, as usual, were of Lucius, and he was listening intently for any sign which might indicate his capture. Presently he heard the boy's voice shouting misleading directions as he practised his simple *ruse de guerre*, and once more at rest upon this point, gave attention to the question, which was now repeated in a more peremptory tone.

'Waal,' answered Ephraim slowly, feeling, as it

were, for his words, 'I heard a fuss, and I was runnin'
to see what the trouble was.'

'I reckon yew must have an outrageous fine bump
of locality,' said another man sneeringly, 'seeing that
yew're making tracks in a teetotally wrong direction.
—Hi! Pete, hurry up with the lantern, and let's have
a look at this coon.'

'Ef I don't keep a level head,' thought Ephraim,
as he heard this, 'I'm a goner, shore. Waal, it
don't matter much, ez long ez Luce is safe, and I
reckon he is, so fur, fer I don't hear any row.—Oh!
Ugh!'

The expression of pain was wrung from him as the
grasp of one of his captors tightened upon his wounded
shoulder.

'What's the matter with yew?' inquired the man.
'My land! My hand is all wet. So's his shoulder.
Quick with the light! Why, it's blood! I guess,
corporal, he war running *from* the trouble, not towards
it. No wonder he war in sech a hurry.'

The corporal stepped up and examined Ephraim's
torn coat and lacerated shoulder by the light of the
lantern.

'Humph!' he ejaculated. 'A nasty rake, and a
fresh wound, too. How did you come by this?'

'I reckon something must hev struck me,' returned
Ephraim, as though he were now receiving news of
his wound for the first time. 'Thar's sech a heap er
things flying around these days, ye can't tell whar
they come from or whar they go ter.'

'This is no bullet wound, though,' said the corporal,
examining it again. 'It's been done by a bayonet.—
Come, you, tell us what happened. Did you meet

the Reb?' For he noted that Ephraim was clad in the Federal blue.

'I 'magine it must hev been suthin' er thet sort,' replied Ephraim cautiously. 'Ennyway, I run up agin suthin' or somebody, and thet's the fact.'

'Where did it happen?' asked the corporal.

'Somewhar round. It mought hev been hyar and it mought hev been thar. I can't ezackly say.'

'Did your assailant bolt after wounding you?' was the corporal's next question.

'I didn't stop ter see,' began Ephraim, when a loud shout close by announced that the question had received a practical answer by the discovery of the body of Sergeant Mason.

'Hi! Help!' shouted a voice. 'Thar's a dead soldier over hyar. No, he ain't dead; but he's got it pretty bad. Help!'

The corporal rushed in the direction of the hail, and the soldiers hurried Ephraim after him. Presently they came to the scene of the late scrimmage, where the sergeant still lay upon his back, moaning faintly.

'Why, if it isn't Sergeant Mason!' cried the corporal, bending over the prostrate man.—'Did you do this?' he demanded fiercely, straightening up and facing Ephraim.

The Grizzly recognised that further concealment was useless, so he answered firmly: 'It war in fair fight, corporal. I reckon ef it hadn't been him lyin' thar, it would hev been me, so maybe it's ez well ez it is.'

'Then I guess you're the man we want,' cried the corporal.—'Boys, this is the pesky Secesh, what's given so much trouble to-day, going round in Federal uniform. I bet it is.—We've got you now, Johnny

o

Reb, so you may as well own up. Who are you, any
how ?'

'I reckon you make me tired with your questions,'
answered Ephraim. 'I shan't answer no more. Ye
ain't the provost-marshal, air ye ?'

'Ho! if it's him you want to see,' mocked the
corporal, 'I guess we won't be long gratifying your
desires.—Hey, boys ?'

A low muttering among the men swelled suddenly
into a shout, and there was an ugly rush in the
direction of Ephraim. The corporal threw himself
in the way of it.

'No, no, boys,' he cried. 'I guess his time is short
enough without your cutting it shorter. Besides, fair's
fair, and the fellow that could get the best of Sergeant
Mason in a tussle must be a stark fighter and a pretty
average kind of a man. Let him take his chance
with the provost-marshal. I reckon it's his business,
not ours.'

The men, appealed to in this soldierly fashion, fell
back, and at the corporal's direction four of them
raised the fallen Sergeant Mason and started for the
camp, bearing him between them.

'Now, you,' said the corporal, 'since you're in such
a hurry, step out, and we'll call on your friend the
provost-marshal. I shouldn't wonder if he was waiting up to receive you.—Fetch him along, boys.'

'Corporal,' asked the Grizzly in a weak voice, 'kin
I hev a drink er water? I'—— The words failed
on his lips, he staggered and would have fallen,
but for the supporting arms of the two men who
held him.

'My land!' exclaimed the corporal. 'I'd forgotten

his wound. Lay him down on the ground.—Hyar, drink this. We may be Yankees, Johnny Reb; but we are not brutes by a good deal.' He held his canteen to Ephraim's lips, and when the latter had satisfied his thirst, rapidly cut away his coat and made a fresh examination of the wound.

'There,' he said, arranging his own handkerchief as a pad over the gash, and binding it in its place with another which one of the men handed to him—'you'll do now till the surgeon can get his paws on you. It's only a scratch, though it's a pretty deep one. Feel better?'

'I'm obleeged ter ye,' said Grizzly, sitting up. 'I'm all right agen now. It war water I wanted.—No,' as he rose to his feet, 'ye needn't carry me. I kin walk well enuff.'

'Are you sure?' demurred the corporal, who was prepossessed in Ephraim's favour on account of his prowess in having overthrown such a mighty man of valour as Sergeant Mason. 'It'll be easy enough to have you carried.'

'I'll walk while I kin walk,' returned Ephraim with grim humour. 'Ye kin carry me after the shootin'. Or I reckon it's hangin' when ye're ketched spyin' around; ain't it?'

'I'm afraid it is,' answered the corporal as they moved along. 'And I wish it wasn't, for you're a brave man, and I'd sooner see you with an ounce of lead in your brain than dangling at the end of a rope.'

'That's real kind of you, corporal,' said Ephraim. 'The selection is very ch'ice; but I 'low the result won't make much difference ter me.'

The corporal seemed to feel the force of this, for he made no reply, and they continued their way in silence until the groups of smouldering bivouac fires showed that they had reached the outer line of the camp. Passing through the long rows of slumbering soldiers, they came at last to the guard tent, and here the corporal, on making inquiries, was referred to the officer of the day, who in his turn directed them to the provost-marshal.

They found that this dreaded functionary had left word that, in the event of the capture of the spy, he was to be awakened at once, no matter what the hour; but as a matter of fact he arrived upon the scene in a very bad humour, for after waiting up till considerably past midnight, he had thought that he might safely turn in, and now his first sweet, refreshing sleep had been rudely broken. That this was due to the strictness of his own orders did not tend to soothe him, for there was nobody to shift the blame upon, and to be reduced to grumbling at one's self is a state that offers little consolation. Yes, there was some one, though, upon whom the vials of his wrath might be legitimately emptied, and the provost-marshal determined that the spy—if spy he really proved to be—should have nothing to complain of on the score of undue leniency.

'Bring that prisoner in here,' he said, appearing at the entrance to his tent.—'Now, corporal, is this the spy?'

'Can't say, sir,' answered the corporal; 'but I shouldn't wonder if it were. I captured him as he was attempting to escape after clubbing Sergeant Mason.'

The provost-marshal, who had seated himself at a small table with a note-book before him and a pencil in his hand, looked up in surprise at this. 'Do I understand you to say,' he asked, 'that this weedy creature actually got the best of Sergeant Mason?'

'It's a fact, sir,' replied the corporal. 'Mason has got a crack on the head that will keep him quiet this long time. Of course I didn't see the fight myself, but this fellow here don't deny that he is the man, and he has a bayonet wound in the shoulder to speak for the truth of what he says.'

'Humph!' muttered the provost-marshal. 'I shouldn't have thought it possible. Well, I'll question him.—By the way, corporal, did you hear or see anything of those other two fellows?'

'No, sir,' answered the corporal, understanding the reference; 'but I heard, sir, that Colonel Spriggs was still out on the hunt for them.'

The provost-marshal's moustache was slightly agitated. So grim a person could not be expected to smile; but his amused thought was evidently: 'Spriggs will take precious good care not to return to camp until Jackson moves from Port Republic, or we move from here.'

For Ephraim, too, the announcement had a special interest, for it showed him that his identity with one of the escaped aeronauts was not, so far, suspected, and hence the provost-marshal could have no idea that any one else had been concerned in the affair of the despatch. Lucius, he hoped, was by this time out of harm's way; but at all events Spriggs was not there to complicate matters by referring to him. The Grizzly was quite prepared to take the onus of the theft of the despatch upon his own shoulders, and he awaited calmly the discovery of the packet. Casting his eyes downwards to his cartridge pouch, he saw with some slight surprise that the flap was unfastened. He had been very particular about the fastening, lest by any chance the papers should be lost, and he wondered whether it had come undone during his combat with Sergeant Mason. He was roused from his meditations by the voice of the provost-marshal questioning him.

'Are you a soldier or civilian?'

'Civilian, sir. I am a factory hand at the iron-works at Staunton. I came into your lines by accident, and 'cause I wanted ter git out agen without comin' ter grief, I put on these clothes thet I found in the wood.'

'Ah! I suppose it was also by accident that, thus disguised as a Federal soldier, you played the part of sentry, and became fraudulently possessed of a despatch belonging to General Shields and addressed to General Frémont? And I imagine that if, by another and very lucky accident, you had fallen in with your friends, the enemy, you would have felt compelled to hand the despatch over to them. It is fortunate that we got hold of you first.'

This was a shot on the part of the provost-marshal, for he had as yet no means of knowing that Ephraim and the man who had stopped Captain Hopkins were one and the same. As Ephraim did not answer, he went on : 'Have you got the despatch, corporal?'

'No, sir,' replied the corporal. 'I was busy attending to his wound and bringing him here.'

'Search him, then.'

The corporal searched Ephraim literally down to

his skin, and to the surprise of no one more than the Grizzly himself, discovered nothing.

'They must hev dropped out while the row war goin' on,' thought Ephraim; for it never crossed his mind that by an accidental exchange of belts the papers had come into Luce's hands. Had he suspected this, he would have felt miserable indeed.

'What have you done with that despatch, you fellow? What is your name?' asked the provost-marshal angrily.

'Ephraim Sykes,' answered the Grizzly, paying no attention to the more important question.

'Psha! Where is the despatch?—Well, do you not intend to answer?' For still Ephraim held his peace.

'I told ye the truth jest now,' said Ephraim at last. 'I war tryin' ter git out er your lines, whar I come without any wish er my own. I hevn't got any despatch, ez ye kin see.'

'What have you done with it, then?' inquired the provost-marshal impatiently.

'I hevn't said I ever had it,' answered Ephraim, anxious to gain time. 'Ef ye air so ready ter accuse me, ye'd better start in and prove me guilty. I'm not supposed ter do it fer ye, I reckon.'

The officer eyed him sternly. 'Justice shall be done, my man; don't you be afraid of that,' he said significantly.—'Corporal!' He gave an order in an undertone, and the corporal immediately left the tent.

In a few minutes he returned, followed by Captain Hopkins, who entered with a look of eager expectation on his face.

'Do you recognise this man, captain?' asked the

provost-marshal.—'You, Sykes, come forward into the light.'

'Recognise him! I should think so,' exclaimed Hopkins, as Ephraim obeyed the order. 'That is the rascal who personated a sentry by the river-bank, stole the despatch by means of a trick, and set my boat adrift.'

'You are certain that you are not mistaken, captain?'

'Absolutely. The interview was too fruitful in consequences to allow me to forget the interviewer. I would have picked this man out of a whole regiment.'

The provost-marshal looked at Ephraim. 'You hear the charge,' he said briefly. 'What have you to say?'

'Waal, I han't denied it,' answered Ephraim.

'You mean that you admit that you took the despatch from Captain Hopkins. I understand you to admit that.'

'It ain't much use my doin' anythin' else, so fur ez I kin see,' returned Ephraim. 'Yes; I stopped him and took the despatch.'

'Good! Your intention, of course, was to deliver it to the enemy?'

'Nary a doubt er thet,' admitted Ephraim.

'By whom you were commissioned to enter our lines and collect whatever information you could?'

'Not at all,' answered Ephraim sharply. 'It war jest ez I told ye. I war a civilian tryin' to escape out of yer lines. But the chance came ter me, and I took it.'

'I need not tell you in return that the taking of that chance will cost you your life; for civilian though you may be, you are probably acquainted with the punishment incurred by a spy. It matters not at all that the paper has not been found upon you, since you have been identified and have confessed your guilt '——

'Guilt!' put in Ephraim quietly. 'I han't confessed to any guilt ez fur ez I know. I don't call it a crime ter try and serve my country, whatever ye may do.'

'We won't go into the question of patriotism either,' returned the provost-marshal. 'Unfortunately for you, when a man is caught serving his country in the particular fashion in which you have elected to serve yours, there is only one thing to be done with him.'

'I'd like ter be allowed ter ask ye, Mister Marshal,' said Ephraim, 'ef thar air none er your men prowlin' around our lines jest ter see what they kin pick up? What's the difference between them and me? Ain't they servin' their country, too, accordin' ter their lights?'

'I'll allow that,' answered the provost-marshal. 'And if your fellows can lay them by the heels, they will serve them as we shall serve you—namely, hang them. But now, my man, seeing that you can't get off, and that there is but one end in store for you, you may as well tell me what you have done with the despatch.'

'It'll make no difference to me, ye say? Ter the hangin', thet is?' queried Ephraim.

The provost-marshal shook his head. 'Not the slightest,' he said.

'Then hang away and welcome. Ye'll git no more out er me.'

The provost-marshal considered for a moment. It was important to ascertain if possible whether the

despatch had reached the enemy or not. Finally he
said : 'Understand me, my man : I am empowered
to deal summarily with cases like yours. I might
condemn you out of hand ; but if you will tell
me truly what you have done with the despatch,
I will give you this further chance, that I will refer
your case to the general in the morning. Speak out
now.'

Ephraim considered in his turn. He did not give
much for the grace of being brought face to face with
General Shields, who he did not doubt would instantly
recognise him as the purloiner of his breakfast and
the *soi-disant* 'Trailing Terror,' and so the matter
would become more hopelessly complicated than ever.
But life was sweet, and if he could gain a respite
of only a few hours, there was no saying what might
happen in the interval. He had risked his life, and
would have done so again, to carry the despatch
to the Confederate General ; but seeing that it was
lost and he could by no possibility discover it, why
should he not simply say so and take the proffered
advantage ?

'Well,' said the provost-marshal at last, 'have you
made up your mind ?'

'I hev, sir,' answered Ephraim. 'But if I tell ye
the truth ye'll maybe not b'leeve me.'

'Say your say, and we shall see,' returned the other ;
'but I seriously advise you not to attempt to put me
off with any cock-and-bull story.'

'Waal,' began Ephraim, 'I 'low I might bluff ye
by tellin' ye thet I'd got thet despatch across the lines,
fer I reckon thet's the idee thet's makin' ye oncom-
fortable ; but if I'd got thet fur with it, I wouldn't

hev been sech a born fool ez to come back jest fer the pleasure er bein' hung. The plain truth is, I don't know whar it is any more than ye do yerself.'

'Do you mean that you have lost it?'

'Nuthin' less. I had it hyar in this pouch jest before thet rumpus with the sergeant at the end of the ditch, and I reckon it must hev fell out somewhar thar.' Ephraim did honestly believe this to be the case.

'If you had had an accomplice, it would have been a simple matter to pass the paper on to him,' said the provost-marshal, regarding him doubtfully.

'Ye may be easy on thet score,' replied Ephraim firmly. 'I got hold er the despatch by myself without the help er any one. I carried it in this pouch, ez I war tellin' ye, and I know thet I had it jest before the row began. Maybe it's lyin' around loose on the ground somewhar thar. I'm tellin' ye the truth and no lies,' he added earnestly. 'B'leeve me or not, thet's my last word.'

The provost-marshal rose to his feet, 'Captain Hopkins,' he said, 'return to your quarters. I will send for you when I require you.' Then as the captain went out: 'Corporal, place this man under guard. Afterwards take your men and return to the spot where you arrested this spy. Make a thorough search of the ground in the vicinity. If you find the despatch, bring it at once to me. If not, come back here with the prisoner at dawn.'

'Very good, sir,' answered the corporal.—'What shall I do about the man's wound, sir?'

'Oh, thet's nuthin',' put in Ephraim. 'I don't know it's thar sence ye tied it up.'

'The sentry can be told to send for a surgeon if it becomes necessary during the night,' said the provost-marshal. 'Remove the prisoner.'

The corporal retired with Ephraim, whom he immediately conducted to an empty tent, before the door of which he set a sentry. Then he unslung his canteen and laid it down on the ground beside the prisoner, and a moment later forced a great handful of biscuit upon him.

'There,' he said good-naturedly, 'you won't starve now, and if your shoulder troubles you, hail the sentry and he'll send for a surgeon. I've told him.'

'Tain't wuth it fer all the time I'll know I've got an arm,' said Ephraim gloomily.

'Oh, maybe it'll not be so bad as that. If we find the despatch, you may get off. I don't say you will; but I hope so, for I like your pluck in standing up to a giant like Sergeant Mason.'

'I'm obleeged ter ye,' said Ephraim more heartily. 'I hadn't looked fer so much kindness from a Yank.'

'Ah, we're not so black as we're painted down South,' laughed the corporal. 'And we're all Americans, if it comes to the pinch, and don't you forget it.'

He nodded kindly and went out, leaving Ephraim alone with his reflections.

They were not pleasant, as may well be imagined. The lad was brave, but it takes a considerable supply of somewhat unusual fortitude to enable one to wait through the dark watches of the night, looking forward to the death which is to come with the dawn, and strive as he would, Ephraim found it hard to put the dismal prospect from him.

'I wish they'd hung me out er hand,' he said to himself. 'It would hev been over by now. It's the thinkin' what's ter come thet makes me sick.' He rose and paced backwards and forwards in his narrow prison. 'God be thanked, Luce warn't with me,' ran his thoughts. 'Ef he's had any luck, he'll be safe in our lines by now. But I wish I knew. I wish I knew. Luce'll be sorry when he comes ter hear er this. We've always been sech friends. Thar's on'y him and Aunty Chris. Luce'll take keer on her; I bet he will. I'd like ter see him once more before I die; but I wouldn't hev him hyar fer thet. By time! no. I wonder will it hurt. I dunno, but I'd ruther they'd shoot me; but I s'pose I ain't good enuff fer thet. Waal, I reckon it won't take long either way. Funny, ain't it, ter hev ter die? I reckon I orter be thinkin' about heaven, 'stead er which I'm hankerin' a good deal after this old earth. Anyway, I'll try and fix my thorts above, ez the minister said last Sabbath. Maybe it'll do me good and make me brave; but I reckon it's none too easy.'

He knelt down upon the ground and covered his eyes with his hand, as if with the sight of earth he would shut out all thoughts of it. Then from his simple heart there welled a passionate prayer to God, not for his own safety, for he considered that as a thing past praying for, but that he might be able to look Death bravely in the face, and meet him as a man should do—that God would take care of Aunty Chris, and bless and keep Luce from harm—'Let him git home! Let him git thar!'—and he was done.

He rose to his feet, refreshed in spirit and steadier in his nerves. Hope seemed to have returned to him, and there was something like a smile upon his lips as he stowed away the biscuit which the corporal had given him in his pockets.

'Ye never know when they might come in handy,' he muttered.—'Hello! What do ye want?'

For the sentry had put his head through the opening of the tent, obscuring the faint light that entered there.

''St!' whispered the sentry. 'Don't make a noise. By time! Grizzly, I'm sorry ter see ye fixed up like this.'

CHAPTER XV.

ANY PORT IN A STORM.

TO say that Ephraim was astonished as this sympathetic remark fell upon his ear, would be to convey a very faint idea of his sensations. For the moment he was simply bewildered. The voice was the voice of a friend, and where in all that great army should he look for a friend just now ?

'Who air ye ?' he attempted to say ; but his tongue clove to his mouth, and no sound came from his lips.

He groped for the corporal's canteen and took a drink. 'Who air ye ?' he said at last. 'Who air ye thet speak ter me like thet ?'

His legs began to tremble under him. He sat down upon the ground and took another sip of water from the canteen. It refreshed him, and he listened eagerly for the reply.

'A friend,' answered the sentry. 'Don't ye be down in the mouth, Eph Sykes. I'm hyar ter help ye. On'y we must go cautious, ye know.'

'Who air ye ?' repeated Ephraim. 'Who air ye ?' He said it over and over again monotonously, like a parrot repeating the words.

'Sh! What's the matter with ye? Don't ye know me? I thort ye would. I'm Jake Summers. Ye know me now, don't ye?'

'Ah! I do thet,' answered Ephraim with cold contempt. 'Jake Summers, the Southern Yankee. The man who quit old Virginny when the war broke out, and took sides agin her. I know ye well enuff now. And ye call yerself a friend. Yah! Git out and leave me alone.'

'Oh, shet yer head, Grizzly,' was the retort, given without a spice of ill-humour. 'What do you know? I reckon we've all got our own opinions, and may be allowed ter keep 'em. I'm not the on'y one by a long sight ez couldn't make up his mind to cut loose from the old Union, ez ye know well enough. I 'magine ye won't deny a man the right ter foller the call er his conscience in this onnatural war.'

'Couldn't ye hev hung on ter the Union 'thout firin' bullets inter old Virginny, ef thet's the way ye felt about it,' answered Ephraim. 'Anyway, ye kin settle up with yer conscience the best way ye please, so long as ye git out er thet. Quit!'

'Eph,' said the man earnestly, 'don't make sech a pizen noise, onless ye want ter wake up them ez doesn't feel fer ye ez I do. I tell ye I want ter be yer friend ef ye'll let me, and not be a fool.'

'Garn away,' replied Ephraim dismally, but not so roughly as before. 'What kin ye do?'

'I'll show ye ef ye'll git up and come over hyar, whar I kin talk ter ye 'thout bein' heard all over the camp,' said the man.—'Eph, d'ye remember little Toots?'

'Ah, I remember him,' answered Ephraim. 'What ye bringin' him up fer?'

'Little Toots, my little b'y Toots,' went on the man with a catch in his voice. 'The on'y one me and Jenny ever had. D'ye remember, Eph, after we thort he war gittin' well from the dipthery, how ye useter come and see him, and bring him toys ye'd made yerself. One time it war a little gun, one time it war a Noah's ark ye'd cut him outern a block er pine, and another time it war a Jack-in-the-box thet useter frighten him every time it come out, and then make him larf till we thort he'd never stop?' The rough voice died away in a sob.

'I don't see what yer meanin' is,' said Ephraim uncomfortably, for he hated to be reminded of his little charities.

'Don't ye? I'll larn ye soon. When we quit Staunton, Jenny and Toots and me, the little b'y he sorter sickened after the old home, and he got weaker and weaker. We'd lost everything, Eph, and we couldn't git him the little comforts he wanted, the pore lamb, and thar we hed ter sit and see him wastin' before our eyes, me and Jenny. Eph, I tell ye, he war always singin' out fer you. "I want Grizzly," says he. "I want him ter bring me a toy." And when he died, Eph, he war jest huggin' yer old Jack-in-the-box ter his breast, ez ef he loved it too much ter leave it behind him. So we put it in with him, Eph, fer we couldn't bear ter take it from him.' His voice choked again, and he stopped abruptly.

'Pore little Toots!' murmured Ephraim sympathetically. 'And so ye lost him, Jake?'

'We did,' answered Jake; 'and we thort our hearts

P

war broke, we did, me and Jenny. And then ter-night, jest now when the corporal brought ye along and sot ye in thar with me ter look after ye, I couldn't believe it fer a spell. And then I thort how good ye'd been ter little Toots, makin' his little life thet happy, and how fond he war er ye and all. And I sez ter myself, I dunno what Eph Sykes hez been up ter; but I reckon ef harm comes ter him while I'm hyar ter keep it off'n him, I'll never be able ter look little Toots in the face when wanst I meet him again. Now ye kin tell, Grizzly, ef I'm yer friend or ef I ain't.'

Ephraim made no answer; but in the dark he groped for Jake's hand and wrung it hard.

'I've got a plan, Eph,' said Jake, returning the pressure. 'It's ez simple ez hoein' a row. On'y we must be quick.'

'No, Jake, I can't let ye do it,' answered Ephraim at last. 'Ye can't help me 'thout hurtin' yerself, and I can't save my life et the price er another man's, 'ceptin' in a fair fight. It's good er ye, Jake, and it's like what I remember ye in the old days. But I can't let ye do it; though I'm obleeged ter ye, all the same.'

'Shucks!' exclaimed Jake impatiently. 'Don't ye consarn yerself over me. I reckon I like a whole skin ez well ez any man. Thar'll be a court-martial and thet; but they won't be able to prove anythin'. Don't waste time. Hev ye got a knife?'

'On'y a little wan,' replied Ephraim, yielding to his persuasion.

'Then take mine, and open the big blade. Now then, rip a great hole in the back er the tent. Do it soft, now. Don't make no noise. Hev ye done it?'

'Yes,' answered Ephraim. 'Am I ter git out thet way?'

'My land! no. Ye'd be stopped before ye'd gone ten paces. It's on'y fer a blind, thet. Now come over hyar. Put yer hands behind yer back ez ef they war tied, and step out alongside me. See hyar, Eph, this has got ter be smartly done, fer I must git back ter my post without loss er time. I'll take the resk. I can't do everythin' I'd like ter do; but I'll pilot ye through the camp, and then ye must make a break fer the woods on yer own account. Ef ye let 'em nab ye agen, ye're not the man I take ye fer. Air ye ready? Then come along.'

With considerable difficulty Ephraim clasped his hands behind his back, owing to the stiffness in his shoulder; but he set his teeth and bore the pain, and while Jake grasped him by the arm, the two of them set out with soft but rapid steps through the slumbering camp.

Here and there a head was sleepily lifted; but the sight of a prisoner at any hour of the day or night was altogether too common to attract serious attention, and only once did Jake open his mouth to inform a sentry that he was taking his charge to the provost-marshal.

Presently they reached the tent where the stern dispenser of martial law slept in blissful unconsciousness that his prey was on the point of slipping through his fingers. Needless to say they did not enter his tent, which was at the extreme end of the camp near the river, but making a slight detour, slipped past it, and almost immediately afterwards Jake came to a halt.

'Thet's all I kin do fer ye, Grizzly,' he whispered.
'Ye must trust ter luck fer the rest. God send ye git
safe in. Give a kind thort ter Uncle Sam sometimes
fer this night's work.' And before Ephraim could
utter a word of the thanks that rushed to his lips, his
benefactor had turned and left him.

'Waal,' thought Ephraim, as he cast himself at full
length upon the ground in order to escape observation,
'thet Jake Summers is a man down ter his boots. To
think of the few toys I give little Toots bringin' about
all this. I never thort when I made him thet Jack-in-
the-box thet it war ter be the savin' er my life. My
land! I kin sca'cely onderstand it.'

As he lay, he rapidly revolved plan after plan for
his further procedure, rejecting them all, till at last he
made up his mind to attempt to reach the hut in the
forest, and conceal himself therein until the day broke.

'It's resky,' he thought to himself; 'but then everythin''s resky jest now. And it's better than wanderin'
round in the dark, when I might plump up against a
Yank before I knew whar I war. Thet window is so
handy, too. Onless they come on me from all sides at
wanst, I kin slip through it nicely and away inter the
woods.'

He stole across the fields, bending almost to the
ground lest any prowling Federal or lynx-eyed sentry
should catch sight of him; nor did he pause to take
breath until he reached the long ditch, at the far end
of which he had waged that memorable battle with
Sergeant Mason, which had, after all, resulted so disas-
trously for himself.

'I wonder whether the corporal has found the
despatch,' he thought, as he rested his back against

the sloping side of the ditch. 'It must hev dropped out somewhar thar. He's a good man, thet corporal, and ef I git cl'ar of this scrape, I won't hev so many hard things ter say agin the Yanks after ter-night. 'Ceptin', of co'se, that pesky Cunnel Spriggs. But then, I reckon, he sorter stands alone, bein', as Ginrul Shields said, a disgrace ter everybody. I wonder whar he is, the critter! Layin' on ter be lookin' fer us, when all he wants is ter be quit er the fight ter-morrer, or ter-day, for I guess it's been ter-day this two hours back. I wonder ef thar will be a battle. It'll simplify matters a good deal fer me ef thar is, fer the Yanks will hev enuff ter do 'thout huntin' me. I wonder whar Luce kin be? I hope he's made our lines all right. My land! I'd jest better quit wonderin' and 'tend ter business.'

He started off again, going warily, and anon reached, without accident, the short arm of the wood, through which he groped cautiously until he came opposite to the back of the hut. Here he paused again, and throwing himself down, crawled on his hands and knees across the short strip of intervening ground. At the window he raised himself up cautiously and listened intently. Not a sound broke the stillness, and satisfied at last, he edged his way round to the front.

'All cl'ar,' he thought. 'Thet's well. Now I'll set down jest inside the door, and then ef anybody comes I kin slip in and away through the window, or out across the open ez the case may be. It's oncomfortably nigh the camp, this cabin; but I 'magine it's the safest place till the mornin' breaks.'

He sat down at the door of the cabin, and pulling

out a piece of the corporal's biscuit, ate it with relish.
Half an hour passed, and the deep stillness acting
soothingly upon his tired nerves, he began to feel
drowsy, and actually nodded once or twice.

'This won't do,' he muttered. 'I must keep awake;
it'—— Another nod, and then he sprang noiselessly
to his feet, wide awake and quivering in every limb.
He heard, or thought he heard, a scratching sound
at the window of the hut.

He strained his ears to listen, ready the instant that
doubt became certainty to flee across the open into
the fields once more.

Again that faint scratching sound, this time a little
louder, and accompanied by a gentle tapping.

'It's a squirr'l, I reckon,' thought Ephraim, much
relieved. 'He has maybe got a knot hole on the roof.'

'Whippo-wil! whippo-wil! whippo-wil!'

Ephraim stiffened into attention again. There was
nothing extraordinary about the sound. It was night,
or rather very early morning, the time when the
whip-poor-wills took their exercise and screamed out
their loud, clear notes; but there was something else.
In the old days at Staunton, which the startling events
of the last four-and-twenty hours had crowded so far
into the background that they seemed removed by
a distance of years from the present, it had been
Luce's custom to come whip-poor-willing down the
little back street where Ephraim lived, to give his
friend timely notice of his approach. Therefore the
sound had a greater significance for the Grizzly.

'Hear thet bird!' he said to himself. 'It's jest
what Luce use ter do. My! I wonder will I ever
git back to the old home again.'

'Whippo-wil! whippo-wil! whippo-wil! Tap, tap, tap!'

Now a whip-poor-will may sing its song at night, but it does not usually perch upon a window-sill and lightly tap to attract attention, and this was borne home to Ephraim when for the third time the cry was repeated, followed by the mysterious rapping.

Ephraim's heart gave a great leap. 'It can't be!' he said, in the silence of his brain. 'It can't be! I reckon I must find out, though.'

He crept noiselessly round the cabin and peered beyond the angle of the wall in the direction of the window.

The space at the back of the hut was darker than that at the front, for the nearness of the woods threw an additional gloom; but Ephraim, staring into the dark, could just make out a figure standing at a little distance from the window with outstretched arm, which rose and fell rhythmically, and at every movement came the light tap, tap of a switch upon the sill.

'Whippo-wil! whippo'——

'Luce!'

'Grizzly!'

There was a rush through the darkness, the shock of a violent meeting, and panting, trembling, almost sobbing with joy, the two friends clung to one another in a fervent embrace.

'Luce!' whispered the Grizzly, the words falling in broken syllables from his lips. 'What ye doin' hyar? I thought ye would be safe and fur away.'

'I didn't know what had become of you,' whispered Lucius back; 'but I imagined that if you had got away you would make for the cabin. It seemed the most likely place. Oh, I'm so glad! I'm so glad!'

'I'm glad too; but I'm sorry ez well, fer I thought ye would be well within our lines. Ugh! Ah!'

'What is the matter?' asked Lucius in alarm, as at another friendly hug Ephraim uttered a low cry of pain.

'It's nuthin', bub. On'y I got it in the shoulder, and ye gripped me thar. Come into the cabin. We'll be safer thet way.'

'What! Are you wounded?' inquired Lucius anxiously, as he followed Ephraim in through the window.

'Jest a scrape on the shoulder. Never mind it. Tell me what happened after ye left me. I reckon ye ran back the way ye had come. I heard ye shoutin'.'

'No, I didn't,' answered Lucius. 'At least, only for a few steps, and then I made a break clean away. And I got through,' he added proudly.

'Through the ring thet was round ye?' queried Ephraim, not understanding.

'No,' replied Lucius; 'through their lines and into ours.'

'What! Ye—got—through—inter—our—lines?'

'Yes; and gave the despatch to General Jackson.'

'The despatch? Ginrul Jackson? Luce, what air ye sayin'?'

'I am telling you just what happened,' answered Lucius. 'Didn't you miss it? The despatch, I mean. I found it in my pouch. We must have changed belts without knowing it in the darkness of the cave.'

'Ye found the despatch, and ye got inter our lines,

and ye gave it ter old Stonewall, I onderstand ye ter say!' said Ephraim, still bewildered.

'I did, all three.' He laughed a low laugh of satisfaction.

'Then why in thunder didn't ye stay thar?'

'Grizzly! Did you suppose that after all you have risked for me I would run away and leave you without trying to find out what had become of you? I had such a time with the General. He didn't know me, not a little bit, and he wouldn't hear of my coming back. But he was so kind, and when he saw how anxious I was about you, he actually came with me himself as far as the outposts to find out if any one had seen you come in where I did. And then'——
He paused and gave another little laugh.

'And then?' queried Ephraim, who had listened to the recital in absolute silence.

'Then I gave him the slip and bolted for the Federal lines. Some one gave the order to fire; but the General—I had told him who I was by that time—called out "Order—arms!" and I got clean away.'

'And how did ye git ez fur ez this?'

'I sneaked through somehow. No one saw me. I heard a shot; but it was not fired at me, and I made for this cabin as fast as I could; for I thought you would be here if anywhere.'

The Grizzly bent forward with his head upon his arms and groaned aloud.

'What is it?' asked Lucius sympathetically. 'Does your wound hurt you?'

'Wound!' moaned Ephraim. 'D'ye s'pose I'm thinkin' about thet et sech a time ez this? No, Luce, it's you. That ye should git off safe and all, and then

start out to come back fer me.   Oh, bub, why did
ye do it ?   Why did ye do it ?'

'Why shouldn't I ?'

'And ye don't seem ter know thet ye've done anythin' out er the way,' said Ephraim in a wondering
tone.

'Grizzly, old stick, wouldn't you have done as much
for me ?'

'Thet's different.   I brought ye out, and it war my
duty ter git ye home agen ef it war anyways possible.   Ye got yerself the best part er the way—inter
our lines, thet is—and now ye've been and run yer
head inter the hornet's nest agen.   And all fer me—all
fer me.   Luce, ye didn't orter hev done it.   I warn't
wuth it, Luce.'   He sprang to his feet and groped in
the darkness for his friend.   'I'll never fergit what
ye've done fer me this day.   Never ez long ez I live.'
His voice faltered, and he wrung the younger boy's
hand in silence.

'Shucks!' exclaimed Lucius.   'It's nothing to talk
about, and here I am now.   It doesn't come up by a
long measure to what you've done for me from the
time you broke into the pile till now.   Besides,
what's the use of being a friend if you don't act
friendly ?'

'Hear him !' muttered Ephraim feebly.   'It's all very
well, Luce.   But I can't fergit it, and I'm not goin' ter
hev ye makin' light er it.'

'Well, here I am now,' said Lucius ; 'and you are
safe, I am thankful to say.   Tell me what has happened to you since last I saw you.   I tell you,
while that fight was going on at the end of the
ditch, I didn't know what to do, I was so frightened.

I thought at first that the miserable Yank had got you down.'

'Don't ye talk so airy er the miserable Yanks,' said Ephraim emphatically. 'I've had more kindness ter-night from one or two of 'em than I kin well begin ter say. Ef it warn't fer a miserable Yank, I wouldn't be hyar jest now.' And taking up his story, he poured into Luce's astonished ear a graphic account of his adventures since his arrest.

'Well,' commented Lucius when the tale was finished, 'you have had a time of it, and no mistake. I hope Jake Summers got back before it was found out that you were missed. He must be a good man. You see now what it is to be a kind old Grizzly, and go around making little folks feel happy. I remember little Toots. And so he's dead?'

'Yes,' answered Ephraim, 'and pore Jake took on orful when he war tellin' me about him. Yes, I do hope it will go well with Jake.'

'I believe they won't be likely to pry into that tent before dawn,' said Lucius. 'There's no reason why they should. They want light to hang a man, I should say.'

'It don't foller,' replied Ephraim drily. 'But thar'll be light enuff soon,' he added, moving to the door and looking out; 'fer the sky is beginnin' ter brighten. It's time fer us ter quit this establishment.'

'Why shouldn't we stay here?' demurred Lucius. 'I should think it would be as safe a place as any.'

'Not when the day dawns,' answered Ephraim. 'Ye don't s'pose that when they begin ter hunt fer me that they're not likely ter give a look in hyar ez they pass by.'

'I imagine that they will have enough to think about without losing time on your trail,' said Lucius. 'I saw certain signs as I came through our camp with the General that something was about to happen.'

'Maybe,' returned Ephraim quaintly; 'but ef they lay hold er me before thet suthin' happens, I wouldn't be able ter take so much interest in it ez otherwise. No; we musn't stop hyar.'

'Where shall we hide, then?' asked Lucius. 'I tell you I've had enough of trying to break through lines.'

'I agree with ye thar,' assented Ephraim. 'Thar must be no more er that sort er fun. We must make a push across the woods and try and reach the mountain. We kin hide thar well enuff, or make our way along it, whichever seems most reasonable.'

'We shall only lose ourselves in the wood again,' protested Lucius. 'What is the good of that?'

'Even so, we'll hev a better chance ter dodge out er sight among the trees,' argued Ephraim. 'Honestly, I think it ain't safe ter stay hyar.'

'Well, go ahead,' said Lucius. 'I am with you whatever you do. You've got the longest head.'

'I couldn't manage ter git the despatch through, fer all my long head,' exclaimed Ephraim admiringly.— 'Come along, then.'

They slipped through the window, and entered the wood in Indian file, Lucius holding on to the skirt of Ephraim's tunic, lest by any chance they should get separated in the intense darkness, for though the dawn was beginning to break, it would be some time yet before the light would be powerful enough to illuminate the recesses of the forest.

As the stars paled in the sky before the approach of morning, two things happened, both fraught with importance to our fugitives, though they plunged along, steering blindly through the wood, trusting to Providence to guide them aright, and ignorant meanwhile of the turn of events. First, Stonewall Jackson's infantry began to move across the foot-bridge which he had thrown over the South Fork ; and, secondly, Colonel Spriggs, tired of the ineffectual pursuit, and resting his wearied men under the mountain not far from the Confederate lines, sullenly turned his angry face once more in the direction of his own camp. Not that he intended to reach it just yet. His plan—a very simple one—was to lose himself in the wood until the growing day should have revealed to him what the enemy were about. If a battle should begin, he would thus be able to keep clear of it ; while, if otherwise, he could fall back upon the camp quietly and at his leisure. But Colonel Spriggs had reckoned without General Jackson, whose plans included the advance of Brigadier-general Taylor's Louisiana troops through the woods by the side of the mountain, and it was therefore not improbable that Colonel Spriggs would find himself in a very warm corner for once in his life before the day was much older.

Of all these facts and probabilities, however, the boys knew nothing as they held steadily on through the pathless woods, hoping and trusting that their luck would lead them out upon the mountain-side, and at the same time keeping a wary eye for possible surprises or openings in the forest where an enemy might lurk.

The light grew stronger and the woods brighter, and suddenly they came upon just such a place, a natural clearing, where the trees grew thinly and the ground was covered with logs and underbrush. To walk across this did not seem the right thing to do; but to their joy they saw the mountain looming in front of them, and knew that at least their faces were in the right direction.

'It'll not do ter cross over thar, Luce,' said Ephraim in a low voice. 'We must skirt it. Sh! I hear a sound. Down ter the ground! Thar's some one comin' up.'

The wood, indeed, at that part was full of soldiers. The Louisiana men were well forward, but unfortunately the boys had no suspicion that their own men were so close at hand, and only reckoned that they had to deal with their enemies, the Federals, who now appeared to be surrounding them. Far away, but rapidly drawing nearer, they could hear the tramp of stealthy footsteps, and now and again the low hum of subdued voices. Nearer and nearer came the terrifying sounds, and lower and lower they crouched, scarcely daring to breathe.

'It's no use trying to skirt it, Luce,' whispered Ephraim, his mouth close to the boy's ear. 'They seem ter be all about us. They'll crowd us out before we know. We must make a dash across the open before they git up, and try and reach thet other belt er wood. We'll be safer thar.'

'There may be more on the other side,' answered Lucius.

'I know. We can't help thet. We've got ter make a break fer freedom, and chance the rest.'

They crawled to the edge of the clearing, and after one moment of anxious listening, rose to their feet and stole swiftly into the open.

But no sooner had they broken cover than Ephraim, who was leading, pulled up short, and with a sharp exclamation of surprise dashed back again.

'What is it?' cried Lucius, following his friend's example.

'Look! look!' whispered Ephraim excitedly. 'Look over thar up in the left angle er the clearing.'

'Where?' asked Lucius, peering out. 'Oh!' as his eyes encountered an all too familiar object. 'That horrible balloon.'

'Bullee!' exclaimed Ephraim excitedly. 'This is whar we came down yesterday, and thar's old Blue Bag ready and willin' ter carry us out er this pesky difficulty. Bullee!'

However willing Blue Bag might be, it was a question whether she would be able to aid her enthusiastic inventor, for what between her travels and the time which had elapsed since she had been hauled down and fastened to the log, a considerable quantity of gas had leaked out of her, not to speak of that which Ephraim had deliberately set free in order to bring about the descent. Still, she floated with a certain amount of buoyancy, and Ephraim believed and hoped that when lightened of every remaining scrap of ballast, she would be capable of rising to a certain height, and of floating them out of the dangerous proximity of the contending forces.

'She wobbles a bit,' said Ephraim, eyeing the balloon critically; 'but I reckon she's good enuff yit ter take us past the Yanks, and thet's all we want. It don't matter whether we come down in Staunton or in

Winchester, s' long ez we git cl'ar er Lewiston. Come on, Luce. Thar couldn't be a better way than this. We 've all the luck this mornin'.'

He had forgotten Luce's little peculiarity in the matter of balloons, and with another joyous 'Come on!' darted again into the open. The next instant, finding himself alone, he stopped and looked back.

Lucius, deadly pale, with a queer strained look in his eyes, his knees knocking together, and his body swaying from side to side, was standing where Ephraim had left him, apparently unable to proceed.

'What has struck ye, Luce?' asked Ephraim anxiously. 'Why don't ye come?'

'I can't,' gasped Lucius. 'I daren't. It makes me sick to think of it. I 'd rather die.'

'Waal,' returned Ephraim, hugely disappointed, 'ef ye can't, ye can't. I 'd fergotten how ye felt about it. No matter, we 'll make fer the woods on the other side. —Ah, by time!'

He rushed back to Lucius and seized him by the hand. 'Thar 's no help fer it, Luce,' he cried. 'Ye *must* come onless ye reely want ter die. I kin see the gleam er bay'nets through the trees on the other side. We shall be headed off. Thar 's no other way.'

He dragged Lucius forward with all his might; but the boy hung back, sliding his feet over the ground like a jibbing pony.

So they went until rather more than half the distance had been covered, and then all at once a loud shout was raised behind them, and Ephraim, looking hastily round, uttered a groan of despair.

Out from the coverts at the far end of the clearing rushed Colonel Spriggs, his face aflame with excitement, and waving his sword as he drew near.

CHAPTER XVI.

OLD GRIZZLY'S SACRIFICE.

AS Ephraim saw their terrible enemy running towards them, followed by a number of soldiers, his heart, stout as it was, sank within him; for Lucius, in the spasm of unreasoning terror which the mere sight of the balloon had induced in him, hung back, a dead-weight, and refused to move in response to either force or persuasion. It is said that a person in the grip of severe sea-sickness would, if informed that the ship was about to sink under him, calmly accept the fact, and welcome the change as a blessed relief from present suffering. If this be true, then Lucius was in very much the same state of mind. The recollection of his balloon experiences filled him with a hideous, incapacitating fear. To ascend, he believed, meant death. Death was behind him in another shape, but compared with the former it seemed absolutely enchanting. These were his thoughts, if he thought at all, and in answer to Ephraim's wild entreaty that he would hurry on, he did but hang back the more, while he muttered huskily words which fell in broken, meaningless syllables from his pale and trembling lips.

Q

While this struggle was going on, the colonel and his men drew nearer and nearer. Spriggs had not recognised the boys at first, but observing from his place of concealment two Federal soldiers, as he supposed, entering the open, had fixed his attention somewhat idly upon them. It was not until the argument began, and he got a good, though distant, look at Ephraim's hairy face, that it was borne in upon him who these seeming Federals really were. A fierce joy filled his cruel heart. He should not have to return to camp empty-handed after all. 'Don't fire!' he ordered his men. 'Run them down and take them alive.'

Relaxing for a moment his efforts to drag Lucius to the balloon, Ephraim cast a glance over his shoulder. The colonel and his men were still a couple of hundred yards away, but coming on at top speed. Thirty paces ahead was the balloon—a veritable city of refuge. One vigorous spurt, and they could reach it and be safe. Life was very sweet, and Ephraim could save his—if he went on alone.

But that was not the Grizzly's way. No such coward thought even entered his brain. Stooping down in front of Lucius, he drew the boy's arms around his neck, humped him on to his back like a sack of potatoes, and staggering to his feet again, stumbled forward, his body bent almost double under the heavy weight and the effort to preserve the equilibrium of his well-nigh senseless burden.

'Throttle me round the neck, Luce,' he cried wildly. 'Twine yer legs around me. Don't give in, sonny! Keep up yer sperrits, and I'll git ye thar!'

Scarcely conscious of what he was doing, Lucius

obeyed, and Ephraim, straightening up under this better distribution of weight, rushed madly on with long, swinging strides.

On came the colonel. Another hundred yards and they were lost; but gasping and groaning, Ephraim had reached the car, and with scant ceremony tumbled Lucius into its friendly shelter.

His eyes were bulging out of his head, and the sweat poured in big drops from off his face. His shoulder, too, was paining him terribly, and the tremendous exertion had caused the bandages to slip, and set the blood flowing again. But his nerves were steady and his wits clear, and he ran swiftly from side to side of the car, deftly unloosing the knots in the ropes that detained it.

Ping! ping! Two balls from the colonel's revolver sang through the cordage, and passed clean through the balloon; but with a yell of triumph Ephraim scrambled into the car, and having cast off the loosened ropes, began madly to fling out the bags of ballast.

Out went the sand-bags, one after the other, till but one remained, and then, as if in response to Ephraim's frantic invocations, old Blue Bag put forth all her remaining strength, and though she rose but slowly, yet after all she rose. Ephraim was wild with delight. He shouted and sang, without knowing in the least what he was doing, and regardless of the bullets, shook his fist at Spriggs as he came panting along. Then there was a slight jerk, and the shouts died away upon the Grizzly's lips, as the balloon stood still. The grapnel, which Ephraim in his eager haste had only torn from its hold and flung to one side, had dragged again under the log, and now held fast.

Ephraim sprang at the rope where it was attached to the car, and tore at the fastening; but the knot was stiff and badly tied, and in spite of all his efforts, it refused to come undone.

Colonel Spriggs took in the situation at a glance. 'Ha! ha!' he laughed savagely; 'I've got you this time. You don't escape me again.—Hurry up there!' he called to his men. 'A dozen of you haul down this confounded balloon. The rest stand ready, and if the rope gives, fire a volley through the car.'

A rush was made towards the balloon, in which a number of men, who had suddenly issued from the woods under the command of a young captain, took part. The remainder of the colonel's forces halted, and a row of deadly, gleaming tubes was instantly levelled at the car, where Ephraim, lost to all sense of personal danger in his anxiety to save Lucius, tugged and strained at the knot till his nails were split, and blood oozed from the points of his fingers. In vain: it would not yield.

'Never mind,' said a voice beside him. 'We are as good as dead, anyway. Better face them and have done with it.'

Ephraim looked round, bewildered. Lucius was standing by his side, pale, certainly, but with a look rather of relief than otherwise upon his face.

'By time!' cried the Grizzly, losing patience for once. 'I can't onderstand ye, Luce. One moment ye're as limp ez a lump er jelly, and the next ye're ez stiff ez the rammer er a gun. Oh, ef I'd on'y kept Jake Summers's knife!'

'Haul them down!' shouted the colonel, grinning like an ugly imp.

He was standing immediately underneath the car, looking up at the boys. A wild storm of rage shook Ephraim from head to foot, and desisting from his useless struggle with the knot, he stooped to the bottom of the car, and raising the one heavy bag of ballast that remained, sent it with unerring aim full down upon his mocking enemy.

The sand-bag struck the colonel between the neck and shoulder, and felled him like a log; but as he measured his length upon the ground, the car sank to earth; strong hands seized and held it fast, and the young captain, who had been looking on in bewilderment at the singular scene, stepped forward, and parting the ropes, ordered the boys, not unkindly, to get out.

'Whatever does this mean?' he began. 'Are you Federal soldiers, or '—— But Colonel Spriggs, rising from the ground, advanced with a face that was absolutely contorted with rage.

'Hold your tongue, sir!' he shouted rudely to the captain. 'I don't know who you are, nor what you want here.—As for you, you scoundrel,' he foamed at Ephraim. 'You filthy rebel, you; I'll teach you! You've played your last prank.' Then, maddened by the quiet smile upon the Grizzly's face, he raised his arm and thrust his fist, guarded by the heavy hilt of his sword, violently in the lad's mouth.

'Take that, you dog,' he cried. 'What do you mean by grinning at me?'

Lucius uttered a cry of rage, and struggled violently with the men who held him on either side; but Ephraim, spitting out a mouthful of blood, coolly replied: ''Twould hev made a cat laugh ter see ye sprawlin' thar. I on'y wish it had broken yer neck, ye or'nery skunk.'

'Colonel!' exclaimed the young captain, stepping to the front. Then, seeing that his superior was temporarily out of his senses with wrath, and fearful of some dire catastrophe, he turned sharply upon the crowd of soldiers, and ordered them to fall in.

The men, drilled to prompt obedience, obeyed at once; even those who were holding the balloon loosing their grasp and joining their comrades, the colonel's men in one group, the captain's in another. Instantly the balloon rose in the air, and the grapnel having been freed in the commotion, soared higher and higher, till at last, caught by a current of wind, it floated over the tree tops towards the south. An hour later it astonished Jackson's rearguard by descending suddenly among them, a collapsed and miserable wreck.

The colonel was striding up and down, muttering furiously to himself. Now, when he looked up and saw the balloon drifting away, his wrath broke out afresh.

'What did you let that balloon away for, you fools?' he shouted. 'Now we have no ropes to hang these dogs with. What did you do it for?' He glared at the men, who naturally made no reply.

'It was by a mistake, colonel,' the young officer hastened to explain. 'It was my fault. I gave the order to fall in.'

'And who are you, sir, to give your orders while I am on the ground?' stormed the colonel.

'I addressed my own men,' replied the officer respectfully; 'I understand that I command my own company. Your men heard the order, and obeyed it at the same time. Hence the escape of the balloon.'

'Who are you, sir?' repeated the colonel. 'Who are you with your "I command my own company?" You won't command it much longer if you presume to take so much upon yourself in the presence of your superior officer. I tell you I won't be answered back. I believe you let that balloon away on purpose.'

The captain flushed deeply. 'My name is Peters, sir,' he answered, 'Captain Peters of the —— Vermont. I received orders to make a detour of these woods, to feel for an advance of the enemy. The scene which has just passed has considerably surprised me. I know nothing of these people, though, from the presence of the balloon, and the fact that they are wearing Federal uniforms, I am led to believe that they are those of whom all the camp is talking. I have no wish to hinder you in the execution of your duty. If you conceive it to be your duty to arrest these fellows, do so, by all means.'

'I conceive it to be my duty,' retorted the angry colonel, 'to let you know that you are too free with your speech, young man. You don't command anything or anybody while I am on the ground, and just you remember it.'

Captain Peters reddened again, but held his peace. He was a volunteer with little experience, and he really did not know whether he ought to be at the orders of a stray colonel, just because he was a colonel.

'We've got a friend in the captain,' whispered Ephraim to Lucius. 'We won't come to harm ef he kin git the whip hand.' But this it did not seem that Captain Peters was likely to do.

'He'll kill us if he can,' replied Lucius. 'Look at his face.'

'I reckon,' returned Ephraim simply. 'The old blunderbuss is mad.'

The colonel resumed his march up and down, probably wrestling with himself; for brute though he was, what manhood there was left in him could not but recoil from the deed he contemplated. For several minutes there was silence, the men standing at ease, and the captain meditatively poking holes in the ground with the point of his sword, and ever and anon casting furtive glances at the two prisoners.

The stillness became oppressive. Only the colonel's hurried footsteps broke it irregularly, and the sound jarred so much upon Ephraim's tense nerves that he felt he must speak at whatever cost.

'See hyar, cunnel,' he called out. 'It's cruel ter keep us standing hyar. What ye goin' ter do with us? Remember we ain't done ye any harm, 'ceptin' thet whack I ketched ye jest now, and any wan would hev done ez much, makin' a break fer freedom.— Cunnel!'

Captain Peters made Ephraim a swift sign to be silent; but the colonel, after one prolonged and malevolent stare, continued his march as though he had not heard a word.

'The pesky critter!' muttered Ephraim. 'Hold up, Luce. He dassn't do nuthin', and he knows it too, right well. Thet's what's makin' him so mad. He'd like ter chaw us up inter little bits, on'y he dassn't.'

He stopped obedient to the captain's signals, but the next moment his roving eye caught the gleam of gun-barrels in among the trees in the section of wood they had left when they ran for the balloon, and here and there a face peeped out and was rapidly withdrawn;

so rapidly that the Grizzly rubbed his eyes and asked himself whether they had not deceived him. 'It looked like 'em,' he said to himself; 'but it can't be. How can it be? Oh, I reckon it's some more Yanks comin' ter see the fun.' He held his tongue, however, and, for want of something better to do, took a piece of string from his pocket, and twisted it nervously round and round his fingers, the while he kept his eyes steadfastly fixed upon the forest opposite. But if he had seen anything, there was nothing to be seen now. Suddenly the colonel halted in his walk, turned, and approached them.

'Now it's comin',' thought Ephraim, twirling his string more rapidly than ever. Lucius stood perfectly still and erect, his hands locked behind his back, and his eyes staring straight in front of him. Whatever his feelings, they did not appear upon the surface.

The colonel's swarthy face was deeply flushed, his black, deep-set eyes glittered menacingly under their bushy, overhanging brows, and he gnawed persistently at his long moustache. It was evident that in the struggle which had been going on in his mind, the evil had conquered the good.

Captain Peters drew himself up as the colonel neared him, and waited silently at attention.

'Captain Peters,' began Spriggs, speaking rapidly in a husky voice, whether the result of shame or of his still blazing wrath it would be hard to say, 'since you seem to have taken a more proper view of your position, I will condescend to explain matters to you. You were right in your surmise that these fellows are those who arrived yesterday in that balloon for the purpose of making observations of our position. They escaped, as you have doubtless heard, and they have been retaken, as you now see.

Captain Peters bowed.

'Well, sir,' went on the colonel, 'I presume you know the punishment in these cases, though your experience is probably not very great.'

He sneered out the last words, and still Captain Peters did not reply, though his brown face became a shade paler.

'We will take that for granted, then,' pursued the colonel. 'Very well, sir, as, owing to your hasty assumption of the command, that punishment cannot be carried out in the usual manner, you will take a firing party fifty yards to the right, set these two rascals twenty paces in front, and—shoot them. The word came out with a snap as though the demon which possessed the man had forcibly expelled it.

'Colonel!' ejaculated the astounded Captain Peters. 'Shoot them! Why—why—— Has the charge been proved?'

'Your duty is to obey, sir, not to ask questions,' said the colonel with a hang-dog look. 'Call your men forward at once.'

'But, colonel,' protested Captain Peters, 'I beg your pardon, but I think I should be informed why I am ordered to do this. You have your own men, and'——

'Obey your orders, sir. It is just to teach you that lesson, and for nothing else,' thundered the colonel, now more violently inflamed than ever, because of the captain's evident reluctance. 'Obey your orders, and at once, or I'll have you disrated. Do you know who I am, sir?'

But Captain Peters held his ground like a man, and ventured on another protest.

'One of them is a mere boy, colonel,' he said.

'Boy or no boy,' returned the colonel sullenly, 'take him out, and shoot him along with that hairy-faced baboon there. He knew what he was doing when he turned spy, I'll be bound.'

'But I don't see '—— began Captain Peters.

'Never mind what you see, or what you don't see, sir,' vociferated the colonel. 'I tell you that they are a couple of rascally spies. I had the proof of it in my hand.'

'Thet's a lie,' interjected Ephraim most injudiciously at this point. 'We came down here because we couldn't help it, not because we wanted ter. He didn't find any proof.'

Captain Peters looked hesitatingly at the colonel, who hastened to say : 'From the pocket of that fellow was taken a paper covered with details of our movements. That of itself is proof enough.'

'Thet's another,' cried Ephraim. 'Thar warn't nuthin' but stale news on thet paper. Don't ye listen ter him, captain. Ye take the resk. We han't had any trial. He dassn't shoot us 'thout'n a trial.'

'Silence!' commanded the colonel.—'It may satisfy you, Captain Peters, since you require so much satisfying, that I have General Shields's express orders to deal summarily with these persons, when and wherever I might find them. Now will you do your duty ? I don't choose to be kept waiting here all the morning.'

This was decisive, and though the captain turned a sympathetic eye upon the prisoners, he had no further objections to advance. 'Company ! Attention !' he shouted; but Lucius broke from the men who were standing on either side of him, and rushed forward.

'Captain,' he cried, 'that man is a liar. Here is General Shields's own order.' He thrust a paper into the captain's hand.

'Bullee!' chuckled Ephraim. 'So ye got thet, too, Luce. By time! thet 'll upset him.'

Captain Peters took the paper and read aloud: '"Colonel Spriggs—If you come up with the two men who escaped from the balloon this morning, you will detain them as prisoners, and bring them before me without taking further action."—This appears to be addressed to you, colonel,' he finished, looking up.

Spriggs advanced upon him, and simply tore the paper from his hand. 'You impertinent puppy,' he raved, 'if it is addressed to me, what do you mean by reading it?' He glanced over the paper and his countenance changed, but he recovered himself. 'You greenhorn,' he continued bitterly, 'did it never occur to you to ask yourself how this precious document came into that rascal's hands? Are you familiar with General Shields's handwriting?'

'No,' answered the captain; 'but'——

'Well, I am, sir, and I declare this thing to be an impudent forgery. Pah! You call yourself a soldier, and allow yourself to be taken in by such a trick.'

'It is not a forgery,' cried Lucius. 'Certainly, the general did not know that we were the escaped prisoners, but he gave my chum the paper, all the same. It's the truth, upon my honour.'

Captain Peters looked puzzled, as well he might. 'I don't understand you,' he began, when the colonel at a white heat broke in again.

'Captain Peters,' he roared, 'do your duty.'

Captain Peters hesitated for the last time. He was very young, very sympathetic, and he did not know his position with regard to Colonel Spriggs. But he did know what would be the consequences to himself of disobedience on what was practically the field of battle. Finally he said : 'Colonel, this appears to be a very curious and unusual case. Would it not be better, if I may say so, to refer it back to the provost-marshal ?'

For an instant the colonel paused. It appeared that one chance more was to be given him. Then his good angel turned away and left him, and a black lie dropped from his lips. His voice became dangerously calm. 'I do not know that I am bound to make explanations to you, Captain Peters,' he said ; 'but I have done so out of consideration for your extreme youth and inexperience. It may be enough for you to know that I carry the provost-marshal's order, countersigned by General Shields, and dated 1 A.M. to-day, to hang these fellows as soon as possible after their capture, should I succeed in taking them ; and that document, sir, is not bogus like the one you have just read. Now, for the last time, will you obey orders ?'

Captain Peters wheeled round and faced his men.

'Company !' he cried. 'Attention ! You will remain drawn up in line. Your orders are to keep a sharp lookout for the enemy. You will take no part in this business, if you are men. That is my last word to you as your captain.' He turned about and faced the infuriated colonel. 'No, sir; I will not obey your orders,' he said with flaming cheeks. 'Do your murderous work yourself, if you must do it. I am

a soldier, not an executioner. There is my sword.
I am prepared to take the consequences.'

'Bullee!' burst from Ephraim, while a low murmur
of approval ran down the line of Vermonters. But the
colonel, livid with rage, said as he almost snatched the
sword from the young officer's hand : ' Very good, sir.
Fall back ! I shall know how to deal with you when
the time comes.—Sergeant Plowes !' A low-browed,
thick-set fellow stepped forward and saluted. ' Carry
out the orders which Captain Peters has refused to
execute, and be sharp about it.'

In every company of men there are some souls of
the baser sort, ever ready to curry favour with those
above them. The colonel had made a careful selection
from his regiment, when he set out to hunt the
fugitives down, and he knew that there was no fear
of his orders being disobeyed, whatever their character.
Had not Captain Peters appeared upon the scene it
would have been all over with Ephraim and Lucius
long ago, but the presence of the junior officer had
inspired Colonel Spriggs with the mean idea of forcing
some one to share the responsibility of the execution
with him. Foiled in this, he fell back upon the men
he had brought.

The sergeant also knew his men, and having named
six, ordered them to step to the front. They did so.
The remainder of the company stood at attention.
Their sympathies were with the prisoners, but the
fear of the provost-marshal was before them, and as
the colonel had absented himself from them for about
an hour after midnight, they could not know that he
had lied in saying that he had seen that dreaded
functionary.

'Fall in between the second and third file,' said the sergeant to the prisoners.

Lucius stepped forward and took his place. His head was held proudly up, and on his pale lips was a set smile. His hands were still locked behind his back, so no one saw how convulsively his fingers were twined together.

'Now then, you,' said Plowes roughly to Ephraim, catching him by the arm.

But the Grizzly broke from his hold, and rushed up to the colonel. 'Cunnel!' he cried, in heart-rending tones, 'stop before ye do this bloody deed. I ain't keerin' what ye do ter me, ez I told ye before. But thet boy thar, thet Luce, he's ez innercent ez a lamb. I made the balloon jest fer ter pleasure him, and he didn't want ter come; but I fetched him along. He's done nuthin'. Cunnel, ez God is above ye, don't harm him.' His voice rose to a shriek. 'Cunnel! cunnel! Hold yer hand. Don't shoot him. He's his mother's only son. He's my friend, and I love him. And I've brought him ter his death.' He covered his face with his hands and sobbed.

'Take him away,' said the colonel abruptly.

'Cunnel!' screamed Ephraim, struggling with the sergeant. 'Spare him! Spare him! Ef ye will, I'll jine yer army and fight against my own side till I drop. Ye'll git one man more thet way.—Oh, what am I sayin'? I don't want ter git off myself. On'y let him go! On'y let him go!'

'For shame, Grizzly!' called Lucius. 'Don't degrade yourself by talking to the ruffian.'

'Oh, Luce, Luce!' wailed Ephraim, suffering the sergeant to lead him away. 'What shall I do? What

shall I do? I brought it on ye. Oh, fergive me!
Fergive me!'

'Files! 'Shun!' cried Plowes, shoving Ephraim into
his place. 'Right face! Fifty paces to the front!
Quick—march!'

The melancholy procession started, Lucius still holding his head high, and Ephraim crying and whining
like a child that has been whipped.

'Don't cry, Grizzly,' said Lucius, taking him by the
arm. 'They'll think you're a funk. I know better;
but don't give them the chance to say so. Don't worry
over me. It's not your fault. I ought to have remembered what my General said. It's a big price to pay
for being disobedient; but it's my fault, not yours.
Oh, don't cry so, dear old Grizzly!'

Their positions were curiously reversed. The soft,
young southern voice was calm and clear, there was
no shrinking in the bright blue eyes, and the quivering
coward of half an hour before now marched to his
death with a step as steady and bearing as firm as
that of any of the cavaliers whose blood ran in his
veins; while his comrade, all his steadfast courage gone,
shuffled along, his gaunt frame seeming to shrivel in
his clothes as he went, and his queer, old-looking face
drawn with the agony of his fear and self-reproach.
Only there was this difference—Lucius was thinking
of himself, and that nerved him. Ephraim was thinking of Lucius, and that unmanned him.

'Files! Halt! Front! Order—arms!' shouted the
sergeant, and the men stood still.

'Now then, you two,' said Plowes, 'come with me.'
His rough heart was touched for once in his life by
what he had just heard, and he muttered as they

marched along: 'I'll make it thirty paces, and ye kin take yer chance.' Such a favour! And having said thus much, he placed them and went back without another word.

Lucius straightened himself up and once more locked his fingers behind his back. 'Hold up, Grizzly!' he said. 'Don't let them think that you're afraid.'

Ephraim bent his lank body and kissed Lucius on the cheek.

'Good-bye, Luce,' he said. 'Maybe God 'll let me meet ye by-and-by.'

He raised his head, and swift as lightning a change came over his face, and a flame of joy sparkled in his eyes as he stared over the heads of the firing party at the woods beyond them.

Plowes had reached his men. ''Shun!' he called. 'At thirty paces—prepare to fire a volley! Ready!'

'Ef I kin on'y gain an ounce of time,' muttered the Grizzly, with a sob in his throat.—'Hold on!' he shouted suddenly. 'I can't abear it. Wait till I blind our eyes.'

'Blind 'em, then, and be quick about it,' returned Plowes sullenly; for he was getting heartily sick of the job he had taken in hand.

'I'll not have my eyes bound,' declared Lucius, pushing Ephraim's hand away.

'It's the last thing I'll ever ask of ye,' stammered Ephraim, scarcely able to speak, and Lucius submitted.

'Now then, sharp with your own,' called Plowes.

Ephraim drew out his handkerchief and fumbled with it in his hands, but all the time he scanned the opposite woods. Then the light died out of his eyes again, for save for the waving boughs that swept

R

gently to and fro in the morning breeze, there was nothing to be seen.

'Now then,' shouted Plowes; and Lucius muttered: 'Have you got your handkerchief on?'

'Yes, sonny,' answered Ephraim soothingly, as he glanced once more towards the woods. 'Thar they air, the boys in gray,' he murmured. 'Why don't they come out? Am I dreaming? It's too late! too late! One of us must go under. I reckon it'll hev ter be me.' Then dashing the handkerchief to the ground beside him, he placed his right arm round Luce's shoulders and roared at the top of his voice: 'Fire, boys! Fire!'

'Ready!' called Plowes, astonished at this mode of address, for he supposed it to be meant for him. 'Present!'——

But ere the fatal word could cross the sergeant's lips, Ephraim swung suddenly round in front of Lucius and clasped him in his arms. The Grizzly's broad back was turned to the platoon, and his body covered the friend he loved from the deadly volley.

But it never came. For before a trigger of the six rifles could be drawn, a line of flame spurted from the opposite woods, and a frightful roar of musketry swallowed up all other sounds. Lucius felt a sharp agony of pain in his right ankle, and then, with a dead, heavy weight bearing him irresistibly backwards, fell fainting to the ground with the wild rebel yell ringing in his ears.

The battle of Port Republic had begun. For the second time Lucius and Ephraim had stood up to the fire of their own men, and this time they had gone down.

'Fire, boys! Fire!'

CHAPTER XVII.

WHAT CAME OF IT ALL.

'WHEN we found him, he was lying completely covered by the body of the elder boy, and if we had not come up when we did, he must have been suffocated. The sergeant of the firing party, a rough brute, who was captured, and who explained the matter to us and pointed out the boys, said, with tears in his eyes, that he had never seen such a piece of heroism. Ephraim had evidently caught sight of some of our men in the wood, and knew that in a moment or two the fight must begin. At the same time he believed that the movement would be too late to stop the fire of the platoon, and even as the word was upon the sergeant's lips, flung himself in front of Lucius, deliberately offering his own life to save that of his friend. As a matter of fact, all his wounds are from our men and in the back ; but for all that, they are as glorious as any received in front by our brave fellows to-day.'

'"Greater love hath no man than this, that a man lay down his life for his friend." It was splendid !'

The full, earnest voice stirred a faint memory in Luce's dull brain. He looked wearily up into the kind face bent anxiously over him. 'My General!' he murmured, and closed his eyes again.

Stonewall Jackson laid his hand caressingly upon the fair, curly head.

'Poor fellow!' he said. 'Will he pull through, doctor, do you think?'

'Oh yes; I trust so,' replied the surgeon. 'His ankle is badly shattered, and he will limp for the rest of his days; but I think we shall be able to save the foot.'

'And Ephraim?' asked the General.

'Ah!'

The mournful sigh smote heavily on Luce's ear. He was still drowsy and stupid from the combined effect of shock and the chloroform which had been administered to him before the ball had been extracted from his leg; but at the sound of that dreary monosyllable his senses quickened, he opened his eyes again, and looked vacantly round.

For an instant the unfamiliar surroundings of the field hospital confused him; but in a flash full consciousness returned, the whole of the terrible scene in which he had lately borne a part rose before him, and with a shriek he struggled up on his mattress, supporting himself upon his hands.

'Ephraim! Ephraim!' he wailed. 'Where are you? You are not dead. You can't be dead. Oh, and you died for me!'

Then, as his eyes fell upon something stretched beside him, very calm and still, he writhed round, regardless of the pain of his wound, and flung himself

upon the quiet form, raining tears and kisses upon
the white, pathetic face.

Was it a dream? The pale lips parted in a feeble
smile, and a weak voice, almost drowned in the groans
of the wounded and dying, whispered faintly: 'Hold
up, Luce! Keep up yer sperrits! I'll git ye thar!'

   .   .   .   .

It was the fall of 1862, and the tender light
of the exquisite Indian summer lay on the deep
Virginian woods and glorified the rolling hills of the
Blue Ridge. In a secluded part of the beautiful
grounds of Markham Hall, a tall, thin young man,
with a white, wasted face, reclined in a comfortable
wheel-chair, dreamily enjoying the warm sunshine,
and inhaling the fragrance of the ripe, red apples
that hung from the laden boughs in the orchard.

Presently a fair-haired boy came through the trees.
In one hand he bore a bowl of broth, and with the
other he supported himself upon a stick as he limped
along.

'Hello, Grizzly!' cried the new-comer. 'How do you
feel now? Here's your soup. Aren't you ready for
it?'

'I reckon!' answered Ephraim, smiling in his own
old way. 'Ef this weather holds, I'll be around agen
in no time. My! It's jest glorious ter be hyar. But
what a lot of trouble I'm givin' ye all, Luce. I ain't
wuth it, ye know.'

Still thinking of others and careless of himself, the
grand old Grizzly. Lucius flushed deeply.

'See here, Grizzly,' he said, setting down the bowl
upon a rustic table, and placing his arm affectionately
round his friend's neck, 'don't you ever say that

again. If there is anything good enough for you in the wide world, the Markhams have got to find it out. Just you remember that. Where should I be to-day if it hadn't been for you? Lying under the ground alongside that pesky colonel, as you called him.' Then as Ephraim was silent, he went on: 'I can't do much, you know, Grizzly, for I'm only a boy, and a lame one at that; but I've got a piece of news for you, just to show that we are not ungrateful. Father has arranged with Mr Coulter that, as soon as you are able for it, you are to go into the works as assistant mechanical engineer. Then, when the war is through, he's going to send you to college, so the loss of the pile doesn't matter after all. Meantime, till you go to college, you are to live with us.'

Ephraim's great eyes swam in tears. He caught Luce's hand in both his own and fondled it.

'Shucks! Luce,' he muttered brokenly. 'What a fuss ter make about a little thing. I han't never took any count er thet, seein' it war done fer you.'

THE END.